...novel.

More praise for *A Ghost's Story*:

'The author has a meticulous eye for historical detail and writes evocatively' *Irish Times*

'Astonishingly adept... mysterious, wry, sophisticated but also brutally honest' *FEAR Magazine* *****

'Genuinely moving' *Financial Times*

'This intriguing novel teasingly moves between truth and fiction with all the inventiveness and unpredictability of the mediums, frauds, and spirits who crowd its pages. The dazzling succession of extraordinary characters and bizarre happenings leaves the reader as puzzled as the dogged Victorian investigators of the "spirit world" – but much better entertained. For as well as being both horrifying and funny by turns, the novel becomes a touching love story of the most unusual kind' Charles Palliser, author of *The Quincunx*

'Lorna Gibb has incredible imagination and verve. We willingly, compulsively go into the labyrinths of this ghost story with .... ying read' Yasm

A GHOST'S STORY

Lorna Gibb

GRANTA

Granta Publications, 12 Addison Avenue

First published in Great Britain by Granta Books 2015
This paperback edition published by Granta Books 2016

A CIP catalogue record for this book is available
from the British Library

9 8 7 6 5 4 3 2 1

ISBN 978 1 78378 036 5
eISBN 978 1 84708 898 7

www.grantabooks.com

Typeset in Ashbury Light by Lindsay Nash

Printed and bound by CPI Group (UK) Ltd, Croydon, CR0 4YY

MIX
Paper from
responsible sources
FSC® C020471

For my mum

PROLOGUE

I am aware.

Of light and dark. Of Shade. Of colour. Of Cold. Of Warmth.
Of movement. Of stillness. Of air. Of soil. Of water and sky.
Of animate and inanimate. Of warm breath. Of cacophony
and quiet and the space in between. Of languages, whispered,
spoken, shouted, cried.
Of the manifold naming of things.

And then.

Of a hospital; a woman lying on the street, screaming, her
legs spread wide; a ship at sea in a heavy storm; a coal mine;
a jungle where a spider crawls on a baby's arm; a young girl
whose skin is the colour of poppies; a workhouse; a glittering
palace; a dank cellar infested with rats.

I try to concentrate, peer at the colours that unfold around me,
begin to make sense of brief scenes that evolve.

I see a city of painted wooden buildings decorated with copper,
burned by its inhabitants, and watch soft, melting flesh ooze

amidst the flames and charred cinders of structures and humanity.

I see a brand-new scaffold. Two men fall from the gibbet and no one weeps or cares.

I see a young woman in a white kimono seated on a mat, her legs stretched out before her. Her feet are tiny, crushed and shaped into the smallest, most perfect of silk shoes, but they are also filled with poison. Her blood pressure is minimal, her heart cannot pump enough blood around her body. In a few seconds she will be dead.

The world shifts again and I see a parched plain. Men with burnished red skin and painted faces beset and overcome white men on countryside that is strewn with corpses.

And then there is chaos, a multitude of battle-weary soldiers, dressed in a ragtag of clothes. They wear long women's skirts, as well as remnants of uniform, snippets of mantilla lace, all tattered now; many feet are wrapped in greying rags, for only a very few of them have boots, despite the thickly falling snow. There is a splash of colour from a red silk shawl. One man has wrapped a woman's blue bonnet around a kneecap; another has made his hands the size and shape of bowling balls with the layers and layers of hessian sack he has fastened around them. They are all worn away by hunger and exhaustion, struggling in the blizzard, without any hope of victory or even of a battle any more. The scant remnant of heat, the life in their bodies, ebbs outwards, freezes on overgrown beards, turns fingers and *toes to numbness and black. A few stagger as their faces twitch and contort and from their eyes blood falls, like too many tears. When someone collapses, another stops to take his clothes, or unwind the tattered cloth that makes his shoes, to use them for himself.*

And just as men fall to the ground, birds drop from the sky, literally thousands upon thousands of them, hurtling down from the white clouds, a rain of feathers and beaks and motionless wings.

Then I see a city, in a sweltering country, surrounded by a sea that shines like a turquoise jewel. It is built in squares. The largest and grandest of these is a bustling place. Fruit of every shape and hue, vegetables, fish, birds singing in cages, at a market that is bright with colour and seems the opposite to all that I have just witnessed. The sounds of the market are a lovely lilting tongue that seems like water in the way that it turns and trills. To the east of the square is a cathedral. It is not an attractive building, solidly built on twenty-four pillars, but it proudly displays the only public clock in the town. In the middle of the north side a fountain bubbles and dances. The clock turns to two p.m.; the bells of the cathedral begin to chime and are echoed by two other churches. I am delighted by the light air, the shining of the sun, relieved that the world might also have this joyousness in it.

But then, and this is when I know how I am cursed, the earth splits in two and the city falls into it. For some it is a tumbling into death, as buildings crumple beneath them; for others it is as if the weight of the earth descends on top of them and they are crushed. And there are many for whom it is a slow suffocation, while they struggle for air, beneath the ruins of broken-down walls.

And finally, I manage to make the images decelerate further still.

*

It is raining on a grass bank that leads to a river. The greens are all muted; lines are blurred and now I find that I feel as much as I can see. My perception has subtly shifted. Before I was watching a dream, a multitude of dreams, unfold before me. Now I am within them.

Something of import lies there: a factory of stone and sweat. The noise inside is deafening, so loud that I feel as if I vibrate with it, and, here too, I know there will be dying. But there is a boy, no more than eleven or so, a lively looking boy, in expensive clothes, accompanied by a girl of about the same age, his father and another man. This last is an officious-looking companion who writes notes from time to time and wrinkles his nose at the smell of unwashed bodies, clears his throat of the cotton threads that catch in it. But the boy, he is different, so different; he looks around and his eyes are filled with tears. I am caught, stopped absolutely in my fast, flickering pace, by his empathy, the first that I have witnessed. He is not a poor child. His father is obviously important to this workplace and shares some of his son's concerns though he is more business-like, more resigned. But the boy is filled up with an emotion that touches me, new to awareness as I am, so that I too am overwhelmed and linger.

There is misery in this hellishness of din and dust and fine threads that choke up human lungs, and I look for the dying which will make this image like all the others. I find it, but not before the boy does. A woman who is still young, not yet twenty, is doubled over, haggard, and he moves towards her. His father calls him back, 'Robert, come away, leave the poor woman.'

And I watch his hesitation. An obedient child, then, but one whose compassion will now make him defiant, though only because he knows that his father will not think less of him for it. The girl who is with them pulls at his sleeve to try to dissuade him too. Her name is Hyacinth. But he goes anyway, heedless, towards the machine, the loom.

The woman is crouched beneath it, making a sound like an animal. Her skin is grey and her breathing harsh and jagged; she is struggling to inhale, grasping at the air with her mouth, and the boy goes to her, determined now, and asks, 'Can I help you, please?'

Such a polite child, all decorum to a woman who is in her last throes, and she reaches to him, one hand on her throat, the other stretching out for comfort, for rescue, the benediction of human touch. He does not flinch. I do not see even the shadow of a grimace on his open, tender face. He takes her hand and holds it steady, fingers weaved through hers, clasped, a shared prayer that he clutches onto even after she is lifeless and gone.

'Poor soul,' his father says. 'May God be with her.'

Tears fall unchecked from little Robert's eyes and his father helps him up, uncurls his fingers from those of the corpse, smiles at his son, but with worry lines furrowing his brow. 'So much compassion, Robert, it will be a hard life for you unless you learn to bear it better.' The girl's face is emotionless but she puts her *arm round her friend's shoulders, reaching up uncomfortably to do so for she is so much smaller than him. Robert's empathy is like a softly glowing light around him against a background that is damp and dreary. It warms the coldness that is me, suffuses my nothingness with gentle heat.*

This boy fills me up with something like yearning. I look into him and I see his vicarious hurting; know him for the rarest, most tender of souls. I wonder what becomes of him, this boy who cares too much, and I strain to look beyond this time, to the years that might stretch ahead. The scene shifts, dissolves into another. A house that is both imposing and soothing is set in a valley of misty, washed-out pastels, caught between undulating hills. There is a light drizzle of early morning rain; the house is soft, as if its edges are frayed by the landscape, but prosperous, the biggest house for miles around.

And inside it there is my Robert, a sickly boy of eleven years. At first I think I have failed to follow his life when I realise that only months have passed since I saw him, on the factory floor with his unashamed weeping. But he is entirely changed. He has been a clever, adventurous boy and now he is brought to this bed and this room, with its chamber pot and rose-coloured walls, a room of stultifying stillness, in a sandstone house, in a landscape that has every colour of grey. I find that I can be in this room with him and know that here too death is close.

I see his eyes twitch behind his closed lids as if perhaps he dreams of me, but of course, I think, that cannot be. I see, in his restlessness, the pain that is inflicted by the touch of even these, the finest of cotton sheets. His hair is cropped short, close to his head. I remember his kindness, his absolute understanding, and wonder if I can make him strong. Somehow I know with every fragment of existence that I have, with every shred of awareness in me, that this is not allowed, is wrong and irredeemable. But I am young, newly aware of the world, and think it cannot hurt this once, and so I try. I try to enter inside him but do not have the skill or years, and so instead I concentrate, focus on sending my spirit energy to his barely moving form. I feel energy drain out of me in a rush and, as I do, he awakes, seems to pull away from the death that has been coming to collect him in his sleep. His eyes open. A pale pink flush spreads across his pallor. He looks around the room as if trying to see what has brought this change, and coughs a little to clear his throat. Robert sees the glass and the water in the china jug beside his bed and stretches towards it. When he fails to reach it, he eases himself up slowly onto his elbows and calls for his mother.

In another room, in another house, in the same misty valley, Hyacinth's mother tries to rouse her with a gentle tug at her bed-clothes. When she cannot, she places her hand on her daughter's brow, only to find that it is already growing cold.

It is 1812.
I remember nothing else for forty years.

The only 'Katie King' text in the Hamilton Collection. The handwriting is very spidery, uncertain, and in a different hand from the later papers. Robert Dale Owen's own description of the illness and his miraculous escape from death in his autobiography, *Threading My Way*, is similar to that presented here. He observes that 'The mental effects of that sickness, carrying me to the verge of death, have never been wholly removed. Since then my emotion seems to lie even nearer the surface than formerly; to be more readily called forth by pity, by admiration, by love.' [AM April 2007]

It is 200 years since the memories of this text and five years since I first read it. I think now that Robert Dale Owen's conversion to spiritualism was related to some perception of this early encounter.

I think of Katie, what it would be like to be aware all that time. Is she happy in her state or not? I should like to be freed from the concerns and needs of my fast-failing body, yet still to be aware. I find increasingly that the time the treatment buys me is not worth the cost it exacts. Perhaps living well for a short time is better than living in this half state of pain and sickness.

Does she see me? Does she know that I believe?
[AM March 2012]

A BRIEF INTRODUCTION
TO SPIRIT NATURE

In the beginning there was me.

Actually, no, that's not quite right. In the beginning there was the idea of me. Better, but still problematic. An idea seems to presuppose the presence of a human who can have it and there weren't humans *in the beginning*.

So, in the beginning of human existence there was the idea of me.

Yes. I like that. It gives me the kind of importance I deserve, the kind that gets forgotten in the flimsy white dresses and pretty little hands that are so cold but so very, very delightful.

I have no physical presence of my own, no body to decay, I am aware only of my thoughts, of a kind of gentle brightness that seems to emanate from them.

I see all things and yet have no eyes, understand thoughts yet have no physical mind with which to process languages, can hear music, the rustle of leaves, the sound of the Adriatic, yet have no ears. It is as if I am dreaming, have dreamt, the world we live in, as if I interact with imaginings. I see some people and know their past, how they have come to this, can watch their earlier life unfold around me, feel them living, although I do not.

But know that as I write this, I feel far more faded than I was when this story began. I have whole days that I do not remember and it seems that I sleep for months at a time. I cannot die. I have never been born or lived, but perhaps I can somehow dissolve into the ether from which my consciousness came. This book is to be the telling of a tale, the preservation of moments of pleasure and pain and loss, set down, so that if my consciousness does vanish, as I hope it shall, they will be known and remembered. The debate as to my existence, or rather as to the existence of my kind, will be seen to be flawed by a chasm that runs through all of the investigations and most of the argument. Essentially this: the use of trickery, and its discovery, shows only that, not more. Because some people create me, imagine me, impersonate me and use trickery to do so, does not mean I do not exist and proves nothing, nothing at all.

In the years when I was developed enough to borrow human bodies, inhabiting them for a few breaths or a thousand, a heartbeat or a short spell of a lifetime, I learned what it is to feel the pleasure of human touching and the heaviness, the terrible weight of flesh that seems in contrast to its utter vulnerability.

I do not know if I had another life, a physical life, before this spirit one. If I did, I do not remember it, in much the way that humans cannot remember before they were born. Robert Dale Owen and Lord Alfred Russel Wallace are the only people who came close to understanding spirit nature. I know only that in the early nineteenth century I became aware of my own existence and could see what was happening around me.

As the decades passed I found I was able to interact more and more with the scenes I witnessed, then after a century or so had passed, I found this ability degenerated again.

I made a name for myself in the mortal world. In fact I made two names, male and female. The male *manifestation*, John, left a book, but all the female me gave to posterity was some wishy-washy photographs in scanty clothes, although I am rather fond of the one where my arms are crossed over my chest. I had just learned how to influence body movement and I took much pleasure in amusing myself. Originally I tried out the arm position to see if it might accentuate rather small breasts, so that they might peek through the spaces above the elbows, pushed up and forward by just the lightest pressure. Now I see that in fact I created the appearance of the newly risen dead, an excellent look for a ghost.

Katie has long outlived John despite his tome. Outlived, an inappropriate verb to use for a ghostly form, but amusing. Katie, the witty phantom, is so much better than all that vapid wispiness and the smell of violets or hyacinth or roses. In the late twentieth century I'd hoped for a more dynamic version of the female me. But no, there I was, still looking like a Victorian waif, in Rome, a city I've always rather liked. It was however very annoying that they pretended to have six men carry me across the stage. The actress who played me was a slip of a girl and I am, after all, weightless. Their display gave the impression that I had somehow put on weight over the years. It seems that I can't modernise and be popular, that the essence of what I am is somehow inextricably linked to hushed Victorian parlours, levitating tables and men of science debating my existence.

It is not ideal but there is some advantage to timeless-ness. This is the third century that I have known and yet, and yet, I can still draw a crowd. John stopped doing that in the 1930s. The female *manifestation* is obviously deadlier than the male (deadlier being a covetable quality in a ghost). Perhaps the embodiment of ghostliness is (eternally?) feminine, very beautiful (I would blush if I could but this is simply a fact), ethereal, cold, on the cusp of womanhood, inspiring sadness and fear of the unknown but also a contradictory reassurance insofar as it has a recognisable form. It is perhaps a kind of default gender, just as God is usually seen as male.

Most importantly of all, though, I learned during more than a century of observation that this abstract entity must arouse desire, always, always that; not a full-blooded passion but a thin longing, stretched out tight over the decades, tense as a violin string on the point of breaking, delicate as narrowly blown glass. Sometimes that desire will be sexual; at other times it will be to know what happens *afterwards*.

Question too much, look too closely, the illusion shatters. But withhold all doubt and you may find a slim ledge, on the edge of a precipice that is the verge of wanting more than you ever thought you could. If you are one of the few who reach it, who can believe absolutely, then, only then, will your yearning for me make you fall into madness.

This page culminates in what is apparently a warning and contrasts with the rest of the typed sheets which are predominantly historical narrative. There are no citations or references to published sources and it appears to be a work of fiction in the fantasy genre. It does however touch briefly, in a humorous way, on some of the themes that dominate the Cesenatico scripts: that of gender, the historical associations of certain kinds of culture, and how modernising does not always lead to a growth in popularity, especially when the period allusions are intrinsically linked with the identity of the theme in the first place. Harrison's *Allusions to a Culture of History* (2006) discusses this at length with regard to fantasy tropes and the prevalence of period scene setting, but I think that it can equally be applied to the séance environment in a historical sense.

The circumstances surrounding the manuscript suggest an elaborate prank, but the intelligence of the writing and the links with the dated and documented historical archives make it worthy of some consideration. On a personal note, I do admit that there are moments when I think it is a slightly ridiculous use of my time. People can be so gullible. However, the Society for Psychical Research has deemed it worthy of investigation and the related archive documents are mainly in the Magic Circle's possession, so inevitably it falls to me. [AM 2007]

I can hardly believe that I wrote these sceptical, ridiculously aloof notes just five years ago. I see now this page is a warning. And I realise that Katie meant it to read as a guide to the other papers, a way of navigating them safely. [AM 2012]

The Magic Circle Library
Everton Street
London
16 Nov. 2012

Dear Dr Gibb

I was very interested to hear of your latest project and enclose herewith, as requested, the complete set of King 'spirit writing' that we have in our archive. They have come to us from various places and the provenance of each is marked thereon. Additionally I have included photographs of the Davenport correspondence that we hold here. You may also find it useful to contact the librarian at the Harry Price Library in Senate House, where there are two further pieces of 'John King' spirit writing, as well as the current archivist at Arthur Findlay College, Stansted Hall, where I know there is at least one further example by 'Katie'.

Our own pieces were transcribed and heavily annotated by my predecessor, Adam Marcus, who began work on a similar project to your own. Sadly Adam died in tragic circumstances before he was able to complete it. We have included his notes as appendices to the document, as they do provide an excellent guide to the various sources the writer (or writers) have used over the years, and have left his comments about the possible identity of the authors within the transcription. You will see his annotations are dated. I do hope that you will bear in mind that while the earlier comments are invaluable, the later ones show the effects of the illness that was diagnosed in 2010. Adam was an esteemed colleague and perhaps if you find his 'guesses' useful it would be nice to acknowledge him in the final book; I'm sure his partner Peter would be very pleased. It would be a shame if the cancer which so blighted his final years should in any way detract from the thoroughness and acuity of his work in better times and I hope you will bear this in mind while reading.

While obviously all clever fakery, the 'spirit papers' intrigue beyond mere curiosity because the time frame of their acquisition, as well as the handwriting, indicates they must have been written by several people, yet each person seems to have taken the trouble to read the previous paper in the sequence so that together they form a consistent, if at times patchy, narrative that spans more than two hundred years. The true puzzle is in the fact that we have accumulated these papers from different sources in diverse countries and have not yet managed to find the identity, or consequently the link, between any of their various authors.

The six sets of typewritten sheets which I have also scanned and attached came from the Katie King specialist bookshop in Cesenatico, Italy. They were found lying on a computer printer over the course of several mornings, despite, as the bookshop owner claims, the building having been empty and locked securely all night. Various well-known Italian 'ghost hunters' checked the shop (there is even a YouTube clip of an Italian TV ghost show that was filmed there) and several sceptical academics tried, without success, to prove it was obvious trickery. They even went so far as to lock the place up themselves and camp outside, thus preventing anyone from entering. A manuscript duly appeared the following morning nevertheless. No trace of the documents was found on the computer itself, just the pile of paper printouts which the owner copied and sent to Adam, at his request.

I suspect this is nothing more than an attempt by the bookshop owner to gain publicity for her small shop. It can't be easy running an independent bookshop these days, let alone a specialist one. I wonder however at the identity of the person that the owner paid to write the pieces; her own English is very basic. There is also the small mystery as to how the writer knew of our collection so that he or she could be consistent with the earlier narrative, in some cases even filling in gaps between the various papers, while following the style. We have only made our collection available to the public this year and you have the dubious pleasure of being the first to see copies of what we have. It follows therefore that the author might have some connection to the original writers. Should you wish to contact them for research with your enquiries, it is probably best to do so via their website: www.katieking.it. You will see from Adam's copious textual references that he treated them as he would any other document.

I wish you well in your endeavour to gather all of these together and can only hope that you have a volume worthy of publication at the end of your labours. Please do not hesitate to get in touch again if I might be able to assist you further.

Yours sincerely,

Bob Loomis

Senior Librarian

From: Dr Lorna Gibb
Sent: 20 November 2012 00:49
To: Bob Loomis
Subject: Thanks

Dear Bob,

Many thanks for all the manuscript copies. I am looking at them in conjunction with some other items of spirit writing of different provenance and date that relate to the John and Katie King phenomena. Firstly there are the three remaining Arthur Husk spirit writings, the so-called 'death pages' which seem to jigsaw with the Cesenatico manuscripts in such a way that I may embed them while carefully annotating for any reader that I have done so, but also three items from the Hamilton Collection and a short but very odd sample from the Stadhuis Museum in Amsterdam.

From my brief initial consideration, these seem to tally with both the Cesenatico scripts and your own various archival writings. This of course is less mysterious than your own coincidences because all, except the Husk, have been available for public perusal for some time now. It is highly possible that someone from the bookshop looked at copies of them before somehow producing their own manuscript. The archival fit is more puzzling, I agree, but I'm sure we will find a logical explanation in time.

Best

Lorna

1. A SÉANCE IN A LOG CABIN

This is a remote place but it is where it begins again.
It is the Year of our Lord 1852.

I see one of the only flat spots for a few miles, a kind of ridge that is also a plateau with a hill, shadowing it at certain times of the day, and a gentle slope at the edge where the children, when they were small, would race each other to see who could roll to the bottom first.

There is a man, dark haired and burly, accompanied by four of his seven sons in his labours, tended by a wife, who carries the youngest boy in her arms, and their only living daughter. The woman and the girl prepare and carry drinks and food while the menfolk are building something which will stand some distance from the farmhouse. Here at this break in the landscape, bordered on one side by thick pine woods, looking out over the softly undulating but barren hills, there is already a farmstead and beside it a small graveyard, carefully maintained. The newest stone is a little over one year old. It says:

Filenia Koons
Daughter of J. and A.T. Koons
Died Sept. 1851, Aged 12 Y 8 Mo 1 day

Beside the graveyard there will soon be a long, low log cabin. There is an earthy physicality about this toil of chopping trees and of encouraging the old piebald horse to drag them across to the already recognisable construction and that physicality is in sharp contrast to the purpose and intent of the labour, which is me, something that is without substance, something that is not of this place at all really, something that does not belong here. And it is this conviction that seems to have brought me back to consciousness again.

The man is called Jonathan Koons and I know that he is in love with me. He thinks of little else. It has not been a bad year for crops, the Koons family account books are healthily in profit, and the motivation behind this venture is not money but passion, bordering on fanaticism.

There is a local church. If you stand on tiptoe and look from the Koons' first-floor bedroom window you can even see its steeple poking up from a dip in the landscape, a few miles from the farmstead. It is a simple place, the focus of Dover Village, Ohio, and until a few years ago, the Koons family, all eleven of them, attended there, fastening the horse to the trap on Sunday mornings and driving out to be reminded of the horrors of Hell that awaited them for even the most minor of transgressions.

But Jonathan is a gentle man, and a forgiving one. He worries and doubts the pitilessness. His children sleep fitfully some nights, terrified by the depictions of the afterlife that awaits them, convinced that they are sinners and will sin. And then they lose Filenia.

She was playing by the creek, unusual for a farm girl who always had chores to do, but there she was, that

fateful afternoon. She wore a white pinafore and blue
dress with little puffed sleeves that were the envy of her
sister and had taken her mother a quarter day to sew.
No one knows what she was thinking but she was skipping, skipping and turning, as if making a dance out of
air. I watched on: fair hair, her end-of-season, darkened skin, Filenia, in all her prettiness and innocence.
But the copperhead snake had young to protect and
saw only this person moving quickly, threatening her
and her family, and so she rose, fast as a whip, right
up from a clump of weeds and river's edge wetness, and
pierced Filenia's thigh with her fangs. Filenia saw the
glint of copper from its shining head for no more than
a fraction of a second, then felt nothing but pain. She
screamed and screamed and shook her leg but the snake
held tight for a time that seemed eternal. Her elder
brother, Nahum, came running, then Samuel, who was
one year younger. They carried her back to the farmhouse. Before they had even reached it, and it wasn't far,
ten minutes' walk, not more, the vomiting had begun,
and the shaking. Those tremors shook her body so hard
that it seemed she was fighting the arms that bore her.
But Samuel held back her hair and Nahum tried to keep
her still while she cried and cried through the heaving,
as wave after wave of bile rose up and splattered onto
the grass. And then it was over. The trembling stopped
and with a half-choked sob and a dribble of pale pink
sick still running from her mouth, Filenia was finally
motionless. Completely. So that the boys, children that
they were, started to cry where their sister had left off,

keening over her body, looking up at the wide expanse
of perfect, cloudless sky, then down at their motionless
girl, a tangle of childish limbs on grass turned yellow by
the late summer sun.

The condolences for the family from the local church led to the
final breach. Children died, of course they did, it was a hard life
full of tragedy and loss, but there was, from the flint-faced minister, the implication that Filenia had somehow sinned. He spoke
of Eve and the serpent, and Jonathan Koons, gentle, bookish
Jonathan, struck him hard across the mouth. The family never
listened to a sermon from him again.

But in a landed wilderness where men and women spend
so much time looking up into the sky or across the vastness of
their landscapes, the sense of longing for the spiritual is strong-
est of all. So Jonathan came looking, and found me.

The stage road that led from Millfield to the state capital
Columbus was rough but often used because it was the only
route available to people travelling to or from the North. It was
frequently blocked by uprooted trees and cascades of boulders
that rumbled down the hill in the all-too-frequent storms. There
were sixty-seven miles of it between the Koons and Columbus,
and in one hour it was unusual to travel more than two and a
half miles due to the condition of the terrain and likelihood
of rough weather. The journey West was as arduous as that to
the North, with a twenty-five-mile stagecoach ride on a pitted,
seldom clear road to get as far as McConnelsville and the possibility of a steamboat. Jonathan and Nahum set off, just six
months after the death of Filenia, for a neighbouring farm,
some eight miles towards McConnelsville.

Spiritualism was slowly gaining popularity; news of a death might bring an invitation to a meeting where the newly bereaved might try to connect with a lost loved one. Samuel Tideswell had a daughter just of an age with Filenia, and now, it seemed, she was suffering from nightmares. These were not just bad dreams but visions of the dead girl, trying to reach her family, panicking because she could not. Jonathan and Nahum took the stagecoach, travelled two days and a night, not, at first, to see a spirit, or because they even believed in the possibility of such a thing, but because there was the glimmer of a chance that Filenia needed them.

The Tideswells greeted them warmly and ushered them into their front room. There would be no more than a handful of people present. This was not a public event and the only account of the proceedings was that which Jonathan subsequently sketched briefly. Filenia did speak, through the young Tideswell girl, of quiet family things and the missing of them.

I was there then, in that simple room with its rough-cut maple furniture and candle lanterns made of tin, somehow understanding what had gone on before. I watched, knowing of the hours of practice spent before a mirror, and a father's pride at his daughter's mimicry. They would soothe a friend and gain a follower to a church that offered hope and salvation, not hellfire and damnation. Did they believe in me? I think they truly did. The spark in the girl, that which you might call imagination, made her feel that her voices really were something other than from herself. The practice was for the show rather than for any deceitfulness. And in this they were a rare thing, for they were true believers, and brought Jonathan Koons and his son to be as them. Filenia's message was an exhortation to them not to shut her out but to speak with her, and other spirits, for they too had the gift.

Jonathan Koons returned to his farmstead and his family but his life had changed irrevocably.

Abigail, his wife, was wary at first.

(It is often women who are more aware of the dangers of wanting anything too much and so it was with the Koons.)

But their surviving daughter, Quintilla, ten years old, quiet and unassuming, dreamt of her dead sister and brought her mother to the faith too.

Nahum imagined, or more specifically convinced himself, that he had been told to build a log cabin where the spirits could speak to an audience; it would be a place that would withstand investigation through its simplicity, its lack of places to hide. Together the family toiled and built the rough log house, stout and solid enough to withstand the weather, just fifteen feet by twelve, in a clearing between the sites of the graves, for Filenia was buried next to her grandfather and the house itself. No other building touched it so that sceptical visitors could walk its perimeter and find no secret corridor or means for anyone to enter or leave the single room where the meetings would be held.

The first visitors came within two weeks of its completion. They were predominantly curious, quizzical neighbours, who pitied the Koons and thought perhaps their daughter's death had driven them to some new eccentricity.

They entered the room and were ushered onto benches at the end closest to the door. Before them was a round table where Nahum, Quintilla and their father sat. On the table was a contraption, the likes of which no one had seen before. It was the Spirit Machine, dreamt by Jonathan one night, a complex arrangement of copper and zinc, a kind of battery to draw spirit energy to the room and to the mediums.

Surrounding the contraption were various musical instruments – a harp, a tambourine, a violin, a tin trumpet and an accordion – and a large bowl of phosphorus. The phosphorus was to make the spirit hands visible in the pitch blackness of the séance. (We are, after all, not corporeal.)

No money changed hands at that meeting or at any subsequent. The Koons were deceivers but with the best of intentions and would have thought it unconscionable to profit from offering hope as if was a saleable commodity.

That first audience watched the miraculous Spirit Machine draw energy from another world into that simple place. They saw those luminous, phosphorescent hands play the instruments, heard a ghostly voice exhort them to belief through the tin trumpet which glowed in the dark, and when they left, they were filled with talk of nothing else.

Their voices spread, like the forest fires that swept across the state in July and August, slow burning at first, then filled with flames of belief that would take everyone in their path.

And so they came, crowds and crowds, on the narrow stagecoach road that wound from Columbus to the Koons' farm, and as they did so, it seemed the spirits responded with new and ever more wondrous demonstrations.

They represented their leaders as 'most ancient angels', of different orders and ranks and claimed to be governed by certain individual spirits, who, in their written communications, styled themselves by the general name of King.

They included the souls of departed human beings who had recently entered the spirit world and bands of dark, undeveloped spirits.

Of course, I had my detractors too: people who said that spirits did not exist or were the devil's work. They spat on the Koons' children, smashed two windows at the homestead, and once daubed the exterior walls of the spirit room with thick white-painted words proclaiming 'Liar' and 'Satan worship'.

(I watched them with scorn. I thought of all the things that might bring them to me. Bereavement, of course, the most noble calling, or the desire for knowledge, although I suspected them too ignorant even for this, and then the ignoble deceit, the careful constructs to satisfy the longing for fame, for wealth.)

When the guests arrived the evening after that vandalism, they saw the two youngest boys scrubbing the walls with lye and felt more convinced than ever. They spoke amongst themselves about how only a true faith, and not any kind of trickery, would persist in the face of such victimisation. Such perseverance was proof of conviction, and that belief, confirmation of my existence. Those guests were from Cleveland, Ohio.

Report of the Cleveland Company

Strange and interesting accounts have been given us of the spiritual manifestations occurring at the spirit room of Jonathan Koons, of Athens County, Ohio. The undersigned recently devoted a few days to visiting that place and witnessing for themselves the wonderful phenomena there produced.

(The writer exaggerated a little here, but this is something I'd want to encourage.)

In the darkness the two successful businessmen and three ladies of quality watched as the trumpet floated up from the table and a spirit voice issued from it. Jonathan was inspired that day, it seems. Despite the trickery, the black-gloved hands, he believed, really truly believed, that a spirit voice was speaking through him, and the spirit's name was John King.

(In fact it was. This was my first aural performance. I achieved it by imagining the words I wanted to say and focusing on the trumpet. Koons was then an uneducated man; I was far more persuasive as John King's voice than he could have been.)

My John King was erudite and devout, impassioned in his pleas for mankind to embrace the church of spiritualism. Jonathan Koons and his trumpet were no more than a vessel for his brilliance. But, inspired, Koons, the farmer who produced an average yield and kept a few cows, read long into the night. In time his John King became an educator as well as an entertainer, more and more distant from the quiet man who presented him to audiences in thick blackness.

Then, in May 1855, a visitor of some import set out on the long journey from New York, culminating as always on that last stretch of bumping stagecoach from Columbus. He did not give his name on arrival at the Koons', although of course the stagecoach driver knew the name of his passenger and spoke with awe to young Nahum when he saw him in the threshing field. When, at the séance that night, John King addressed Mr Charles Partridge by his name, it seemed to that noted enquirer that it was the first of the miracles that he would witness. For Jonathan and Nahum Koons, the stagecoach driver had been no less than a messenger from God, a spirit communication by day and in sunlight, without the paraphernalia and the mystery of darkness.

Charles Partridge was ushered into the hut with thirty or so of the other people who had congregated outside. Almost as many remained behind, unable to get a space in the cabin, which seated thirty at most. These were mainly visitors from the surrounding area; it was expected that they would return and gain admittance on another occasion, but many lingered on so that they could listen to the spirit happenings within, even if they could not see or participate in them. As soon as the congregation had been admitted the door was fastened shut, rendering the room pitch-black, the only window having been shuttered up beforehand.

The watchers jumped with fright when a tremendous blow was struck on a drum, more like the blast of a cannon than a prelude to any music, apparently from somewhere beside them, and then were further discombobulated by echoing beats of bass and treble drums in the same area. The noise increased over a period of minutes until some of the guests seemed on the point of leaving, although whether through fear or through discomfort at the sheer volume of the cacophony it was impossible to know for sure.

The din ended as unexpectedly as it had begun, although the reverberations seemed to make the air vibrate around them. A trumpet-like instrument, long and brass, illuminated by the application of phosphorus, appeared before them, and through it a friendly spirit voice introduced itself as John King and bade them welcome. Mr Partridge was especially delighted to be singled out by the voice for some words about his investigations into and writings about spiritualism.

'Are any particular manifestations required this evening?' the voice politely enquired and then, when there was no reply from the spectators, asked if Mr Koons could kindly play his violin and thus lead the spirit orchestra. Each instrument then followed the violin. The harp, accordion, harmonica and guitar played complex and very quick harmonies while the time was marked on the tambourine, triangle, drum and bells.

But the instrumental music, while it delighted the visitors, did not enchant them as the spirit singing would. Distant, sweet, obviously feminine voices were heard and gradually became louder, as if approaching from a long way off. These melodic, other-worldly singers seemed to surround the rapt audience. Mr Partridge had attended séances all over the country and yet never before had he heard such harmony. Their beauty and their talent, Mr Partridge later wrote, was beyond that of which humans were capable. For him, there was no doubt that the voices were angelic spirits, led by the quivering soprano of John King's daughter, conveying holy sentiment that no words or discourse could ever hope to.

(*Actually, it wasn't John King's daughter at all. Obviously spirits don't really have sons or daughters, and you will see later just how tiresome it is when we are labelled with human relationships. This was me again. I didn't actually go into the child. I was nowhere close to being mature enough to do so yet. Rather I imagined her voice as an ethereal, perfect sound and then marvelled at my own abilities when her wobbly, slightly off-key singing was transformed. I admit I was also having a little experiment to see how effective a feminine presence might be. I was surprised by my own success.*)

A solution of phosphorus lay in a bowl on the table in front of the benches. Through the trumpet, John King encouraged his fellow spirits to coat their hands in the solution that the audience might see part of their earthly form. This they duly appeared to do, and disembodied hands and lower arms moved above the small crowd. One small, gentle hand reached out and Charles Partridge was able to clasp it within his own, finding it very like a human hand but colder, with a tremulous motion that reminded him of the dying more than of the dead. The quivering delicacy of its paleness seemed to somehow belong with the purity of the high, perfectly pitched voice, the memory of which still touched some longing within him.

A larger, more masculine-looking hand appeared and began to write on a paper that was on the table before them. It was none other than the hand of John King and he closed the meeting, as he had become accustomed to doing, with a short sermon, given through the trumpet, in which he exhorted everyone to listen to spirits, commune with them when they could and be charitable in all things, including their dealings with doubters.

Afterwards the cabin door was opened to reveal Mrs Koons, with a lit torch, ready to lead the visitors to their accommodation for the night.

Conviction, and the call to conversion, had more power when uttered in a male voice, and John King's message had been compelling. But the enchantment of the séance, the moment that touched the journalist's heart, had been when the true voice of John King's unnamed spirit daughter sang most exquisitely. When Charles Partridge returned to New York, he wrote a piece in the *Spiritual Telegraph* that told the country what he had seen and where he had done so.

(I had my first name: John King. And also that other feminine

voice, the one that brought longing and touched the heart, name-less but powerful, an idea that might arise again in another time, another place. But not yet.)

Visitors poured in from further afield. A party from Kent County in Michigan and Nashville Tennessee arrived doubtful and left with the idea of me, the longing for me, in every ounce of their being. They had been lodged and fed for more than two weeks and night after night seen wonders they could not deny. There was no cost for the hospitality, no charge to watch the séances, only kindness and absolute faith.

Michigan, September 25 1855

It seems to me utterly impossible that anyone who takes up his residence with either of these families, partakes of their simple, yet abundant hospitality, observes their own intense faith and devotion to their angelic guides, their affection for, and confiding trust in the spirits who surround them . . . living literally with the spirits, like mortals, and yet, for one moment dream of their being guilty of deception, as having the will, even if they had the opportunity for fraud in this manner.

While the testaments and endorsement of the séance brought fame to the Koons and an ever-increasing number of converts, it also brought detractors and penury. The farm suffered from their spiritual devotion and the neighbouring church, whose steeple they could glimpse from the upstairs room, denounced them as evil and in communication with the Devil. Perhaps in explicit refutation, the communications from the meetings were compiled in a book called *Communications from Angels*.

(I was never really convinced that writing this book was a good project. I do like the idea of being seen as angelic (so much nicer than the alternatives) but this was a rather weighty tome, full of rodomontade.)

Two years after her death, Filenia left a message at a séance for her mother, telling her to 'rejoice in the fullness of love' rather than grieve. Women in the audience that night wept openly, yet all they had seen was the small, palely luminous hand writing on paper in the darkness. I could not help but think how much more moving it might have been if there had been a glimpse of the little girl, perhaps a brief memory of those minutes in the sunshine, just before her death.

The power of the local church, the established religion, prevailed. The three smallest of the children should have attended school in the township until they were ten at least, but they were ostracised and ridiculed. Joshua, just five, was made to spend one whole lesson on his knees before a roughly hewn wooden cross, begging God for his parents' salvation, that they might turn from the wickedness of their sinful ways and return to the local church.

Jonathan and Abigail took their children out of school and encouraged them to listen for the spirits speaking to them. I waited and watched as their young imaginations soared towards some idea of me. This was good work, not bad. Nahum found that even keeping his lips still he was able to find a voice within himself and project it from a point in the room. He saw it as a gift from God.

Despite the rumours in the city that true mediumship was to be experienced in Ohio, the numbers dwindled with time. People were put off perhaps by word of the angry crowds that gathered around the meeting hut some nights, shouting abuse and invoking God's wrath.

I disdained those hordes who could not understand that there was real faith behind the necessary artifice. I wished them fear and questions they could not answer, a dread of death, of Hell, of everything that might come hereafter. Because, for all their trickery, the carefully constructed illusion, the apparent *intent* to deceive, what the Koons offered was hope. No spirit in Millfield Township ever condemned an onlooker, nor indeed gave an account of the horrors of the afterlife. Instead they spoke of a spirit world with educated, entertaining hosts and singing that might make you forget your cares. But ultimately their motivation meant nothing. The farmstead did not survive the harsh winter of 1859. The visitors came whenever the roads were passable and those mouths to feed took their toll on the already diminished resources of a family of ten. When they lost the homestead and the land, when even the plot where Filenia was buried had to be sold off, they travelled for a time, an evangelical roadshow bringing the spirits to the people. But these performances were less convincing. Away from the cabin and the carefully constructed staging at its centre, the encounters seemed clumsy and contrived. Even my interventions did nothing to help.

Audiences dwindled until there was no one at all. Abigail lost her faith and went back to her parents, taking all the children except Nahum, who refused to go.

Jonathan and his son settled finally in Jefferson County, Illinois. Their prospects were diminished; their apartment was shabby and bare. Charles Partridge wrote to him there, hoping for some spirit message, still longing for that unearthly voice.

He enquired as to Koons' beliefs now that such hardship had befallen them. Jonathan replied for both himself and his son, 'We have a faith that is as strong as a granite pillar. A communion with spirits that is more precious than gold. It is a blessing, a gift, not a burden.'

Jonathan Koons was among the best of my believers and a rare, rare thing, although, in my detachment, it was a long time before I would realise that.

Stylistically this is different from the other manuscripts and reads like a chapter from a non-fiction book. However, the author seems to have quickly abandoned this style in favour of a more immediate and engaging one in the later Cesenatico typescripts, where the inclusion of dialogue makes them seem like chapters of a novel. Already, in this first account, there is an example of one of the signature quirks of the narrator, the hinting at what is to come to build suspense. Here it is the phrase 'it was a long time before I would realise that'. Examples in later manuscripts become increasingly reminiscent of Victorian penny dreadfuls. The tone in the bracketed insertions is somewhat arrogant and therefore irritating. I am not predisposed to like it much.

The names of all the surviving children listed in the 1860 FCI Census are: Samuel, Quintilla (the only girl), Roland, John, Cindello, George and Joseph-Britton. Nahum was by then married and living elsewhere, as was another son, Frank Marcellus. In 1852 George was a tiny baby and Joseph-Britton wasn't born until 1853, which means that only four of the sons could have helped to build the log cabin. This is noteworthy because of its accuracy; other accounts often miscalculate the number of children at the property at the time.

The inscription given is on the actual grave which is now on the property of the Tinkham family. Mrs Shirley Tinkham was most obliging when I contacted her and furnished me with several photographs of the headstone and surrounding area. I discovered Mrs Tinkham through the Find a Grave website where there is a photograph of Filenia's stone at http://www.findagrave.com/cgi-bin/fg.cgi?page=pv&GRid=97905113&Plpi=68025138

I believe this might have been an inspiration for the author. Additionally the text shows good command of contemporary sources. The quotes and references in this chapter are from:

- Emma Hardinge Britten (1870), *Modern American Spiritualism: a twenty years' record of the communion between earth and the world of spirits*
- 'Astounding Manifestations at Koons's Spirit Room', *Age of Progress*, 29 Oct. 1854, Cleveland, Ohio
- And finally, of course, Koons' own book: Jonathan Koons (1853), *A Book for Skeptics: Being Communications from Angels*, State Library of Ohio rare books collection.
  [AM 2007]

Katie is little more than an observer here, primarily a narrator rather than a participant in her early encounters with humanity. It is touching that she is pleased when she is able to imagine a voice for the first time, and now I find her *pride*, her pleasure, in being thought of as angelic, somehow make her sympathetic. [AM 2012]

THE CONTRACT

It is, I think, a kind of reward for recognising the Koons that gives me back the visions which I thought I had forfeited. They flicker briefly and then settle so that I am able to see some minutes of the time I had thought lost to me.

He is grown now, Robert, the compassionate child, and with him is a woman. What manner of person is he? I ask myself. What have I done? I am watching a marriage contract being made. It is April, 1832, and I am seeing Robert, an adult, with his fashionable whiskers and a nose that is slightly too large for the rest of his face. He has sandy hair and a portly body, not a physically attractive man, yet still I feel that warmth infuse me, something that I can only call gladness.

He stands beside the woman. I admit that they seem well matched. She too is plain, with brown hair severely tied in a tidy knot, and wears a high-necked dress the colour of dead geranium leaves. The colour gives her pale skin an almost yellowish tinge but her face is lit up by love and by some other emotion, a kind of quiet fervour that seems to echo his.

The room is domestic, not public, a reception room in a wealthy family home, but it is clear that the couple are pledging themselves to each other in some non-conformist way.

This is a contract, not a ceremony. There is no preacher or priest standing before the couple, just an officious-looking man who might be a clerk. There are no more than thirty guests – family of the couple, perhaps a few close friends – and none of them is dressed as if for a special occasion. The couple's declaration to each other is simple and heartfelt. I find that I am moved by the equality of it. After this wedding, the woman, whose name is Mary Jane Robinson, should be his property by law, his chattel, yet Robert declares:

Of the unjust rights which, in virtue of this ceremony, an iniquitous law tacitly gives me over the person and property of another, I cannot legally but I can morally divest myself. And I hereby distinctly and emphatically declare that I consider myself, and earnestly desire to be considered by others, as utterly divested, now and during the rest of my life, of any such rights.

It is a noble act and I am pleased that the boy I saved has grown into a man who would think of this. But then, as if this is too much for me, that I should take pride in something so forbidden, the image goes. The glow that has suffused me stays for a few minutes longer, but when I am no longer in his presence, I find that it too dissipates, and the coolness that is my essence, and which I normally do not heed, becomes a trembling chill. I am icy, detached and shivering. I ache for his warmth but know not how to find it.

These early papers show some romanticism and are thus much less amusing than the later writing. I suspect their author is younger, perhaps a teenage girl, given their floweriness, although obviously she is well educated. They lack the witticisms and dismissiveness of the Cesenatico scripts. Perhaps the writer of the scripts found the style of the spirit writing too difficult to sustain, or too overdone to be appealing to a contemporary reader over the length of a book. Thus, while the subject matter of both documents fits perfectly, the tone does not.

Her adoration is touching, though, and the subject of it curiously original. The son of a celebrated philanthropist, Robert Dale Owen, one-time US Senator whose failed social projects and deluded spiritualist dabblings brought him more ignominy than fame, seems an odd choice for such adulation. The dating of the paper belies the style of the text in parts too, an interesting conundrum. Could it have been written on different occasions, years apart? The quote is from Owen's marriage contract. [AM 2007]

A SÉANCE IN A HALL OF ENTERTAINMENT

Charles Partridge proved to be an ambassador of the best kind. His article, with its praise, its utter validation of the existence of the spirit John King, came as reprieve to a family of five living in Buffalo, New York.

(When I first saw them, they were seated together around a table in their front room. Without skill, but with a great deal of artifice, they were trying to find me.)

The Davenports were well-to-do. Ira Davenport Senior was a chief of police, well regarded by the local community – or rather, he had been much respected there until recent events. His two sons, Ira Erastus and William Henry, were just two years apart. With their black-brown hair and ruddy skin, to people who did not know them well they appeared to be twins. However, their physical similarities were contrasted by an absolute difference in temperament. Ira was gregarious and emotional, while William was studious and withdrawn.

Their sister, Elizabeth Louisa, was three years younger again and might have been a changeling with her fair hair and translucent skin. The events that had wrought such a change to the family's reputation were the concoction of these three intelligent young minds.

Elizabeth, known to everyone as Lizzie, at just ten years old, had become fascinated by the growing craze for communication with the dead. Bored by her afternoon pursuits of embroidery and tapestry, she turned to her mother, one afternoon in 1844.

'It seems to me, Mama, if the Fox sisters are able to communicate with the dead, then other people should be able to do so also.'

Her mother smiled indulgently but said nothing.

'I should very much like to try. Perhaps Ira and William and I could sit with you and Papa and see if there is any message from Aunt Sylvia?'

'Let's see what your father thinks.'

In the evening, Elizabeth found that her suit had been picked up by her brothers, and their bemused parents sat with them around the oak table in the basement workroom. The room had the scantest of lights, with the main lamps being turned off and the only illumination coming from candles flickering on the mantelpiece and in the centre of the table.

(In houses at this time there were generally two rooms of the kind now referred to as 'living rooms'. The upstairs parlour was rarely used, and relaxed family gatherings tended to take place in a downstairs sitting room. I always feel a little sad that the only place one can really see this arrangement nowadays is in the Merchant's House Museum in New York. Sadly its former inhabitants were firmly in the grasp of the more established Christian church and so did not invite spirits to what would have been a perfect place to entertain, but nevertheless it gives modern visitors the effect of that time perfectly. Needless to say, I am something of a connoisseur of museums.)

I found myself bemused by the wilfulness of these children and decided to intervene. I had, as I have recounted, interfered a little at the Koons séances, but this was a very different occasion, much more intimate, and I was starting to feel that I might actually be able to influence proceedings far more than I ever had before. It is true that the children had made preparations of their own. Ira had a piece of wood held between his knees and had practised cleverly manoeuvring the tablecloth with it. William was already a gifted ventriloquist, and while he seldom spoke in everyday life, he was, in contrast to Ira, positively garrulous as a thrown voice.

Elizabeth had a knocker strapped around her thigh, hidden under her long skirt, and by lifting her knee up from the seat could make rapping sounds on the underside of the table.

Mr Davenport watched on indulgently at the rather clumsy attempts of his children to replicate a successful séance. Their mother restrained a smile and was more than a little proud at the obvious effort they had put into it. But it was clear to me that no one was going to be really convinced. I interposed. I confess that being new to this whole enterprise I probably overdid it. I concentrated hard and raised the table just above the family, amusing myself with the shocked expressions of the youngsters, and then when I saw half-concealed smiles from the parents decided to raise it several feet higher, so that in effect there was only a very small gap between the top of the table and the dangling crystals of the small chandelier hanging from the ceiling. Everyone now looked aghast and so, to amuse myself, I jiggled it a little in the air, unfortunately smashing a rather pretty candlestick which had been gracing it by causing it to fall from this great height onto the floor.

Mr Davenport jumped to his feet in alarm and proceeded to light the room in as short a time as he possibly could.

Fearing public ridicule, the family pledged to keep the matter to themselves, but Mr Davenport mentioned it in passing to a colleague and in no time at all there were visitors to the upstairs parlour, requesting an audience with the talented Davenport children.

The family held regular meetings. The children honed their skills and I found no need to assist. But success can breed envy in small communities and soon the bullying began. At school, William was the most studious of the children and as such had often been singled out for name calling. Ira's intervention quickly quelled any threats. But this was different. It seemed that all the children had become bullies and all the bullies acted as one, and it wasn't just William, but Lizzie too, who found her hair pulled and the word *witch* scrolled on her books.

Mr Davenport had had enough of it and so, accompanied by his wife, he went to visit the parents of one of the instigators. He found the parents as unreasonable as their offspring and a feud began.

In only a matter of weeks the crowds who had gathered in the Davenports' parlour to commune with the dead had turned into a braying mob. They clustered in small groups around the stolid terraced house and heckled anyone who tried to enter. The Davenports, they claimed, were frauds and cheats of the worst kind, preying on the bereaved, pretending to have skills that they did not. Rainy nights seemed to keep them away and the family found themselves longing for downpours. It was on one such October evening, in the basement room, with his family around him, that Ira Senior produced a copy of the *Spiritual Telegraph* and began to read aloud:

At the close of the session, the spirit John King, as is his custom, took up the trumpet and gave a short lecture through it, presenting the benefits in time and eternity of intercourse with spirits; exhorting us to be faithful to our opportunities and charitable towards those who are in ignorance and error, he closed with an impressive address with a benediction, and bid us 'good-night'. I am aware that these facts so transcend the ordinary experience of mortals that few persons will be prepared to accept them as true on anything short of their own witness.

Several points about the article were raised by Ira Senior.

First the spirit 'King' seemed to be of a particular kind who graced many other spirit rooms besides the Koons'.

Secondly the list of people who had travelled to see the Koons, and who then bore witness to the events they had experienced, was comprised of men and women from several states as well as Ohio, including Indiana, Pennsylvania and New York.

Finally, Ira Senior concluded, it seemed to him that there was a message for them inherent in this séance, as if 'King' knew about their tribulations, was telling them to move above it, and forgive their oppressors.

Ira placed the paper on the table and looked expectantly at his wife and children. For a few seconds no one spoke.

Then Lizzie broke their brief reflection. 'Well, Papa, it seems a simple matter. Since he is such a clever spirit, we must speak with this John King and ask him what to do.'

The following evening due preparations were made to conduct a séance. There was to be only one specially chosen, invited guest, Mr William Fay, a medium who also conducted séances in the area and who had become a good friend to the family.

The table was bare except for a long metal speaking trumpet of the kind that had been used with such success in Ohio. At the dimming of the lights, a glowing hand appeared – in fact a wax one covered in phosphorus and supported by a long wooden mechanism, a bit like scissors, which Ira had devised and now controlled under the table. The seated assembly were accustomed to this kind of manifestation and waited for any words of advice that might be imparted to them.

Ira Senior spoke up, 'Spirit, are you there? Will you converse with us?'

'I am.' William's ventriloquist skills were admirable. The voice seemed to emanate precisely from the point where the bell of the instrument widened out.

'What is your name?'

'John King. I have counsel for you that you must heed.'

'What, then, is that counsel?'

'That you will take your boys from here and travel, that they will allow many to share in their wondrous gifts, and in so doing avoid the danger that lies in wait here.'

'I can't allow that,' Mr Davenport attempted to reason with the trumpet. 'They are but children still. Perhaps as a family we could move to another town. Would that do?'

'No. You must heed me. The boys must go about the world and give others the chance to hear me and follow me. If you do not allow them to go, they will be taken.'

Everyone at the table turned suddenly as little Lizzie piped up, 'What about me? I have gifts too. I was the one who wanted to speak to you in the first place. It's not fair, the boys have all the fun.'

I had a brief second where I thought of intervening on Lizzie's behalf but decided against it. The brothers were doing an excellent job on their own.

(In any case the United Sates really weren't quite ready for a girl as precocious as Elizabeth to go on a tour of the country.)

'Ssshhh!' Mrs Davenport patted Lizzie on the head. 'You're still a baby, and a girl. Your father must decide what is best for the boys, but no ten-year-old daughter of mine will travel around the country like a theatrical person.'

The voice, momentarily silenced, began again. 'The boys must share their gifts. Perhaps when she is grown we will call for Elizabeth too, but not yet, not now.'

'I cannot, will not, allow it.' Mr Davenport had raised his voice slightly, a little annoyed at the female chatter.

At this last pronouncement the trumpet began to thump itself against the table as if in protest. Ira Senior moved towards the lamp and the trumpet appeared to rise up into the air before falling onto the table with a loud clatter. It seemed that John King did not like to be thwarted.

The brothers appealed to their father that perhaps they should follow the advice of John King, but he was adamant. They worried about the warning that they might be taken, but Ira would brook no discussion. If people wished to see their talents, then they could come to them. They were not going to travel round the country like a freak show.

For a few days, nothing happened. The boys went to school and were treated badly. The rain gave way to hail and then to the first flurries of snow as winter settled over the town. Then one morning neither boy showed up for school. Mrs Davenport waited for them to come home but they did not and the alarm was put out. Assuming some human mischief had befallen them, Ira Senior called on his colleagues and neighbours to organise a search. Elizabeth clung to her mother in the downstairs room, tear-stained, repeating over and over that the ghost must have taken them.

When the telegram arrived, Mrs Davenport ran out onto the street without a wrap, despite the newly settled snow and the glass spindles of icicles hanging from the windowpanes.

She found her husband in the park close to their house with half a dozen other men. She ran towards them and her husband reached out to catch her as she slipped. 'Ira, thank God, Ira, they're safe! They're with my father.'

Ira Senior immediately set out by railway to collect them from their grandfather's house in Mayville, Chautauque County. After their initial joyful reunion with their father, the boys' story unfolded gradually. They remembered walking to school at nine in the morning, then they recalled waking up several hours later lying on a snow bank in a field, with no tracks to show where they had come from nor a path to indicate where they might go. William had recognised a steeple in the distance as being that of Mayville, the town where their grandfather still lived and where their mother had been raised when she first arrived with her family from Kent in England.

They struck out for his house, where they were received with amazement and from whence the telegram was speedily dispatched back home to inform their parents of their safe whereabouts.

The boys could give no explanation as to how they might have travelled there. No train had run at that time that might have taken them, and no conductors had any recollection of seeing them. Ira found the boys weary, with feet that were covered in blisters but without any memory of the long walk that might have caused them. He feared the intervention of the spirit and later, back at home in the downstairs parlour once again, the disembodied voice of John King confirmed what he had suspected. There would be a tour after all.

It was decided that some new features would be necessary to distinguish the brothers' tour from those of the many other spiritualists travelling round the country. My John King personality would guarantee a certain number of followers, but there was an immense difference between presenting a meeting in a front room or small local hall and appearing in the theatrically styled public venues that would be available to them.

There was the additional consideration that, at least for the first few months, Ira Senior should travel with his sons, so they would have to generate an income significant enough to compensate for his leave from his post. Taking money from an audience always made mediums more vulnerable to charges of fraud, and it was decided that a new apparatus would be devised that might circumvent potential accusations. Their father was pragmatic: the boys would need to rely on their skill as ventriloquists and conjurors if the spirits failed to materialise when requested. Although Ira had an unquestioning faith in his sons' abilities and believed they would not deceive him, he also knew that they were skilled practitioners in the arts necessary to compensate for an uneventful night.

(Ira later told Harry Houdini that his parents died still convinced that their sons had 'superhuman' powers and with an unshakeable faith in the existence of the spirit world. I find a certain irony in this.)

Now that they had managed to obtain their father's acqui-escence for their tour, Ira and William were determined to make a success of it. Of course, they had no belief in any spiritual powers but instead were slightly wary of each other, thinking that the occasional inexplicable event, like the floating table and the broken candlestick, was the result of a brother or sister playing a trick on them. This resolute refusal to believe in any kind of supernatural cause amused me immensely and led me to make several small interventions in the coming months that bewildered the boys and also became a source of some small friction between them.

Ira, who was exceedingly skilled with his hands, set about designing their newest apparatus.

In effect it was a large box made out of bird's-eye maple wood and perched on top of three tripods. The front of the box could be opened or closed using the three doors fastened to it. The space inside was large enough for two benches, one at each end, and several musical instruments – a violin, a flute, a drum, an accordion – all of which were placed in the central part of the cabinet.

The act involved the boys being tied firmly to the seats and then shut in the cabinet. When the musical instruments began to play it demonstrated the presence of spirits within the cab-inet because, obviously, the boys, being tethered, were unable to touch the instruments. It was a simple but very effective device and required only that Ira and William further hone their con-juring skills so that they were able to escape from any number of complex bindings and knots. The voice of John King would be heard prior to the musical display, introducing the events that were about to unfold, from some corner of the room, far from the cabinet that held the boys. In some shows the doors were removed and replaced with a curtain that showed from its continual movement the wild and varied activity that was taking place behind it. In every case, after the ghostly visitation, the curtains would be drawn open and the doors swung wide, to reveal Ira and William still firmly bound to their places.

I admired both the simplicity of the ruse and the skill needed to pull it off. It also allowed me some scope for duplicity because, within the darkness inside the cabinet, each brother was unsure of the precise second when the other brother had freed himself, so a little interference from me, a brief burst of spirit energy through the flute, say, could have them bickering long into the night.

The cabinet was dismantled and packed into a crate with the other paraphernalia associated with the show, and Ira and his sons set off on a tour that was to become their new way of life.

The first state they headed for was Ohio. The Koons' success meant that the spirit John King was well known throughout the state and his name featured on many of the playbills that advertised the arrival of a new act in town. However, after the first few shows, word spread, bringing much bigger audiences but also public demands for testing. This period, in 1856, and for several years following, would come to be known as the Years of the Binding Tests.

Toledo in Ohio was a busy port on Lake Erie with a growing population that was already over 13,000 strong. It also benefitted from being the hub of several railway companies, which made it an ideal base for manufacturing industries who wanted to transport their goods across the country. But Toledo was also well known for its gambling networks. Faro gaming tables were installed in saloon back rooms across the city, and bookmakers who would take bets on everything from trotting races to a presidential election touted for clients on side streets and amongst their circle of known clients. A Toledo cabinetmaker helped the family add some intricate decorations to their cabinet and spoke about them to a bookmaker to whom he regularly gave and lost large sums of money on the horses. This bookmaker, Howard Reynolds, decided to take advantage of the Davenports' popularity by establishing a book on whether their performance would bear the scrutiny of various members of the town hall.

The show was to take place in the ornately decorated town meeting place, a shabby building whose decoration seemed at odds with the flimsiness of its structure. In the event, the surge of crowds that arrived there, brought both by the possibility of winning a wager and by curiosity to see if Ira and William really did commune with spirits, meant that the venue had to be moved to a large vacant storeroom in the vicinity of the docks, so that everyone might be accommodated.

Ira and William were anxious to guarantee success in front of such a large audience, as well as profit from the wagers they had themselves placed with some help from an old police friend of their father's. They therefore took a new precaution. Beneath the cabinet they made a small space, not big enough for an adult but capacious enough for a child. It would be invisible to the audience, who would merely see a decorative rim running around the side that was presented to them. For a sum that was slightly more than they might have liked, the brothers found a willing boy whose skill at contorting his limbs had already garnered him success at a circus, and acquired his services. He was called Anthony, a rather remarkable boy that I should have liked to see more of but sadly never did, since he chose to continue his career in the circus, rather than in pursuit of me.

The expectant crowd watched on as two sea captains took more than three quarters of an hour to fasten the brothers to their chairs. One onlooker later remarked that it was unlikely that the brothers would have been able to loosen the bonds without the benefit of a knife.

The cabinet was closed. John King introduced himself and Anthony quickly escaped from his hiding place and proceeded to present a short musical display of some considerable skill. When the cabinet was opened the boys were still in their places, and the flabbergasted audience went off to claim their winnings or shrug off their losses, squabbling among themselves over the nature of what they had witnessed together.

The tour was not an unmitigated success, however. To compensate for cynical crowds and the occasional mechanical failure, Ira Senior became adept at spreading stories that conflicted with any less favourable accounts so that the truth was often lost in a mire of invention and publicity.

One such occasion followed the university testing episode.

(It was the first time that any of my mediums were the subject of a university study, and while in this case it was a rather unprofessional and haphazard one, it was nonetheless flattering to be considered worthy of the attention.)

Two Harvard professors, Agassiz and Peirce, publicly challenged spiritualists to undergo their tests and the Davenports took them up on the offer. Agassiz irritated me. He was one of those men whose vision of the world holds a wealth of contradictions that they cannot themselves see. He was, of course, absolutely certain in his belief that spirits did not exist and that any displays of so-called spiritualism were trickery and charlatanism. And yet he was a devout creationist, believing in an invisible God who had brought order and structure to the world, so much so that he dismissed the newly popular theory of evolution, finding it contrary to his religious ideals. It seemed to me that given his religious beliefs he might at least have had a more open mind towards other spiritual possibilities.

Despite Ira Senior's protests that the boys were too young, Agassiz and two of his colleagues subjected the brothers to a long oral examination, a sort of viva voce of their activities. I watched this to see how the boys might handle themselves and was ready to intervene if need be. My boys readily agreed to any manner of binding. Handcuffs were suggested, then twine. Finally rope was settled on, great lengths of it, not only to fasten the limbs of the boys but to tie them to the cabinet sides. Holes were bored in the walls of the cabinet and the rope was pulled through the holes and tied so that the knot was visible to everyone watching outside the structure. At this point, the boys did protest. William called out, 'It hurts. Could you loosen it a little, please?'

But Agassiz said no, suspecting a ruse. It was the perfect trap. Even if William and Ira had managed to undo their fastenings, the outside knots still held them fast to the walls. In a final flourish, Professor Peirce then went into the cabinet with the bound boys and closed the door behind him. Ira had already decided that they would have to claim that the combination of their discomfort and the negative atmosphere generated by the presence of such a scornful disbeliever made cabinet activity impossible, but he went along with the charade so that it did not seem too obvious.

However, they had not allowed for me. No sooner was the door closed than I drew the interior bolt. Peirce jumped and immediately felt for the boys to see if by some miracle they were free. They were not. A tambourine began to rattle. It wasn't a musical display as such but I did manage to produce enough energy for a hum from the accordion and a bang of the drum. Peirce started shouting and Agassiz banged on the door from the outside and called, 'What's going on in there? What's happening? What trickery?'

Peirce seemed to recover his wits. Fumbling in the pitch-dark, he produced a small phosphorus ball from his pocket and lit it. In the ghastly green glow that filled the confined space, he caught the briefest of movements as the tambourine fell to the floor, but both Ira and William remained where they had been fastened, although they certainly looked more afraid than they usually did at their stage shows.

Peirce unbolted the door and stepped out. The cabinet was opened up and the boys were unfastened. They were in complete accord. The professors had witnessed the antics of John King for themselves and now they would have to testify to their abilities.

The boys' confidence was misplaced. No report was written up about the events that had transpired that day. Neither professor could understand what they had witnessed but they were still not prepared to countenance that it might offer proof of another world. They made no public statement of any kind and subsequently claimed that they had exposed the boys in flagrant trickery by the light of the phosphorus. But they had not. For once the story that supported the boys' claims was true; the deceit lay with those who claimed otherwise.

*

This experience unsettled the boys. The brothers had always suspected each other of tomfoolery when inexplicable events occurred, but now they were at a loss. Ira, who had something of a spiritual bent, began to believe that, despite their own trickery and skill, there might be some truth in this business of ghostliness after all.

Ira's newfound belief led him to view other spiritualist acts in a different light. Both brothers still attempted to uncover and understand the nature of the illusions they came across in a practical, workmanlike way, but Ira also started to look for signs of the numinous.

When he first encountered Augusta Green, with her carefully coiled hair and open expression, he thought he sensed a change in the atmosphere, an indescribable but nevertheless real sensation that hinted at the supernatural. Perhaps this was why he also felt immediately in her thrall.

Augusta was not especially well known or successful. She travelled around her home state, Michigan, and generally conducted her meetings in smaller venues, in private houses belonging to the wealthy, or in hotel public rooms that could be hired by the hour. Her skills were as an actress rather than as any kind of conjuror, and she was far more devious and manipulative than her delicate frame, pale skin and childlike features suggested. She did not charge for her meetings but donations were freely given and made for a reasonable if somewhat unpredictable income.

(She was described in the press as 'a remarkable medium – a delicately, finely organised being'. In practice her physical delicacy and pronounced femininity made her male voices far more

believable, because it seemed impossible that she could manu-
facture them. At times I am amazed at how the most ridiculous
facts serve to convince people of something while at others the
most robust proofs and demonstrations do not.)

Ira happened on her meeting one afternoon while William snoozed between an early and a late show. The hotel where they were staying, and where the séance was being given, was a ramshackle old building with ornate decorations that made it seem more like a brothel than a suitable place for a spirit-ual encounter. Nonetheless, Ira had heard good things about Augusta's abilities in the bar the night before, and with the longing born of a lifetime of trickery, he hoped that she was genuine. Ira, quite simply, wanted to be amazed.

Despite the tawdriness of the surroundings, there was an atmosphere of expectation. Only eight people sat around the oval table and Ira, used to much larger audiences, reflected that this would be a hard way to make a living. Surprisingly for such a gathering, there was enough light to make out the room and its inhabitants, if not in detail, at least distinctly. One chair next to Ira was empty, but on his other side a heavy woman with blotchy skin dabbed at her eyes with a linen handkerchief. She was not the only one. Another woman sobbed from time to time, producing a fine lace handkerchief to wipe away her tears, while a third did not actually weep but looked as if she was likely to at any minute. The rest of the group were men, who looked uneasily at each other and then even more awkwardly at the women in their midst.

The smell of lavender seemed to drift into the room carried on the lightest of breezes, and with it came a small, incontro-vertibly beautiful woman with bright red hair and creamy skin.

Her natural colouring was highlighted by the austerity of her gown, a high-necked, heavy black velvet dress that seemed to swamp her. The room was silent except for the occasional muffled sobs of the woman with the lace handkerchief. Augusta walked around the table and sat in the empty place next to Ira. The lavender scent became almost overwhelming and Ira had a vivid image of his grandmother, who had dried lavender flowers on sheets of white cotton right up until the month before her death. Always the more emotional of the brothers, he shuddered a little.

(None of this was anything to do with me; the smell was from a small, carefully hidden phial of lavender oil. Needless to say, I am a connoisseur of good quality essential oils.)

Augusta spoke, and her voice was loud and confident and seemed incongruous somehow in the face of her physical delicacy. 'We must hold hands. I ask all of you gathered here that whatever happens you will remain like this, handfasted, until our visitors have left us. Do I have your word?'

The company murmured their promise. When the required position was taken, Augusta began a soft hum which soon gave way to a louder one, ending in a half cry before she fell face down onto the table, as if in some kind of sleep. The assembled witnesses looked at each other and then back at the apparently unconscious medium. A minute passed, then two, and just as they were starting to wonder if anything was going to happen, Augusta sat bolt upright, eyes fixed and staring beyond the party at the table, as if at a figure standing just beyond them.

Her lips parted and the voice that emerged was so unmistakably, undeniably male that even Ira, who had a long acquaintance with his brother's skills at ventriloquism, looked aghast.

'I am John King. I have a message from Mary-Anne.'

The woman next to Ira tightened her grip on his hand, as if in fear that he might break the magic of the circle.

'It's my daughter, Mary-Anne. My dearest child.'

'She tells me she is well and that you must not worry for her. She is at peace now, with all the colour and shine that she had before the consumption took her life from her.'

Ira tried to squeeze the woman's hand to show some kind of sympathy but received a look of utter contempt in return.

'I have a message too for my good cousin, Ira.' And Augusta turned slightly towards his chair as she spoke. 'There will be a surprise at your next meeting. Something you do not expect to happen will occur, and something you do hope to transpire will not.'

Ira found himself both impressed and questioning. It was not surprising that she had recognised him – they had been playing across the state for the past three months – but to use the name of his own spirit against him in this way was ingenious, and he could not fathom how she might interfere with the careful choreography of their show.

For my part, I was much less overwhelmed by Miss Augusta. She seemed to be a woman in search of a man, no more, no less, and I was rather depressed by the cheap way she was going about the hunt. She had no spiritual leanings whatsoever. Rarely have I encountered someone with such utter conviction in her own disbelief in anything at all beyond the confines of the physical world.

(I must also add that I had rarely met anyone less interested in anything apart from herself.)

Ira was obviously quite taken with her, and while I could

understand his attraction, I was a little disappointed in his readiness to succumb to this, the first real attack on his bachelorhood. I was determined to see if I might play a trick on Augusta to confuse her out of her embittered cynicism and disbelief. Now was not the time, however. The séance was winding up, having passed without incident, and Ira would be alert and impatient to see how John King's premonition might come to pass.

The boys had recently changed their act. Now they were not only bound to their seats but also to each other. While this looked like a far more difficult arrangement to be extricated from so far as the audience was concerned, it was in fact easier for the brothers. As the rope was wound round one of them, the other would pull back, thus always ensuring there was some slack in the rope between them, which facilitated their escape.

Their next performance was held in Armoury Hall, Coldwater, Michigan, and Ira was delighted to see Augusta in the second row of the audience. As always, they invited two people from the audience to tie them, and Ira invited Augusta to be one of them. The atmosphere was uneasy in the audience, although neither brother was able to pinpoint exactly what was different from usual. Once they were secured and the cabinet was closed, the boys loosened themselves and William picked up the voice trumpet so that he might announce the presence of a spirit. However, before he had a chance to say anything at all, a loud female voice filled the space and addressed the spectators.

'I am afraid that John King will not be with us tonight. Instead, I, his daughter Katie, will try to entertain you.'

The brothers were somewhat flummoxed by this, but Ira remembered Augusta's message. He picked up the flute that had been carefully placed on the floor with the mouthpiece touching the chair leg so that they could find it in the pitch-black, and began to play.

The female voice began to hum along to the tune.

William, regaining his composure, began to bang loudly on the walls of the cabinet, but as he did so, the front door was pulled open from the outside. The two brothers – one with the flute in his mouth, the other punching at the air in front of him so that he stumbled, both completely free of any binding – were in full view of the audience. In front of them stood a preacher, who had opened the cabinet door to expose them.

The preacher shouted but was inaudible above the din of the audience, who now swarmed towards the stage. William grabbed a sword from the armoury wall and swung it in front of himself and his brother.

'Where is the harlot?' The preacher pushed his way into the cabinet to look for the female accomplice who had presented herself as Katie. Finding no one, he turned to rail at the brothers again.

I should have intervened, could easily have rescued the performers from their embarrassment, but I did not because, for once, I was distracted. In the second row from the back, fourth seat from the end, there was a small man with sandy hair. He sat with a notebook and an earnest expression. I looked again, but the emotion that rose through me answered my hesitation. Robert Dale Owen had come to see the Davenports. He was interested in my world, so much so that he was writing about it. This man, the most human and committed of atheists, was looking for the spiritual, and I was so taken aback by the sheer delightful improbability of it that I did not help him to find it when I had my opportunity.

(In fact, I later discovered that it was not so surprising. Robert's father, Robert Owen, was a celebrated philanthropist who had greatly improved the lot of factory workers at his mill in New Lanark, Scotland, while also developing the first scheme for infant childcare. Owen Senior was the man I had watched at the factory who was concerned by his son's tenderness. Despite decades of atheism, he converted to spiritualism four years before he died. Robert was exploring his late father's beliefs and hoping for a message.)

The people swarmed angrily but then a female voice went up, somewhere to the left of where Ira and William were trying to hold off the crowds.

'Help, please, please, help! Oh, get off me, you brute!' Somehow this voice, with Augusta's well-bred nuances, was so loud that it was heard perfectly among the din, and for a moment the crowd was distracted from the focus of their ire.

It was enough. Augusta, who was in fact right next to the brothers, grabbed Ira's hand and weaved her way through the melee, with William trying his best to follow them, towards a concealed panel at the back of the room where she knew there was a staircase that she often used in her own performances.

I saw them escape safely, but, more significantly, I watched a solitary figure close his scribblings and make his way to the exit at the back of the room.

That November in 1861, I failed the Davenports. The disturbance was widely reported across the state as proof that they were fraudulent hucksters. Yet the regret I felt for this setback in their career was nothing to my utter dismay that I had surely given Robert nothing but doubt.

Augusta took the brothers to her family home and they made

preparations to travel onwards to Richmond, Indiana. However, Ira had no wish to leave their saviour and before they left, he asked Augusta if she might do him the honour of becoming his wife. She accepted, and instead of continuing with their tour, both William and Ira remained in Michigan until 22 February 1862, when the couple were wed.

Augusta surprised me by proving to be a good wife to Ira. She was solicitous and kind; the only point on which they differed absolutely was her refusal to believe in any kind of spirit world. The marriage contract had brought the gift of shared secrets, professional trickery unmasked, and both Ira and William greatly admired the skill Augusta had shown in her profession, a talent that had even deceived Ira, albeit briefly.

However, although Ira was fully aware of the power of illusion, he still believed in his heart that there was some truth in the notion of a spirit world. This was in part due to my interference, which neither of the brothers could account for, but which William resolutely believed was Ira's doing, a kind of long-term joke that he would never admit to.

It troubled me that Augusta should attempt to dissuade her husband from his faith and so I decided that once again I would interfere with these two boys – no longer boys but men now, yet still, in some way, children to me.

Within one year of their marriage, sadness came to Augusta's life with the death of her father. He had been a kindly man, and – just as Ira Davenport Senior with his sons – had retained a conviction in his daughter's supernatural abilities that was both touching and deluded.

He was not young and his death was neither protracted nor unexpected. He sat in his armchair, looking at a new programme that his son-in-law had prepared for a forthcoming tour, and drifted from this world into the next. Augusta was distraught. Her mother had predeceased her father by several years and now she found herself an orphan in the world. After the funeral the couple retired to Augusta's room in her father's house and Ira held her while she wept. Her sorrow moved into shared tenderness and, as is often the case following a bereavement, lovemaking reaffirmed the life and love of those who were left behind.

The pain of loss gave way to knowledge of new life in waiting, and Augusta informed Ira that she would not be travelling with them on their next tour because she believed she was with child. She remained alone in the home they had made together in Chicago, Illinois, while the brothers' tour took them first to New York, then to Wisconsin.

Now, with her swelling belly, and company only from newly made friends and kindly neighbours, I saw a vulnerable Augusta, one who might be more susceptible to faith, who perhaps could be brought to share her husband's belief in me. I began with a dream.

(There is a point in the night when mortal sleep patterns change: the eyes move restlessly, the brain is active; it is known now as paradoxical sleep, because the brain becomes active as if awake. Only at this point is it possible to suggest ideas to another consciousness, and these ideas – my ideas – then manifest themselves as dreaming. It does not require a great deal of effort; the skill is in being able to observe the point during slumber at which it becomes possible.)

The child in Augusta's belly would never live, this I knew with certainty, and so I sent her an image of the coffin that would carry her unborn baby. And just to make it more poignant, I made her dead father carry the tiny white coffin and place it at the foot of her bed.

The day following the first of the dreams, she dismissed it as superstitious fancy. She spoke sternly to herself and wrote a letter to her husband saying that she was becoming silly in her confinement, given to morbid fancy. The second night I repeated the dream, but this time her father was seen to weep for the loss of his grandchild. The sight of her lost, beloved father in tears was more than Augusta could bear. She feared for her child with a superstitious dread that no doctor – and she summoned four different local practitioners – could assuage.

Ira sent friendly, domestic letters about the choice of decoration for the room that would serve as a nursery, and about the christening they would have. Augusta replied that it was all pointless, that the child would be dead, that she knew not how she could foresee it, but that it would be so.

And then something occurred that I swear was not of my doing, and the dream changed again. Now Augusta's father arrived carrying not a child's coffin but one for a full-grown adult. The spectre placed the coffin by her bedside and even spoke, lest there be any doubt, saying simply, 'There, daughter.' He left the room – the dream of a room – and returned again, but this time with the child's coffin that had grown so familiar to Augusta, placing it on top of that which he had carried for his daughter.

Ira was worried when Augusta sent him news of this latest dream, but he put the fancy down to his wife's pregnancy. The tour was doing well, and with the child on the way they would need some money to shore them up for the first few weeks after the birth, when he planned to stay at home. In one of his letters he wrote:

Dearest One,

It is only normal that our loss should lead to this misgiving. Be assured that I shall be with you both soon and that when I lie beside you, the babe resting between us, you will see these imaginings for the dark fancies that they are.

But instead of preparing a christening, Augusta was making arrangements for the death she felt sure awaited her in a matter of months. She ordered a coffin for her baby – small, white, lined with silk of the palest pink – and for herself she requested a box of poplar wood, lined with dark red.

She went into early labour towards the end of June. A midwife and a doctor were called and attended immediately. They heard her screams as they came up the driveway, and as they were ushered into her room they saw that the bed was stained with her blood. It was not an easy dying. Augusta tried to push out the baby, retaining some small sliver of hope that it had all been an illusion, and that at the end of all this pain, there might be new life. But all that came from her was the corpse of a baby girl. The metallic smell of iron filled the room, her screams changed to weeping, as more and more blood followed the dead child, and the sheets became saturated. The midwife placed her hand against the forehead that thrashed against the pillow, then was still. The doctor pronounced Augusta Davenport dead at half past seven in the morning on 29 June 1863.

But to Ira too I had given a dream. It was my warning, a

preparation for the pain I knew would possess him. From a cloudy sky a bird had descended, a beauteous, colourful thing, with a sweeping tail and rainbow-patterned wings. The bird became his wife, who lay beside him and fell asleep, but then would not waken. He knew it for a premonition of her death, and despite his brother's scepticism he set off for home that night, interrupting the tour.

When he arrived, the funeral arrangements were completed. The burial service took place in Augusta's home town of Adrian, Michigan, and the prayers were led by the spiritualist minister that she had requested.

(Augusta's grave is in a very cheerful sort of cemetery, not one where people are often given to imaginings of the spiritual kind.)

Ira would believe until his death that her spirit awaited him in a world beyond, and, despite his own carefully crafted mastery, he sought her voice, her image, her touch, at the home of every charlatan in the country during the months immediately following her demise. So it was that Ira became a convert as a result of my dream – a desirable but completely unintentional side effect.

The 'spirit narrator' seems to have taken some of this account from Nichols' 1864 book, *A Biography of the Brothers Davenport*. The quote about Augusta I managed to track down to Powell's (1864) *A Sketch of the Lives of the Davenport Brothers*. The letters, however, are more puzzling from a scholarly perspective. They are all here at the Magic Circle but prior to our acquisition were in a closed collection. For the sake of completion I include their references in this note:

- Augusta to Ira Davenport, Feb. 1863, Chicago, Illinois, 134/727
- Augusta to Ira Davenport, u/d, Chicago, Illinois, 134/729
- Ira to Augusta Davenport, May 1863, Wisconsin, 134/736.

The obvious conclusion is that the writer had some connection to the previous owners, members of the extended Davenport family, so I intend to try to contact them. The grave of Augusta Davenport, born 1841, died June 1863, is in Oakwood Cemetery, Adrian, Lenawee County, Michigan, Plot B11-39. It is, as the narrator suggests, a bright and lovely place.

This chapter marks the development of what I will refer to as the 'dream abilities' of the entity but also of a sinister side to the narrator's character that has been missing in the earlier accounts. The very human emotion of jealousy inherent in her dislike of Augusta seems in direct contradiction to the ghostly character she is purporting to be. Her triumph at Ira's conversion highlights her callous disregard for Augusta and the baby. This is unpleasant stuff.

There is some consistency with the Koons chapter: once again the writer is somehow brought into the presence of a certain group of humans because they call the name King.
[AM 2007]

The owners of the private collection which had housed the letters until 1990 are now deceased, and without descendants, so it is impossible to ascertain whether the writer of this piece had access to them or not. [AM 2008]

In retrospect I find my remarks about jealousy very badly thought through. Surely Katie's concern was the result of her ability to correctly deduce the selfishness inherent in Augusta before her marriage and her wish to protect the Davenports from it. She doesn't say she caused Augusta's death, only that she had a premonition of it. Given the repercussions of her early interference when Robert Dale Owen almost died, it would have been unwise for her to try to intervene.

And the dreams. Now I know what stuff those dreams are made of. [AM 2012]

Spirit Writing Fragment Two
1863, Magic Circle Collection

I see a man writing a letter. He looks to be sixty or so, but his face is not ravaged by wild living. The furrow lines that mark his brow are those of care; his face is crumpled with concern but lit by the brightness of his eyes, shining, questioning eyes that ask so much.

I know that it is him. This is a much better sight than the glimpse I had across the crowded hall in the midst of the melee of discontent. The compassionate child from the factory, the generous husband, grown more serious, is writing:

Can you look forward to the future of our country and imagine any state of things in which, with slavery still existing, we should be assured of permanent peace? I cannot. We can constitutionally extirpate slavery at this time. But if we fail to do this, then unless we intend hereafter to violate the Constitution, we shall have a fugitive slave law in operation whenever the war is over. Shall the North have sacrificed a hundred thousand lives and two thousand millions of treasure to come to that at last? Not even a guaranty of peace purchased at so enormous a cost?

He asks, no, he demands that slavery be abolished, and I feel a flicker of pride in my youthful wrongdoing. I wonder why

I see this now, when I half expected punishment for the dead woman and her dead child, and not solace. I wish that my part in this might be recorded for posterity.

The dating of the original of this spirit writing is as stated and it was donated to us from a private collection in the States. No one has accessed it here, yet the 'Italian' author must have known of its existence. Perhaps, astonishingly, there is a family link between the nineteenth-century writer in the US and the present-day Cesenatico one. Surely this kind of practical coincidence is far more likely than any fanciful and absurd alternative. Unfortunately the owner of the collection, despite his great wealth, is reclusive and now suffers from an extreme obsessive-compulsive disorder that makes it difficult for him to leave his home or even to communicate in any meaningful way by telephone or electronic means. [AM 2007]

A SÉANCE IN REGENT STREET

By 1864, the Civil War made touring impossible for the Davenports and there was also the question of conscription. The obvious place to go was England; it was the place of their mother's birth and spiritualism was enjoying a surge in popularity there. William Fay, their old friend and fellow entertainer from Buffalo, would accompany them because the voyage would be too much for their father, whose health had suffered from their travels.

(I confess to some small interference in this matter. Scotland, the site of my first interception and the Owen family triumph, would be close by. I might not be able to control my flow of information yet, but I could at least influence the people to whom I was associated and tied to at this time, and who seemed to bring me into being.)

On 27 August 1864, the Davenports set sail from New York on the *Britannia*. I was content to go but had no choice over my attachment in this period; it was as if some invisible thread bound me to those who called for me, as if they had brought me into being. It was a joy to see them, with their easy confidence and surety in their success, waving from the ship as it sailed out, the sun glinting on the water, shining on their wide smiles. They docked first at Glasgow on 9 September but moved quickly on, finally reaching London two days later, ready for their first private séance at the home of Dion Boucicault, whose celebrity would guarantee them good media coverage from the outset.

(The Glasgow stop was a brief moment of hope for me. I would have 'caught my breath' if such a thing had been possible.)

Dion Boucicault and his second wife, Agnes Kelly, had only recently returned to London society and acquired a new apartment in Regent Street. Their attainment had been a rapid turnaround from the bankruptcy that had threatened to overtake them just one year previously and they were revelling in their newly regained position. For the most part it was due to the outstanding popularity of *The Colleen Bawn*, Dion's play in which Agnes played the title role.

The séance was not, as some papers claimed at the time, an attempt by Boucicault to see if the brothers were genuine or not. Boucicault would have done everything that he possibly could to ensure the meeting went well; he wanted to be remembered as the man who brought the newest and best act to London.

The first séance was held in the new Boucicault home on 28 September. The brothers and Fay were completely recovered from the voyage and adequate time had been allowed for the press to be made aware of their arrival. Michael Faraday, who would have been a most exciting observer, and one that I would have taken immense delight in bewildering, declined to attend with a letter:

Gentlemen – I am obliged by your courteous invitation, but really have been so disappointed by the manifestations to which my notice has at different times been called, that I am not encouraged to give more attention to them; and therefore leave those to which you refer in the hands of the professors of legerdemain. If spirit communications, not utterly worthless, should happen to start into activity, I will trust the spirits to find out for themselves how they can move my attention. I am tired of them. With thanks, I am very truly yours.

M. Faraday

Ira penned an invitation to Cromwell Varley, the telegraph engineer and innovator, who accepted with alacrity. Having been warned that any specific mention of ghosts or spirits might cause enmity and adverse publicity from certain quarters more inclined to remain in the favour of the clergy, the brothers were careful not to claim any psychic abilities in their publicity leaflets. They stated simply that, in their presence, certain 'physical manifestations' took place. The beholders could watch and judge as to whether they were achieved by natural or supernatural means.

The séance was an intimate event, in Boucicault's large drawing room, where the furniture had been removed to make room for the twenty or so attendants and the Davenports' cabinet, which was assembled there. All that remained was the chandelier, a small table and sofa, and twenty-six cane-bottomed chairs.

The tricks were no different from usual but seemed to gain an added conviction from the intimacy of their environment. The instruments – a guitar, violin, tambourine, two bells and a brass trumpet, which had been purchased only that morning especially for the event – were played loudly if not always tunefully, and the brothers were shown to be tied securely at the end of the performance.

However, instead of the usual rapturous applause, there was only some restrained clapping as well as a few remarks about how skilful the boys were at knots. This was clearly not going to be as easy as they – and indeed I – had hoped. Ira and William remained fastened in their chairs; the crowd started to lose interest and turned to each other to discuss the event, while Lord Bury, one of the audience members, stood as if to approach the cabinet and either examine it or release the boys. I did what I had been too distracted to do in the séance where they had last come to grief. I concentrated very hard, picturing in my mind a small, white, delicate hand, such as might belong to a dead girl or young woman, and was very pleased when it manifested, floating in the air, just in front of the tethered brothers. It was a little hazy, but the quivery nature of its appearance just seemed to add to its ghostly nature. This immediately drew the attention of the onlookers back to the cabinet with much delight and surprise, and far more conviction. The gathering was an unqualified success.

Boucicault wrote to the *Era*, listing the attendees and attesting to their witnessing of the most inexplicable event. In particular he wrote, 'a very white, thin, female hand and wrist quivered for several seconds in the air above. This appearance drew a general exclamation from all the party.'

For the rest of the year we were engaged, with much success, for public séances at the Hanover Square rooms, as well as private ones at the houses of various members of the gentry around the capital. However, the press showed much less enthusiasm than the public. The *Standard* dismissed them as 'vulgar jugglery', a particularly offensive phrase, because it hints at the cheap sleight-of-hand work performed on the side of the road. The Davenports were *prestidigitators*. The *Spectator*, ignoring my haunting and lovely manifestation of a hand, put it all down to a kind of cheap escapology. The *Daily News* (and here I have to pause to collect myself) went so far as to say:

> It is both surprising and deplorable that persons of education and standing should not only countenance but welcome and applaud such efforts and that influential organs of opinion should be found ready to give them direct encouragement. (*Daily News*, 8 October 1864)

The *Morning Star*, snobbish to the last, dismissed the meeting as 'tedious, dull and vulgar'. Only the *Globe*, while being equally condemnatory, threw out an interesting challenge, and one that I would certainly have needed to help the Davenports take up:

> We say, let the brother conjurors make their money; but if they are to be put to the test, let the test be applied, not by men of science, but by a board of conjurors under a competent chairman. (*Globe*, 8 October 1864)

Vilification by Fleet Street did not have the slightest effect on the financial awards and satisfaction brought by public fandom, at least not in London. As well as the cabinet performances, Ira and William organised tabletop séances for smaller rooms.

The mechanics of the trickery used in these had changed very little from when they were children in their parents' parlour. A dummy hand covered in phosphorus could float in the air with the help of some fine thread and a pulley operated by foot. Wooden instruments could be controlled by movements of the feet or legs to make the table rise, rock or sound as if it was being rapped. However, there was one piece of machinery that had been damaged during the trip.

William had designed a small wooden scissor-like contraption with a hammer on the end which fastened onto each kneecap (he was already seated at a table covered in cloth when the participants arrived). By moving his knees together and apart, he could concertina the hammer up to hit the underside of the table with whatever frequency was desired. One of the legs had broken in transit, and on the recommendation of Boucicault, William took it to a local craftsman, John Nevil Maskelyne, who also had something of a reputation as a conjuror. This young man was curious about the purpose of the piece of wood, but William evaded his questions. On leaving, he handed him a five pound note, almost twice the cost of the repair, saying pointedly, 'I'm sure a smart fellow like you could use the loose change. And in return, just forget you ever saw me.'

There was other trouble on the tour, unrelated to any garrulousness on the part of the conjuror. Both Ira and William were always adamant that their tour itinerary was controlled by the desires of their guiding spirit, John King. The north of England had little appeal for me, but I seemed to be able to do very little to dissuade the brothers from going there. I saw it as an unnecessary detour on the road to Scotland, but both men seemed to like the gentle landscapes and the down-to-earth nature of the people who crowded into working men's halls and small assembly rooms to see them. But this practical frame of mind was also their undoing, for after a few successful shows in York and Manchester, they found that in Liverpool, the audience was far from enthusiastic and went so far as to tear the cabinet to pieces, just to prove that there was some trickery concealed within. Similar occurrences in Huddersfield and Leeds drove the brothers and Mr Fay back to London with a new companion they had acquired along the way. Robert Cooper was a writer and owner of the *London Spiritual Times* magazine. He had become impressed with the Davenports following their very first meeting at Boucicault's apartment and had subsequently joined them on part of their tour with the intention of writing a book about their travels.

I was anxious to have some control over the next leg of the tour and so turned my mind to how best to effect it.

(I am non-corporeal and can't really speak in the way that a human might. I have to implant anything I would like to say into someone's head and then get them to pronounce it for me. Commonly called 'direct voice' mediumship, it can lay the medium open to all sorts of charges of trickery and acting. Of the two brothers, I decided that William could be used to better effect. I would have to make him firstly hear me in his mind and then use his ventriloquist skills so that it would sound as if the words were coming from a disembodied spirit, as in fact they would be, at a point in the room that was not obviously the same as the one occupied by his physical body.)

A meeting was arranged at the Great Western Hotel in Paddington. Mr Fay, the brothers and Robert Cooper convened in the downstairs lounge to discuss where they might next travel. Ira proposed that they invoke John King and ask for his advice, so the party retired upstairs to the suite of rooms the brothers had taken.

The speaking trumpet was placed at the far end of the room and the gentlemen seated themselves on two rush chairs and a blue plush chaise and sofa which were all clustered around the fireplace. For once, the fire was left burning, although all the lights were extinguished. It was February and the snow of the month before had still not fully melted so that a chill pervaded the room even when it was sealed.

There was silence at first, then, as anticipated, a voice came from the tube. However, it was not the one they had all expected. To their astonishment, this voice was undeniably female, and very insistent.

'I am Katie,' I said.

Ira cleared his throat and asked if she had seen the recent problems in the north, and if she had a recommended course for them to follow.

'Scotland,' I replied. 'France and Ireland.'

'France?' Cooper sounded hopeful. In truth he was sick of the pervasive British dampness and lack of light and had visions of an elegant Parisian court.

'Yes, but that too will be beset with difficulties, and it will be a brief stay.'

Ira was starting to get annoyed with William. He couldn't pursue it because Cooper was there, but he had thought the agreement was to try and go somewhere warmer, not further north, where it was sure to be even wetter and colder, and probably more hostile, than where they had just come from.

(For my part I find the human preoccupation with the weather extremely tedious.)

I concentrated and did not waver. 'Scotland,' said the voice, a very sweet, lilting voice, but determined nevertheless.

When the lights were once again put up, the gathering discussed what they had heard. William seemed genuinely surprised, and Ira was puzzled; Fay and Cooper were utterly convinced. Cooper would later write how the voice haunted him, for it was so clearly not that of a ventriloquist, but of a practical, earnest, honest woman.

It was decided that a trip to France would be followed by a visit to Ireland, and then to Scotland.

The French trip was brief, not because of me, but rather because of the bureaucracy needed to perform there and the very late acquisition of the necessary licence. It was not, however, without some small success, and the Emperor and Empress commissioned a private meeting in the Palace of St Cloud in which I took no part whatsoever because the brothers were performing beautifully.

Ireland came next, and, fearing that the fatigue induced by the gruelling tour of over two hundred different venues might lead to a change in plans, I found it necessary to reiterate my intention that we go to Scotland. I decided to try a different approach, sensing that a message from John might be heeded better than one from Katie.

During a stop off in Dublin, when William Fay had retired to bed with a small dram of whisky, I decided that he might make an interesting subject for an intervention.

In his dream that night he saw John and Katie King as two separate physical entities in a lascivious embrace. Before he woke, John spoke to him and said that he had a message for the brothers. At breakfast the following morning, Fay announced, 'John wants to speak to you. He came to me after I got to bed last night.'

(He did not elaborate on the nature of my dream, which had pleased him but did not seem a suitable topic for breakfast.)

As soon as they had finished eating, the gentlemen retired to the Davenports' room. Finding that the flimsy curtain offered little in the way of darkness, they nailed a rug over the window. This was far more complicated than it sounds, and after several attempts I was getting impatient. I had William intervene, in the guise of John King's voice, which bellowed, 'There, that will do – that's dark enough.'

Ira rushed to place the horn on the bed so that John's voice might be amplified and then returned to the others, who stood gathered in front of the rug hanging precariously from the wall above the window frame. Cooper reached a hand up to hold it over a chink of light that threatened to destroy their efforts.

Fearing that he was becoming too concerned about the rug again, I addressed him directly in my deepest, most commanding voice. 'Cooper, I want you to go to ...' I paused, thinking quickly, 'Russia, with the brothers. You have done good work in this country, but it is no use stopping any longer – get on to Scotland first, as fast as you can, and then go straight away to Russia.'

(Russia was a spontaneous choice for me. At that time I had only scant notion of any dealings that the Imperial family had, and of none that might interest me.)

For dramatic emphasis, I made the horn levitate from the bed and crash onto the floor. Cooper and Fay looked astonished; William and Ira regarded each other warily. Seeing that each looked as perplexed as the other, Ira assumed that it really was a message from the spirit world, while William worried about the fact that he seemed to be projecting a voice that had a mind of its own.

The areas around Edinburgh and Glasgow were not what I had expected. The audiences in the small surrounding towns were far too similar to those in the north of England and I found that I had to add to the act on several occasions just to keep unruly crowds at bay. But the cities themselves were graceful. In Edinburgh we had the biggest success of the tour, in the Assembly Rooms, just as spring was thawing out the grassy slopes below the castle and flowers were pushing through earth that was soft again.

In Glasgow I saw Charlotte Street, where Robert was born, and I studied its elegant Georgian town houses, searching for any remnant of his past that might bring him closer to me again. We went to Lanark, a small market town near Glasgow but surrounded by gently rolling hills, and I vividly recollected that first vision I had of him close by, in New Lanark, in that sandstone house against the blurred landscape of rainy weather.

The people of Lanark were a cheerful lot, and it seemed that Robert's father's mill, New Lanark Mill, had brought prosperity to the region and a kind of contentment that we did not see elsewhere on our travels. Or perhaps it was just that I wished it to be so, for none of my travelling companions remarked on it, or even seemed to notice. Cooper, in fact, was glad when we left Scotland, making only a passing reference to it in his book, although acknowledging the great success of our Edinburgh engagement. The next destination was to be Russia, and the journey would be an arduous one for the Davenports and for the stalwart Mr Fay. Cooper, bemoaning the bleakness of the weather, even in the summer months, could not face the thought of a winter visit to an even colder clime and declined to join them.

A few sections of this chapter rely greatly on *Spiritual Experiences* by Robert Cooper, London (1867) and the author has obviously quoted freely. For example, the letter by Faraday appears on p. 113 of Cooper. However, the letter written by Boucicault to the *Era* is more obscure and indicates again the scholarship of the writer. A copy can be found in the University of Kent Special Collections in the Templeman Library.

The philosopher Eduard von Hartmann's 1885 *Der Spiritismus* presents an understanding of the issues around the form a spirit might take. His description of the related effects closely resemble those presented in this section. Hartmann posited the existence of a 'nervous mediumistic force'. This force could move or transform objects and create physical or voice materialisations. However, Hartmann discounted the possibility that this was a spirit entity, but claimed it was the psychic power of the medium which he or she was able to use to create 'mental pictures' for the participants of a séance. The medium thus created a 'dream theatre' for the observers. Hartmann's description of a power working through the medium is excellent, but trying to disprove the existence of one fantastical belief system – spiritualism –

by using the equally ridiculous notion of psychic ability, is hardly sound argument.

Similarly, more recent works, such as De Groot's *The Reality of Psychic Phenomena* (2003), persist in the idea that what is often claimed as a haunting or spirit manifestation is the result of human psychic ability rather than an indication of any other kind of life form. The Cesenatico texts assume the veracity of both phenomena.

The reader is also given an explanation for the frequent use of ventriloquist tricks in séances at the time, one which highlights the spirit's factual existence (ventriloquism is not just trickery but a device for communication within the text itself) while reinforcing the point of the earlier chapter that the presence of chicanery does not in itself tell us anything about whether ghosts do or do not exist. [AM 2007]

Now rereading this I find I am moved by the fact that she could not yet be independent, and that her period of freedom to move of her own volition was so brief in what is such an interminably long state of being. I am fascinated by the ruses she adopts in order to guide the Davenport group and puzzled as to why she chose Russia, especially given what transpired there. My notes from my first reading seem ponderous and misguided. I understand the rationality I held so dear, but it is as alien to me now as the thought of ghosts or telekinesis were to me then. I believe. I know that Katie exists. I make no attempt to defend my conviction because it would be pointless. No logical arguments are needed when one is possessed of absolute certainty. I am like a religious convert who feels he has known God and cannot deny the existence of something that, for him, is as irrefutable as water or sunlight or soil.

My faith in this other world gives me hope for what may come after this, something I never expected to find. Perhaps there are worse things even than death in this universe of ours. I find comfort in the notion and try to explain it to Peter, but immediately regret it. He looks worried, afraid that I am half mad with the sickness that corrodes me. His eyes well up; he is not yet used to accepting the inevitable consequence of my illness. To speak of it brings him only pain and so I don't.

[AM 2012]

LANARK

I am dragged back, without comprehension, to see a small, busy market town, and recognise it as Lanark, that ancient dwelling place where I might sense the spirits of thousands upon thousands of years past if such a thing were possible. It does not look as it did on my recent visit with the Davenports. It is Lanark in 1816, fifty years ago, to the day. There is thick frost and bright blue sky rather than the grey drizzle that usually covers the town, but despite the bitter cold, the streets are lined, in some places four rows deep, with not only the townspeople but others who have travelled considerable distances to be there for this event. Brightly coloured bunting hangs across the rows of facing cottages, and the Provost's lamp – the ornate gas lamp that stands outside the front of the Provost's house at the very top of the High Street – displays a Russian Imperial flag.

The Clydesdale Inn, an excellent coach stop with good fare for travellers, displays both Scottish and Russian flags as well as a large banner with a picture of King George III.

The High Street slopes steeply down to St Nicholas Parish Church and the square, where a village band is preparing to play. It is a motley array of instruments – some fiddles, a trumpet, an accordion, a selection of types of drum, and in front of these, two men wielding bagpipes.

When the music starts up it takes me by surprise. The mournful note of the pipes is in contrast to the celebratory music which causes some of the crowd who are gathered to jig where they stand. They are simple country dances, constrained by the throng, but there is a joy in seeing a handsome boy of twenty or so swing a girl with ash-blonde curls by the arm, so that she laughs.

On the brow of the hill, I see the cause for all this celebration. It is a magnificent procession, the likes of which I'm sure that no one in this company has ever seen. There are four high-stepping black horses, with saddles that are inset with gold, stark against the crisp white trousers of their riders. These men wear jackets, as dark as their chargers, but with gold braid on the lapels, cuffs and collars, as well as along the arms and down the front. High black hats with glittering embellishment catch the sun, and many among the crowds stare, open mouthed, at their splendour.

These riders give way to four more, in uniforms of scarlet and dark grey. The plainness of the trousers is broken by a bright red stripe on the outside of each leg, which perfectly matches the jackets of this next quartet. This time the epaulettes and flashings are silver, as is the chain that hangs around the tall fur hat, topped with a thin white feather. Miraculously, the feather stands almost upright, swaying only slightly in this, the stillest and coldest of days.

Amidst this second group of four is a young man on a white horse; his uniform is similar to those of his companions but highlighted by gold, not silver. His skin is pale, almost translucent, and his eyes are a light grey colour that suggests a softness, belying his obvious rank and importance. His sandy, almost red hair *might be native to this Scottish town, yet everything else – the high arched cheekbones and thick lips with a pronounced cupid's bow, the assurance of his bearing and his ease with the opulence around him – betrays his identity. He is Grand Duke Nicholas, younger brother of Alexander I, also known as Alexander the Blessed, Emperor and Autocrat of all the Russias. He is here at the request of Robert Dale Owen's father, and having heard about the New Lanark social experiment, for who in Europe has not, he has come to the town to see it for himself. As the procession reaches the church, the door swings open and I see my Robert and his father come out of the gloom into the brightness of the day.*

Despite the freezing cold and the soft flakes of snow that are beginning to descend from the sky which is somehow still blue, still clear, I am, again, suffused with gently warming heat.

Owen smiles benevolently at the musicians, and the Grand Duke rides towards him, pausing only to lean over and hand the band leader – an elderly man waving a small baton at the assemblage – a ten pound note. The Grand Duke arrives at the church door and dismounts, and the two men lead him into the church.

I see the party later, when the streets are cleared and the sky is dark, and a light dusting of snow, like sprinkled fine sugar, covers bunting and decorations and stone. The Grand Duke, two of his men, Owen, his wife and four children, including Robert Dale, are now all seated at dinner in Braxfield, the house of my earlier dreams. There is a long oak table that easily accommodates the Owen family as well as the Grand Duke and his two attendants, one of whom is his interpreter. The Grand Duke is enthralled by Owen's description of his social experiment at New Lanark, and very taken too with Robert, the enthusiastic eldest son, who is filled with zeal for a future of good works and philanthropy. He has grown well, is now a strong boy of fifteen, with little trace of the sickness that he suffered just four years before. His face is not a handsome one; I recognise all the same attributes I saw in his older self that might be called plain. But he is like a religious convert, so bright is his fervour to make the world a better place, and Nicholas, who is after all no more than twenty years and six months old, is caught and captivated by his eagerness and ideology.

The food is wholesome fare but seems to please the Grand Duke with its simplicity and freshness. It is a merry gathering and I am filled with pride in this life I have saved.

The Grand Duke suggests sending two million men to Russia from the surplus population that Britain is believed to have, so that he might create similar manufacturing communities.

The children he has seen that afternoon are a delight, with their dancing and education, clean clothes and good manners. Owen's children are exemplary and he asks that they too come to Russia with him and the surplus men, so that he might learn from them.

Owen shakes his head, says he is happy where he is, that he is pleased with the happiness of his workers, delighted by the financial rewards his experiment is bringing him, and that his children are too young to leave home just yet. Robert Dale moves as if he will interrupt, but a look from his mother silences him. The interpreter, to break the temporary awkwardness, jokes about the crest which decorates the silver plate at table. It resembles the double-headed Russian eagle, and Owen immediately insists that the Grand Duke take it as a keepsake, to remember what he has seen in New Lanark and to inspire him when he returns to his home. Robert Dale looks upset; his mother appears close to tears; yet still the silver is wrapped and given to the Grand Duke's man at the table. I watch as the Grand Duke and his companions retire to their room, see Robert's eyes fill with tears at his mother's distress and at the loss of something which has brightened the imaginative games of his childhood. I am saddened, and more surprisingly, moved by the human sentimentality of his sense of loss.

This account is a fuller version of events than that presented in Owen's *Threading My Way*, though the various mediums responsible for most of the spirit writing relating to both John and Katie King seem to be very familiar with the work.

In a letter from Robert Dale Owen to J. N. Tifft (1866) he remarks, 'I have often wondered what small influence we might have exerted on the future of this most tyrannous reign had we chosen otherwise' (Robert Dale Owen, Miscellaneous Papers, 1844–70, Special Collections, the Filson Historical Society, Louisville). However, Owen later reminisced in his autobiography that the youthful boy he met showed no propensity towards his future atrocities: 'If my impressions, such as they were at fifteen, are trustworthy, there was nothing at that early age in the future emperor to indicate the arbitrary and cruel spirit which, in later years, marked his subjugation of Poland, and his armed intervention against the Hungarian patriots; nothing in the appearance of the youth of twenty to prefigure the stern autocrat who was by and by to revive against his own subjects the capital punishment which had been humanely abolished by the Empress Elizabeth.'

Robert describes his mother's feeling and his own

sympathy with it in *Threading My Way*. 'My mother, good, sensible matron, took exception to any such proceeding. In the case of a friend to whom we owed kindness or gratitude, or to anyone who would value the offer for the donor's sake, she would not have grudged her nice forks and spoons, but to a possessor of thousands, a two days' acquaintance, who was not likely to bestow a second thought on the things! – in all which I cordially agree with her, especially when I found William Sheddon, our butler, lamenting over his empty cases, the glittering contents of which had often excited my childish admiration.' The writer's remark 'brightened the imaginative games of his childhood' suggests again his or her familiarity with Owen's book. [AM 2007]

Last year, on a visit to my parents in Scotland, I pursued these references and found both Lanark and New Lanark to be largely unchanged. The Clydesdale Inn, which was favoured by Dickens and Wordsworth, still exists as a 'Wetherspoons' pub and is believed by many locals to be haunted. The resident ghost purportedly takes the form of a young woman who wanders the narrow corridor of the upper floor listlessly, ceaselessly pacing back and forth, back and forth, dressed in a long, tattered grey dress that trails along the floor behind her. Unsurprisingly, given the popularity and concomitant commercial success of haunted pubs, there have been several sightings reported by the owners and some of the staff, always on winter nights and almost exclusively when there is or has recently been snowfall in the town.

These 'spirit writing' pages were donated by the former
owner of one of the New Lanark 'mill cottages' in 1950; her
great-grandmother had passed them down to her. I tried to
make contact during my stay to see if I might glean information
as to their authorship but was told the last family member died
without issue ten years ago. I realise now that I was careless
in my earlier note too, and that the dating is also an issue,
because if the spirit writing is from 1866 as it states, then it
could not have relied on the Owen account, which was not
published until 1874. It is a puzzle that can only be solved by
assuming that the writer knew Owen or someone in his family
who was present at the events described, or perhaps Owen
made earlier writings that foreshadowed those of his book
which were known to people in his circle. The recently opened
New Lanark archive is a veritable trove of information about
the Owen family and, as none of it is yet available online, I
took time to look at the various manuscripts and see if the
archival information corroborated that of the ghost scripts
generally or indeed offered some solution to the question of
the dates. However, while no source was able to help me
account for the dating anomaly, I was unsurprised to find
that all other document content dovetailed perfectly with the
information in the scripts. The author has obviously made
considerable effort to build consistency between the fictitious
narrative and the known facts. [AM 2009]

Finally, in the last weeks, I return to Lanark. I look up at the dereliction of the first floor of the Clydesdale Inn, in marked contrast to the cheerful, welcoming lounge and bar below. Despite suspicious, questioning looks from passers-by, I stare and stare at the broken window panes, hoping for a glimpse of shabby silk, a hint of movement from a tired but restless spirit. But it is not wintertime. She is only ever seen in months of snow. I have seen my last winter, and despite the fact I love the sun beyond all things, I am sad, so very sad of it.

[AM 2012]

A SÉANCE FOR THE CZAR

St Petersburg was a grand city. There is no other word for it. The buildings seemed bigger and more set apart from each other, as if so designed that the traveller might better admire the splendour of the architecture. Despite the ninety hours of travelling that preceded our arrival, Ira and William were immediately invited to give a series of private séances for members of the nobility around the city.

A séance was also held for the press, who took great delight in John King's ability to speak Russian. William had spent much of the trip learning a series of exclamations in that language, as well as the ventriloquism techniques necessary to make them. They were very different from those required by the English language and I was impressed by his diligence and perseverance. His new skills paid off and the press were unanimous in their praise of the brothers' obvious spiritual abilities. It was, they concluded, impossible that the brothers could escape from the bindings tying them to the benches within the cabinet, and yet instruments played, and a voice, definitely not that of a human being, offered instruction and amusement in their own language.

The Davenports' success brought still more invitations: the spirit cabinet was set up and dismantled at the home of an admiral, the winter quarters of a count, and the residence of the French Ambassador.

This latter event included in its audience of fifty invited guests the brother-in-law of Emperor Alexander II, Count Scroffenhoff. The Count, as well as the Ambassador, was invited to spend an hour examining the spirit cabinet before the show began, so that they might attest to the genuineness of the events they were about to witness. The Count tied the knots that bound Ira to his bench; the Ambassador secured William on the opposite side.

When the instruments played and the female voice that introduced itself as Katie addressed them in fluent French, they found themselves 'perfectly satisfied as to the inexplicability of the manifestations'.

Finally the most important invitation of all was sent. On the evening of 9 January 1866 they were asked, by special request of His Majesty, to perform in the Winter Palace for the Emperor Alexander II and other members of the Imperial family.

The meeting was to take place in the Concert Hall of the Palace, a huge space for the thirty or so guests that had been invited. The absolute magnificence of the room outshone even the Palace of St Cloud. It was white, and the snow piled high against the tall arched windows seemed to complement it. Five huge chandeliers bearing hundreds of candles and thousands of droplets of crystal brightly illuminated the interior against the darkness, which waited outside for all but one or two hours each day. Pairs of marble statues representing classical figures stood on the cornice, below ornate white bas-reliefs stretching up to the ceiling.

The séance was scheduled for eight in the evening. The brothers arrived at five to assemble the cabinet and ensure all was in place, while still allowing time for any Imperial family member who might want to inspect it for signs of trickery. Princess Dagmar, the betrothed of the Crown Prince, requested that she be allowed to see inside, and after entering cautiously to look at the instruments which lay on the floor, as well as the ropes that would bind William and Ira, her interpreter said that Her Highness found the cabinet to be an ingenious space.

The performance was no different from any other, except it was the Crown Prince himself who fastened both Davenports into their places. The music played by the apparently player-less instruments was a simple Russian folk song that delighted the assembled crowd. John King spoke a little, in Russian, about the beauty he had witnessed in St Petersburg and Katie delighted the women in the company with her praise, in French, for their fashion sense and style. At the end of the show, the doors were swung open and the brothers were revealed to be still secure in their respective posts. The Emperor and the Crown Prince came forward to release them, and as they did so the Emperor asked if he might have a private audience with John King. Ira and William agreed and offered to be tied again, but Nicholas II declined, saying that he was interested in hearing what their spirit guide had to say, not in further questioning the veracity of their abilities, in which he had no doubt.

The Czar entered alone into the cabinet, with William and Ira, and the door was closed behind him; the three were now in pitch blackness without even a chink of the dazzling brightness that illuminated the waiting spectators. William had practised French for hours in preparation for an eventuality such as this. But while I was an admirer of the Davenport skill and talent, it had in no way prepared the brothers to give political advice, and so, although the Czar's utter conviction did not make it necessary for the purpose of belief, I spoke through William once again.

In this obscurity, with the murmur of the assembled audience outside still audible through the cabinet walls, I spoke to the Czar. He seemed, somehow, much more vulnerable in that setting. Beneath the grand costume of white with gold brocade, I detected a nervousness, a fear of what he might learn from this exchange, or perhaps he was afraid of another assassination attempt, given the close escape he had had only some months previously. He was sitting in the middle of the space between Ira and William, and John King's voice, when it spoke, seemed to come from just a few inches in front of him, as if he and the spirit were in close, intimate proximity.

'Two years before you were born, your father visited Scotland. Do you know of this?' I made sure that John King's French held no trace of any secondary accent.

Alexander II, Czar of all the Russias, had a tremble in his voice when he spoke.

'Yes, I do. It was one of the last things my father spoke of before he died. He made me promise to abolish serfdom because he said that what he had witnessed in Lanark showed him a better way. He regretted many things.'

'And you did abolish it?'

'Yes, just five years ago. I am known as Alexander the Liberator.'

'So what knowledge do you now seek from me?'

'I wish to know what my future holds.'

I concentrate and John King replies.

'You must look again to the kindness your father saw with Robert Owen, although it may not be enough to save you from the upheaval that will tear your country apart. Think of an elected parliament, a new system of government.'

'And will there be other attempts on my life? I was almost assassinated this year.'

'Yes, there will even be one next summer, but it too will fail.'

Alexander cleared his throat. William sniffed a little as if he had the beginnings of a cold. It was, for less than a minute, as if the Czar waited for the ghost to speak, and the ghost waited for the Czar. The chatter beyond the spirit cabinet seemed to have become quiet and the only sound remaining was that of the three breathing men. The slight awkwardness and expectation was finally broken when Ira announced that the spirit was no longer in communication with them. I spoke no more that day.

Our return to London the following year might have been an anti-climax, were it not for the fact that the capital now had a plethora of John Kings, none of which were anything to do with me, but which, because they invoked my name, I was able to witness. Not only there, but in many parts of Britain, my voice was reported in the spiritual press, speaking in a wide variety of suitable regional accents. I did interfere once, briefly, at a séance in Bangor, with a splendid table levitation for an elderly medium in reduced circumstances, who presented a rather doddery impersonation of me.

The Davenports eventually settled on a series of appearances at the Hanover Rooms, arranged by the prominent spiritualist Mr Benjamin Coleman. There was, however, a competing attraction.

The Egyptian Hall in Piccadilly was one of the best known

theatrical venues in the city. Built in 1812, it reflected that period's fascination with everything relating to the pharaohs. It had formerly been a museum, able to display the very largest of exhibits within its exotic interior, with representations of the pyramids, the Sphinx and a wide variety of Ancient Egyptian deities. The façade served as an advertisement, with a pharaoh and his queen standing above the portico, and below them two sphinxes seeming to guard the doors, which were shaped like the entrance to a tomb. While the brothers had been touring mainland Europe, a new attraction had begun to feature regularly on its stage.

William caught sight of a poster advertising the show, which proclaimed:

The Royal Illusionists and Anti Spiritualists.

He turned to Ira, at first with some puzzlement, but then with dawning recognition of the likeness depicted there. One of the protagonists of the show, John Nevil Maskelyne, was the very same man who had fixed his table-rapping apparatus when they had first arrived in the city.

There was an afternoon performance at three. William and Ira were not expected at the Hanover Rooms until eight, and so, without any consultation between them, they found that they were heading past the milliners and the Homeopathic Chemist, into the so-called 'Home of Mystery'.

They took their places in the auditorium, which was almost completely full by the start of the show, and sat dumbfounded as the people around them collapsed in paroxysms of laughter. It was blatant pastiche. Maskelyne and his companion untied themselves from the trickiest knots, rapped under tables with a device identical to William's, and most heinous of all, were visited by a ridiculous-looking man, dressed in a turban, claiming to be John King.

(This led me to a strange state, one that was far from my usual detached observation, and which I think might be described by you as humiliation.)

Worst of all, William and Ira eventually joined in the laughter. As they made their way out past the grand purple and gold interior pillars, they congratulated each other. The civil war was over; they would be going back to America in less than three weeks; this show could only add to the attention they would receive before their departure.

When the brothers and William Fay returned to America, I did not accompany them. I found myself once again in the Egyptian Hall, knowing with certainty that there would be a death.

Again there is that hint of Victorian pulp fiction in the rather cheap way the writer builds suspense in that last sentence. While mostly managing to achieve a kind of pastiche of the period that is fairly literary, these attempts to tantalise the reader before a new chapter, or to hint at a forthcoming event, seem to me to be more an irritating quirk of the writer than a successful literary device.

Sources: the first quote about their Russian success 'during which time they received the most conclusive and satisfactory tests, [and] expressed themselves perfectly satisfied as to the inexplicability of the manifestations' is taken from Cooper again.

In case researchers are not familiar with this period in history, I now add a little background to put this account in its proper perspective. Before his assassination in 1881 by the People's Will party, Alexander II had drawn up plans for the Loris-Melikov Constitution. This would have created an elected parliament, or *Duma*. His anti-reformist son, Alexander III, abandoned the plans immediately on succession and it was not until 1905 that Russia had a parliament of the kind proposed by Alexander the Liberator. [AM 2007]

A chance meeting with a professor from UCL SSEES (School of Slavonic and East European Studies), part of London University, led me to the collection of 3,000 letters between Czar Alexander and Princess Catherine Dolgoruky, sold by Christie's, as reported in the *Telegraph* of 19 May 2001. The exchange inside the cabinet is referred to briefly, but very specifically, mentioning New Lanark and a new system of more democratic government in one letter between them, u/d 1868, Summer Palace, St Petersburg Private Collection. The letter is mostly in French but I am grateful to Natalya Danshov for her translation of the Russian asides within it. Either the Cesenatico writer made a very lucky guess or was aware of the correspondence, although the current owners insist that only two SSEES scholars and I have thus far had access to them. [AM 2009]

A MOCK SÉANCE

It is the first day of the new year of 1867. It is freezing cold and the Regent's Park lake is thronged with men and boy skaters, exercising, showing off to wives and mothers and sisters who watch from the banks. The sun will be bright for less than an hour because the time is well past three, and so the skaters glide and pirouette, determined to enjoy the last rays of light.

The park ducks huddle together on the island in the middle of the lake, as if to stay warm. A man from the Humane Society, the organisation that watches out and helps those in danger of drowning, and also recovers bodies from the lake, skates out close to the island. The ducks come towards him, as if expecting food, but when there is none they retreat again to the western edge. The currents of the Tyburn flow fast beneath the hardened surface.

Another man from the society skates out to join him and, using small mallets, they both proceed to crack the ice around the island. Afterwards they will say that it was to protect the birds from the ever encroaching skaters.

A man of around twenty or so, in a navy overcoat, spins on one leg. James looks better here. Without the ridiculous turban and the glare of the lights, he is a handsome lad. A girl watches on, smiling at him, her hands buried in a fur muff that hangs by a cream silk ribbon from her neck. He is one of hundreds, but she sees only him. James notices small fissures in the ice and thinks it is late, he will go back to the shore, to where Helena is waiting to hold and admire him.

But then water spurts up beneath the cracks; the ice is broken into tessellated sheets; the thought of returning to the bank becomes collective panic as everyone tries to leave. The weight of the crowd makes more cracks appear; one man and two boys, his sons, fall between the sheets. A Humane Society man lays out a ladder across the fractured surface and some manage to use it to get across.

James falls but is able to hold on to an island of ice, just a yard or so across. He pulls himself up onto it, shivering and drenched, and cries out again and again for someone to help him. Helena is screaming now. He can still see her, standing between two kindly strangers who are attempting to soothe her. He wonders if he can steer the ice like a boat to safety, but as he has the thought, it cracks again and this time he goes under, carried by the current, swept swiftly beneath what is still hardened surface, gasping for air at the cracks, then doing nothing at all but moving, borne far out towards the sea, trapped like a specimen under glass.

The following day, when it is light again and they are able to recover the bodies and lay them out in the Marylebone workhouse, forty men and boys in all, James's body is not among them. Only Helena, in her mourning gown of black, with her long jet earrings hanging like dark teardrops, an outward manifestation of her utter sorrow, is able to tell John Nevil Maskelyne what has happened to her beloved. And he has been missing from the show for three afternoons and evenings before she is able to do so.

RECONCILING SPIRIT AND FLESH

Maskelyne was devastated by the loss of his oldest and dearest friend. Yet in spite of his grief the shows continued, with only one interruption a week after the event, when a three o'clock performance was cancelled so that the cast and crew could attend a memorial service for James. Maskelyne's scepticism was absolute. His friend's death did not see him waver in his complete lack of belief in anything at all. The service was a palimpsest for those who did believe, and he sat through it knowing that James would not have appreciated this invocation to a God in whom he also had never believed.

Instead of channelling his sadness into some attempt to reconnect with his dead friend *(as I had hoped he might)*, he threw himself into his work.

(I was learning that it was not easy to predict human reactions, which were frequently neither rational nor well considered.)

Maskelyne was tireless in his dedication to rooting out fraud and replicating it so as to prevent even the faintest suggestion that any spiritual interference might be involved. His show became more and more popular as he incorporated an ever-increasing number of tricks from the séance parlours and medium shows all around town. The Davenports had, at one time, been tied up while holding handfuls of flour, to show that they could not possibly have released their bonds because their hands were full. Maskelyne incorporated this into his own act, even publishing a letter describing the method he used:

> I simply put the flour upon the polished seat of the cabinet and wiped my hands with my handkerchief. When the knots were untied I scraped the whole of the flour into my left hand, dusted the seat and returned the handkerchief to my pocket. I then put a portion of the flour in my right hand and came out of the cabinet showing flour in both hands.

As a tribute to his lost friend, he added:

> My late colleague and I did a much better trick under the flour test. We played a cornet duet with the flour in our hands. We held the cornets between our knees and manipulated the valves with our thumbs. 'Home Sweet Home' was our favourite duet. This I would finish with a cadenza and a shake, holding the first valve down with the left thumb and shaking upon the second valve with my right thumb. The doors of the cabinet were opened immediately the duet was finished. Not a particle of flour was spilt, and the seals upon the knots were unbroken.

Another medium who had caught Maskelyne's interest during his researches was Mrs Mary Marshall. With her niece Mary Brodie, she had attracted a small but faithful following at regular séances held at her home in 23 Red Lion Street, Holborn, since early in 1859. At that time the *British Spiritual Telegraph* had made much of her spirit writing, words that mysteriously appeared on blank slates during dark séances. More recent articles in celebrated spiritualist periodicals such as *The Spiritualist* and *The Medium and Daybreak*, describing John King's frequent speeches during her gatherings, had brought her to greater prominence.

Maskelyne was too well known to visit a séance without being recognised, so instead he offered a challenge to Mrs Marshall. He would attend one of her meetings and demonstrate publicly that he was able to reproduce anything that she did there, by mechanical means, thus showing that no spiritual entities were involved.

(This is a common challenge and one that is flawed in its logic. Just because you can replicate something by human trickery does not preclude the possibility that the same effect might be, and in fact has been, achieved by spiritual intervention.)

Mary Marshall's demeanour was that of an overweight, lower-class, rather stupid woman of the kind who would be happiest in the kitchen or engaged in some simple household task.

(I realise this sounds unkind; it is however an accurate description. I had nothing but admiration for Mary Marshall, a woman who took what little she had to begin with and really did what she could.)

But while she was portly and plain and came from humble origins – her mother had been a maid of all work and her father a drunk – she possessed intelligence and cunning and was well aware of just how useful a misleading mien could be. Her usual manner of dress seemed in defiance of her years and her underlying character. When I first saw her, she was wearing a shiny blue silk gown, cut revealingly low in front, so that her wrinkled bosoms were bare to just the tiniest fraction of an inch above the areolae of her nipples. It might have been alluring in her younger years, but Mrs Marshall was close to seventy and the sight must have made some humankind queasy, to say the least. The look was completed by a very generous application of rouge on top of white powder and a garish red lip stain.

Maskelyne came from a respectable Cheltenham family, but he was far too much of a trickster to be taken in by how she presented herself. Nonetheless, he retained the narrow views and prejudices of his background, particularly in relation to the female sex – something that Mary Marshall was wily enough to use (and something that I would take some pleasure in exploiting).

It was a grey day without wind, without extreme cold, a nothing sort of day. Mrs Marshall's warm and cosy interior, with its red walls and inviting fireplace, seemed a place to relax and chat in, rather than somewhere to summon and commune with the dead. She ushered Maskelyne in, with his companion, a completely unmemorable man of the same age and class, whose name I have now forgotten. After presenting them with tea and excellent biscuits, which they enjoyed by the fire, the two were seated at a table with Mrs Marshall and her niece. I wondered briefly at the absence of a Mr Marshall but then realised he had died some months before when I heard the condolences offered by Maskelyne and his companion.

Some newspapers lay on the table at one side, but as the rest of the room was far from tidy, they did not seem out of place. A slate was handed to Maskelyne and he examined it. It was clean on both sides and bound at the edges. He readily agreed that there was nothing strange about it at all. Mary – let us be on first-name terms – told him to take the slate and place it face down on the table with his palms upon it. She encouraged him to rest his head upon it and send a message to his friend in his mind, giving very careful instructions as to what position he should adopt, which he most rigorously followed.

Mary then placed her own hands on the table and began to hum. The sounds gave way to words and she invoked, 'Spirit, come to us, let us hear from John Nevil Maskelyne's friend. He is not a believer. Show him your power.'

Maskelyne sat up from the table when Mary informed him he might do so and the slate was examined, but there was no sign of any writing. Mary sighed and blamed Maskelyne's extreme scepticism, saying that the spirits did require some encouragement and would he please try to keep some kind of semblance of an open mind.

She took the slate from him and stretched it under the table towards him, then asked that he take it from her and hold it against the underside of the table so that the spirits might better write without his scorn. Maskelyne held the slate there for a few minutes, then, at Mary's request, brought it out once more. The words were clear and bright.

'I am in spirit now. We were erroneous in our assumptions. James.'

I saw Maskelyne's brow furrow with something close to anger but, well-mannered young man that he was, he controlled himself and waited while Mary cleared the table of the newspapers, which it seemed would be in the way of the second part of the meeting.

What followed was truly awful. The voice of John King, undeniably feminine, even if 'thrown' very well, spoke to the assembled party and gave various message to Maskelyne and to his companion. I wondered that Mary had achieved any success at all with her 'John King' séances given the amateurishness of her presentation and the fact it was so clearly a woman trying to disguise her ventriloquist voice as that of a man. Then I remembered that, until a few months ago, Mr Marshall would undoubtedly have taken some part in these events and had probably been far more convincing as a jovial male ghost.

Maskelyne did not even deign to point out the inadequacies of the voice manifestation but instead focused his attention on explaining to the small company just how Mary had carried out her slate-writing trick.

Obviously there were two slates, one of which had been prepared with the so-called 'spirit message'. When Mary passed him the blank slate under the table she had substituted the other which she had on her lap, which he acknowledged she had done very smoothly and professionally. Thus, when he held the slate to the underside of the table it already bore the writing that was meant to surprise him. The other slate, the blank one, had been removed under cover of the newspapers when Mary cleared the table for the second part of the séance.

Mary looked close to tears. Maskelyne was not an unkind man. Despite his fury at the message that purportedly came from his friend, he was not without sympathy for this widowed woman who seemed genuinely upset at his explanation. Even if he had been unmoved, there was momentarily an image in his mind, surprising and poignant, of his mother, standing as Mary did, her eyes filling, after the death of one of her eight children.

(This, of course, was another, very tiny intervention on my part. So small, in fact, that it is almost not worth mentioning. I do so only for the sake of completeness.)

He asked Mary if his analysis was correct, and the tears came.

'Yes, sir,' Mary snuffled. 'Yes, indeed, but I do speak to spirits. It's just since my Edward passed over they don't seem to come any more, and I need to make a living. Perhaps you might come again, and I promise to use no trickery.'

He agreed readily, although afterwards wondered that he had done so. He and his companion would return in one week's time, on which date, Mary claimed, she would have a better chance to contact her spirit guide, John King, again.

The young men made their farewells, but I remained in that snug parlour with the young woman and the old, wondering what mischief I might make for their return. However, I was about to have the tables turned on me.

(I particularly love that phrase and the way it has outlived the popularity of the activity; it is like a ghost of the thing itself, haunting our language.)

When the door was closed, Mary turned away from her niece to the empty room and spoke quite distinctly, without any trace of the tears that had so upset her minutes before.

'I know you're there. Who are you? Is it you, Edward?'

Of course there was silence, and I immediately thought, This woman is a lunatic, deluded rather than deceiving – a very poor choice for my dealings with Maskelyne. I would have to think again. However, she insisted.

'You're not my usual, are you, dear? Now don't be afraid. I know you're here. What manner of spirit are you?'

Worst of all, now she seemed to be looking right at me.

(There is of course nothing to see, I am only essence, but nevertheless it was most unnerving to have someone stare at the area which I thought of myself as inhabiting.)

I moved. She turned to exactly my new position and began again.

'Now, now, I do know you're there, dear. Do send me a message of some kind.'

The niece looked worried and went to Mary's side. 'Come now, Aunt, you're overtired. The gentlemen have gone now.'

Far from being soothed by this, Mary seemed quite put out and retorted to Miss Brodie, without any trace of the rather maternal, sweet woman she had appeared to be, 'You silly, silly girl. There is a spirit here. Now leave me to try and speak to it.'

'Now, Aunt Mary, come along,' and the steely tones of the young woman far outmatched the annoyance of her relative. 'We will have to call the doctor if you persist in these – these fancies.'

How ironic! Two women trying to make a living by espousing spiritualism and using trickery to create its effects, one of whom seemed to have some genuine sense for spirits, and the other who clearly thought her companion was mad. Miss Brodie was far too conceited for one so ignorant of the ways of my world, and so, with a little concentration, I made the gas lamp sputter, then, when her attention was drawn towards the little side table it sat on, I made a book, which was placed beside it, levitate some inches from the surface. Miss Brodie screamed. Really, it was hilarious. This was the closest I had come to amusement in these past decades. She was overreacting to something that could easily be achieved by trickery because it was not she herself who had planned it. Mary, on the other hand, was leaping up and down, looking far younger than her sixty-odd years and shouting, 'See, I told you, there is something here! Now you will need to listen to me. Edward always used to know. Now I do too.'

'Really, Aunt Mary -' the niece seemed to have regained her composure - 'don't you think it's ridiculous to go to these lengths to try to convince me of the impossible? It's time we went for our afternoon nap. You're overtired.'

Miss Brodie then bodily steered her aunt out of the room and up the narrow staircase while Mary continued to babble, 'It doesn't matter what you say; I know they're back. They're back, I say.'

In the upstairs bedroom, the two women lay under quilted covers. But while Miss Brodie, helped by a little nip of whisky from the decanter by her truckle bed, fell asleep immediately, Mary lay with her eyes wide open, peering into the darkness as if trying to see something that could not, of course, be seen. When she finally did sleep, I watched. I waited for that slight ripple of movement behind her closed eyelids and I brought her a dream, one that I hoped might rescue her from the ruin that was sure to happen if she continued with those disastrous John King presentations.

(This dream was my initial attempt to reconcile the physical characteristics of the medium with the essence of the spirit she represents, but to do so while still retaining, and indeed increasing, followers. Mortals make many judgements and assumptions based on appearances; it seemed sensible to operate within these constraints.)

When Maskelyne returned at the appointed time, he did so bearing a copy of the *Spirit Times*, which was headlined with news of the city's latest attraction. The Mary Marshall who greeted him on arrival was a transformation of the woman he had seen just one week earlier. The showy dress was gone, as was the heavy powder and paint. Instead Mary presented herself as someone might wish their grandmother to be: she wore a navy, high-necked dress under a white starched apron, and her hair, hitherto dishevelled, was neatly pinned back into a bun. She had transformed herself into the perfect medium to present the spirit of Mrs Katie King, an elderly ghost who could soothe the bereaved with kind words and a cheering message from the hereafter.

Maskelyne proved immune to the charms of Mrs King, however, and, despite the fact that I did help with a little linguistic ability that was clearly beyond the medium's intelligence or education, he remained sceptical. The tricks that I was able to perform to aid her seemed to be no more than those he could recreate by mechanical means. Finally, as he was leaving, in a fit of something that you might call impatient rage I levitated the hall portmanteau. Not just a little, either – I raised it to the ceiling. Then, just to show there wasn't some invisible string guiding it through the ceiling, moved by some hand in the room above us, I turned it round three hundred and sixty degrees before replacing it exactly where it had been. Mary could barely contain her utter delight; the annoying Miss Brodie looked very discomfited; Maskelyne was appalled.

Nevertheless, for the rest of his life Maskelyne continued to eschew any belief in the supernatural; I did fail absolutely in my attempt in that regard. However, he did concede publicly, in an item for the *Pall Mall Gazette* that shocked and even disappointed some of his followers, that he had witnessed 'movements of furnishings' which 'I believe, in my own mind, must have been some psychic or nerve force which ... neutralised the law of gravitation.'

(Thus, while he grudgingly accepted that something

inexplicable had occurred, he did not admit the rational and obvious reason that it had done so.)

A Wondrous Experience
To the Editor of the 'Spiritual Magazine'

Sir,

It may perhaps interest some of your readers to learn that a few days ago I went, with friends, to visit Mrs Marshall at her home. My friend, Mr____, undertook to conduct the séance, and asked to whom the spirit then present desired to communicate. The voice addressed me and gave its name as Mrs Katie King. It went on to make great assurance of communications with my late brother. Messages there from were spelt out correctly by means of letters placed on the table before us. First, there was the place where my brother had passed to the spirit realm, Para; then his Christian name, Herbert; and lastly, at my request, the name of the mutual friend who last saw him, Henry Walter Bates. On this occasion our party of six visited Mrs Marshall for the first time, and my name, as well as those of the rest of the party except one, were unknown to her. That one was my married sister, whose name was no clue of mine.

This encounter, inexplicable within our current assumptions, add to my conviction that there are, other (and perhaps infinitely varied) forms of matter and modes of ethereal motion, than those which our senses enable us to recognise.

If the small minded people who equate the practice of Spiritualism with Diabolical communication, were asked what motive they could give for Satan to send a much wished for communication from the spirit of a dear departed brother, there is no reply they could possibly give.

Yours, &c

Alfred Russel Wallace

Dec. 1869

Alfred Russel Wallace was on a voyage of scientific discovery. It was not dissimilar to that which had led to his paper on the theory of evolution, a proposal he came to independently of Darwin and which had first been publicly presented as a theory espoused in two separate papers, one by Darwin, the other by Wallace, just over ten years before, in 1858.

(I must emphasise the brilliance of A. R. Wallace; he is all too frequently ignored in favour of the hagiographic literary devotion to Darwin, a man who understood nothing at all about spirits and cared less.)

Mrs Marshall, through her guide Katie King, would nurture his curiosity, convert it into conviction, and in doing so, cause the most accurate and perceptive study of spirit life that has ever existed, even up to this present day, to be written and published.

(This is, of course, Miracles and Modern Spiritualism *(1896). It is not praise that I give lightly, because Robert Dale's wonderful but less scientifically precise book,* Footfalls on the Boundary of Another World *(1860), would be my preferred reading. I take great comfort from the fact that Wallace pays tribute to my Robert Dale Owen, as well as to his brilliant if flawed work in the introductory chapter of his own later book. Perhaps, I like*

to think, one would not have been possible without the other, and I may therefore assume credit for both insofar as without my intervention in the young Owen's illness, neither would ever have been penned.)

Wallace was a kindly soul; his precarious finances and insecure upbringing gave him an empathy towards some of the women who practised as mediums. He was quite prepared to countenance the possibility that someone without formal education might, and in some cases did, have abilities that he could not fully comprehend, much less possess.

The letter referred to their first meeting, and, on the cusp of the new decade, Wallace found himself becoming a frequent and very welcome visitor to Mary's home. I did not interfere much, and Mary's initial enthusiasm and ebullience at her knowledge of my existence turned into a quiet frustration as realisation dawned on her. Yes, she could perceive that I was in a room with her, but without having any power whatsoever to encourage me or discourage me from participating in her activities. I might surprise her by an inexplicable movement of a table that she had not prearranged to move (with her unseen threads or carefully concealed hands or knees) and yet, at other times, when she was most anxious to make an impression or recover a trick gone wrong, I would not intervene in any way, even though her senses told her I was present. She puzzled long over whether I was aware of her, as she was of me, because my interactions with her seemed so arbitrary in their timing and delivery.

(Over the centuries, there have been very few humans with an awareness of my presence. This was my first overt experience, although it did bring the realisation that probably Robert Dale,

as a sick child, had had some perception of me. At this time, I was very anxious to remain independent. Had I responded to a request, it might have led to an idea that I was somehow 'doing the bidding' of the medium, one that I could not bear to countenance.)

Often Mary wished she might broach the subject with Wallace, who was both learned and a believer, but it would have meant admitting to trickery at times, which she was loath to do, lest she lose a faithful and high-profile supporter. I did, however, oblige Wallace with a spectacular display on one particular visit, because even then I recognised him as a champion of our faith.

In March 1870 he arrived at the home of Mrs Marshall for an evening séance, accompanied by his elder sister, Fanny Sims, who was a committed spiritualist, as well as two other acquaintances, one of whom was a barrister. When they arrived, a fifth visitor awaited them, the chemist William Crookes, who had recently been persuaded of the possibility of a spirit world by his scientific observation and investigation of the exceptionally clever fraudster Daniel Dunglas Home.

(Despite his great fame as a medium, D. D. Home does not concern us here because he did not involve me, 'King', in any of his 'events'. I refuse to call them séances; Home was a skilled parlour magician, nothing more, and a man without even a vestige of spirituality.)

Crookes had begun working on a series of articles for the *Quarterly Journal of Science* about his experimental investigations and would be one of the most important figures in the development of my public persona, just a few years hence.

Once the five had assembled in the parlour, they began a thorough examination of the room, following Mary's invitation to do so. They checked assiduously for hidden wires, trap doors and other paraphernalia commonly used in mediumistic deceit. The only query, made by Crookes, concerned the lightness of the table. Mary explained that as her spirit guide was an elderly woman, they found that the energy required to move a heavier table put her under unnecessary strain.

(This is a perfect example of how illogical even the most brilliant men can be at times. I do not understand how they can accept that a spirit, who in their minds is representative of a dead person, could suffer from the effects of ageing. Credit is due to Mrs Marshall for her quick and clever response.)

Crookes, Wallace and the rest of the party readily accepted this, and when they were all satisfied that no devices were concealed, four people sat around the flimsy table, where they were joined by Mary and her niece. The lawyer did not sit with them but instead observed from an armchair by the fire, so that he might have a different view. The light was left turned up; this was a fairly new arrangement for a séance and one that was responsible for much of Mary's newfound success in recent months, because it seemed to demonstrate a lack of opportunity for trickery. The proceeding opened with a message, through Mary, from Mrs Katie King.

Wallace described the subsequent events:

1st. A small table, on which the hands of six persons were placed (including my own and Mrs Marshall's), rose up vertically about a foot from the floor, and remained suspended for some twenty seconds, while my friend, who was sitting on, could see the lower part of the table with the feet freely suspended above the floor.

2nd. While sitting at a large table ... a guitar which had been placed in my sister's hand slid onto the floor, passed over my feet, and came to Mr C., against whose legs it raised itself up till it appeared above the table. I and Mr C. were watching it carefully the whole time, and it behaved as if alive itself, or rather as if a small invisible child were by great exertions moving it and raising it up. These two phenomena were witnessed in bright gaslight.

The first of these was easily effected by means of a device hidden up the sleeves of both Mary and Miss Brodie. They had taken their places opposite each other at the table and the devices, really long pieces of wood at an angle, ran under their sleeves to the wrist. When the women placed their palms on the table, a small flick of the wrist released a second piece of wood which passed under the table, enabling them to lift it easily together. This simple contraption had the added advantage that, with practice and care so that the device didn't show, it was also possible for the medium and her assistant to raise their palms just a fraction from the surface of the table and thus demonstrate further that spirits were at work.

The guitar was even more obvious and involved a very fine thread and some inconspicuous foot shuffling. Maskelyne would have been far harder to convince, but these participants seemed content.

Given the gravitas of the gathering, I decided to take part, even though an intervention was unnecessary. It involved Mary Brodie and a piano. As an interlude during the proceedings, Miss Brodie took her place at the piano and enthusiastically banged out a couple of songs that were popular at the time. In this instance, she chose to entertain us with George Leybourne's 'Champagne Charlie' and a pained version of 'The Last Rose of Summer'. The events that followed were described thus by Wallace in his account:

> Afterwards, when she returned to the table from the piano where she had been playing, her chair moved away just as she was going to sit down; on drawing it up, it moved away again, this time causing her to fall to the ground in a very undignified manner. After this had happened it became apparently fixed to the floor, so that she could not raise it. Mr C. then took hold of it, and found it was only by a great exertion he could lift it off the floor.

The participants declared themselves convinced that spiritual entities were at work. The barrister was distressed by what he had witnessed and did not attend another séance, although some years later, in February 1874, he published an article in *London Society,* where he stated:

> It was difficult for me to give in to the idea that solid objects could be conveyed, invisibly, through closed doors, or that heavy furniture could be moved without the interposition of hands. Philosophers will say that these things are absolutely impossible; nevertheless it is absolutely certain that they do occur.

Wallace did not continue to visit Mary Marshall; he was convinced as to her abilities and found no need to test her. But his experience with her strengthened and cemented his faith.

He vociferously challenged critics of spiritualism, and in a conversation with Lord Alfred Tennyson, at that time Poet Laureate, shared his conviction that Maskelyne's tricks were surely performed 'partly by the help of mediumship'. He reasoned that Maskelyne, the medium, would have to compete against many others practising their art, whereas Maskelyne, the magician, who did not admit to his supernatural talents, could make an excellent living as a unique kind of entertainer.

Instead, Wallace turned his attention to another medium, Agnes Guppy, who was much on my mind because, without any encouragement, she too was now presenting the voice of a matronly ghost. There were two Mrs Kings in London, and one of them was a fraud.

> The narrator's voice seems to be more intrusive in this manuscripts than in those that precede it, as if it is growing in confidence. There are no fewer than fifteen comments in brackets on the narrative presented which, even allowing for the length of the section compared to some others, is a significant increase. This development seems to coincide with a noticeable increase in the influencing abilities of the protagonist, as well as the first time she is actually perceived by a medium (although of course she speculates that Owen as a child might have done so too). Her tone continues to be somewhat superior and a little irritating in its condescension.
>
> Maskelyne reminds me of Derren Brown, the popular

twenty-first-century stage and television illusionist, who challenges and exposes those who profess psychic ability. At times Brown replicates the kind of acts performed by these frauds in a most convincing and compelling way, making it clear that his effects are achieved by human skill rather than spirit intervention.

There are numerous sources used throughout this section, namely:

- 'Maxim vs Maskelyne: A Complete Explanation of the Tricks of the Davenport Brothers and their Imitators', *Strand Magazine*, 1876
- *Spirit Times*, Nov. 1868
- *Pall Mall Gazette*, 1868.

There are frequent references to Wallace's *Miracles and Modern Spiritualism* (1896). Of course Wallace formed the theory of natural selection independently of Darwin and co-authored the first ever paper on the subject.

The letter from Wallace can be viewed online: 'Wallace, A. R. to the Editor of the *Spiritual Magazine*', WCP Identifier WCP3070.222, Wallace Letters Online, 31 Nov. 2013. There are many such letters on this site, all quite interesting because they form a catalogue of the many phenomena that could be seen at the various circles in London during the period, and which are referred to in the Cesenatico papers by their author. [AM 2007]

It seems that in the world of this spirit I must question everything. Clever trickery and showmanship are not what they claim to be. I realise now that Derren Brown is psychic. He pretends to use trickery and illusion so that he appeals more to the scepticism of a modern audience while his method also guarantees a successful career free from exposure when the spirits do not behave as he might wish.

Katie amuses rather than irritates me these days. Now I wish I could have seen the piano scene for myself. She does not suffer fools, and I like her all the more because of it.

I don't speak to Peter about any of this. It would sound as if my illness makes me mad, but I have such certainty, such unquestioning faith. I am born again into a world I barely recognise, just as death beckons me to leave it. I look up at the sky and I know that by searching those vast times, those vast spaces, I will find her.

I long impatiently for more of her, more understanding. I would make those fifteen interjections fifteen thousand and scour each one of them again and again so that I might know her better in the time that I have left. [AM 2012]

I LEARN TO READ

It is through my association with Wallace that I learn of Robert Dale's book on spirits. Now the note-taking that I witnessed at the Davenport séance points to a far greater interest and commitment than I had hoped for, one borne out by Wallace's admiration for him.

Books, I find, are easy for me. I can absorb the contents through quiet concentration. It is not dissimilar to the way in which I read people and ambience, but this new discovery makes me both calm and excited. Calm, because I no longer have to long forlornly for dreams that do not come when I most wish for them, just to have any news of him at all. Excited because I understand far more of what is happening around me and to me. I am restless for a time, wandering through the libraries of the houses I am led to, subsuming what I am into a world of other people's words.

Most of all, I am moved by two passages in Robert's book that I return to again and again. My Robert writes in his Footfalls on the Boundary of Another World *(1860):*

But if that spiritual body, while still connected with its earthly associate, could, under certain circumstances,

123

appear, distinct and distant from the natural body, and perceptible to human vision, if not to human touch, what strong presumption is there against the supposition that after its final emancipation the same spiritual body may still at times show itself to man.

This passage is followed by tales and recollections of visions of apparitions, and behind each of them, I sense Robert's longing that he might share the experience of the tellers. It is as if he is asking me for something and I wish for nothing more than to be able to bestow it upon him.

The second piece that catches me is his offering to me. It is his clever attempt to understand me, and helps me to see how my perception of my own existence might be as it is. The man who has been the subject of many of my thoughts, and all of my desires, for the better part of a century, is philosophising about what I am and in such a way that gives me hope he might be correct in his imaginings:

But if the change instantly succeeding the momentary sleep of death be far greater than that we have imagined in a creature lying down, at night, an infant and awaking, next morning, a full-grown man, and if, in this latter case, identity would be lost, how much more in the former!

The body is gone: what continuous links of identity remain? The mind, the feelings. Transform these, and *every* link is severed connecting, FOR US, a Here with a Hereafter. It is not WE, in any practical sense, who survive, but others.

In his words, I see an argument that might convince all men as to my reality. At first it is a fancy, no more. Now that I am a faded phantom, who can no longer interact or influence, I know it for a lost opportunity, a possibility that might have saved me from the worst fate I can imagine: to cease to exist in a world that does not believe I was ever there at all.

This is a more recent paper than the others in the collection; it's from the early twentieth century. The writer is much less overtly romantic than in the earlier pages and presents the impression of greater maturity, more thoughtfulness, and quotes accurately from the cited works. This 'spirit writing' was the work of 'Euan', one of the mediums who assisted the Canadian physician and psychic researcher Thomas Glen Hamilton. 'Euan' also quoted extensively from Robert Louis Stevenson, despite claiming never to have read his works. [AM 2007]

This passage moves me now, although it did not when I first read it. I used to find her (and note that I say 'her' although it could have been written by a man, I suppose) annoyingly self-obsessed. With my illness I find my concerns match those of the writer. I too am afraid that when I die, and when Peter and my mother die, there will be no one left who remembers I ever existed at all. How I have changed. [AM 2012]

A SÉANCE IN TWO PLACES

Wallace had known Agnes Guppy for some years. Before her marriage, Agnes Nichol, as she was then, had been the house-mate and companion of his sister Fanny. Even in those days, Agnes had shown considerable ability in the séances that she conducted for friends. Now that she was married to a very wealthy man, Samuel Guppy, who seemed to bask in his wife's success, her séances had become the most popular in the city.

(It's worth noting that in 1871, Samuel was eighty-one years of age, more than double Agnes's thirty-one years.)

One obvious reason for this was the numerous gifts given to the sitters by her new guide spirit, Mrs King, as a token of her affection, and also as comfort in their time of sorrow. Another important distinction between Agnes and Mary Marshall was that, with her wealth and society connections, Agnes was able to operate as a private, rather than a public, medium. Public – or professional – mediums like Mary charged an entrance fee for attendance at their sittings, which was the basis of their livelihood. Private mediums operated within a closed group of friends and acquaintances and entry was completely free, but by invitation. As the fame of a private medium spread, the circle of invitation widened, but at no time was money charged for her services. Popular opinion was suspicious of those who charged, thinking that they would be far more likely to be fraudulent than someone who offered their gifts for free.

Agnes, although much younger than Mary, was physically similar, in that she was very overweight, with a generous bust that she would nuzzle against her male clientele in a mothering gesture. The London *Echo* of 8 June 1871 referred to her as 'the stoutest woman in London'. Her Katie voice was louder than that of Mary, and also more domineering, more appealing to the kind of man who likes to be controlled. This guaranteed a loyal following among that type, while her generous bestowal of flowers, often exotic ones, and her discreet references to matters of the heart, made her a favourite medium for women of all ages.

The *Report on Spiritualism of the London Dialectical Society* (1871) was put together after a group of distinguished gentlemen had visited and tested mediums in the city. One of those involved was Wallace, and the document included a statement of his belief in the supernatural talents of Mary Marshall. Agnes Guppy was miffed not to have been included and wrote to both Wallace, through his sister Fanny, and another contributor, William Volckman. Agnes also invited Wallace and his sister to visit her home.

Much of Agnes's skill lay in the fact that, despite her physique, she was quite an agile woman, although the sitters were always led to believe otherwise by her ponderous movements, laborious breathing and difficulty in even standing up from a chair. When the gas lights were off, however, Agnes Guppy was quite capable of silently, carefully placing a chair on a table, over the heads of the participants, and manoeuvring herself to climb up after it. When the guests were invited to light a candle, they would be amazed to see her sitting on top of the table around which they clasped hands, having levitated there, as they believed, with the help of Mrs King.

Wallace and his sister were immediately treated to a display of this kind, shortly after their arrival at the Guppys' elegant home in Highbury Hill Park. Wallace was flabbergasted *(I was too, but at his extreme gullibility rather than the Guppy spectacle.)* He wrote:

> You know the medium's size and probable weight, and can judge the force and exertion required to lift her and her chair on to the exact centre of a large pillar table, as well as the great surplus of force required to do it almost instantaneously and noiselessly, in the dark, and without pressure on the table, which would have tilted up. Will any of the known laws of nature account for this?

(I find it very difficult to be impressed by someone whose only talent is to manipulate their body. Surely the majority of humans have a fully functioning one all of their lives, albeit of a changing size, and therefore have a long time to get used to contorting it. It's not as if you're learning a new and unnatural skill, like, for example, ventriloquism or knots.)

Agnes's other tricks, which included producing beautiful bouquets of flowers whose scent would fill the room, depended a great deal on this 'pillar table', a drastic departure from the usual four- or six-legged pieces that were standard fare in séances across the country. Its shape allowed the hyacinths and lilies, and at one time even a sunflower, complete with stalk, to be secreted. A foot switch, concealed by a Persian rug and easily activated by Agnes, caused a door in the table to open and the flowers to rise up.

It was not especially ingenious but the gimmick of the flowers and, on occasion, small dogs, drew in the crowds. Unlike Mary and Miss Brodie, Agnes also sat as part of a circle involving two other mediums, although she was the only woman in the group, a position she was careful to maintain. Her two confederates, Frank Herne and Charles Williams, were obvious charlatans, who had not spent the necessary time and effort to acquire the skills needed for truly successful mediumship. Despite these limitations, Herne and Williams were a moderately successful partnership and relied on those whose conviction required very little in the way of substantiation.

(Note when I say 'moderately successful' I am being generous: both of these men only began mediumship in 1869 and were far too ambitious for their mediocre talents and inexperience.)

Their collaboration made all sorts of new activities possible, including transportation, a first for spiritual circles, and one that guaranteed Agnes renown. In June 1871 Herne and Williams sat in Soho for eleven guests, eight men and three women, bringing the total number of participants to thirteen, believed to be a propitious number for spiritual inducement.

(This is obviously superstitious nonsense. Why should a spirit care if there are four people or thirteen? The main issue is the desire of the participants to find us, and their efforts to do so, as well as, most importantly, what we feel like at the time.)

A very male-sounding Katie introduced herself to the assembly after the room was darkened, and one of the circle joked with her, saying, 'Katie, why don't you bring Mrs Guppy to us?'

Obviously this participant was a plant, a friend of the mediums, who had been invited to set up the scene so that they could have their display. Another sitter, a merchant from Birmingham, retorted, 'I hope not! She is one of the biggest women in London!' The voice of John King interrupted to tell Katie he was sure that she couldn't do it, but within seconds, while the company were tittering politely at the possibility, there was a heavy bump and some screams from the women.

A match was struck by Herne and illuminated the sight of Agnes Guppy sitting in the middle of the table, in a house dress, holding her account notebook in one hand and a pen in the other. Amazement quickly became concern because Agnes appeared to be in some kind of trance. When she came round after just a few minutes, she was disorientated and started to cry. She told the audience that the last thing she could remember was that she was sitting at home in Highbury, working out her household finances for the week.

(Maskelyne gave an accurate description of the occasion. While having no spiritual awareness, he is a good chronicler, so long as no actual supernatural participation is involved, because of course he refuses to admit the possibility.)

This event led to much religious hyperbole, and the flight of Agnes Guppy was compared to the 'catching away of Philip the Evangelist by the Spirit of the Lord' and to Elijah being taken up to heaven.

(I was surprised by this leap of the imagination, but the workings of the human brain continue to astound me.)

The spiritualist press were delighted and extolled Guppy's talents to their readers without qualification. *Punch* marked the occasion with a more cynical poem:

There is a lady, Mrs Guppy –
Mark, shallow scientific puppy! –
The heaviest she in London, marry,
Her, spirits three long miles did carry.

Upon a table down they set her,
Within closed doors. What! You know better,
And we're all dupes and self-deceivers?
Yah! Sadducees and unbelievers!

A friend of Agnes attested to her presence in Highbury and her sudden vanishing. Wallace dubbed the event a 'modern miracle'.

(Again, I find this lacks acuity on his part and find myself disappointed in the credulousness of some of my followers. Wallace is a particular case, because I admire the astuteness of his scientific consideration of spirit nature immensely, but I am also saddened by his manipulation at the hands of people who really are not in any way his intellectual equal.)

Agnes Guppy's renaissance brought an end to Mary's success. Mary Marshall's followers diminished, as did her income. I still visited from time to time to amuse her with my existence, but her paltry audiences, and the disdain of the spiritualist press, meant that even my occasional interventions did nothing to re-establish her. The last decade of her life was blighted by poverty and discomfort, yet her utter joy at being able to perceive me never diminished, never wavered. When she did die, it was in a small rented room, having lost the cosy house in Holborn in the late 1870s. She spoke her last words with her rheumy eyes fixed on the very spot where I sat, a solitary presence by her bedside. She smiled directly at me, murmured, 'Farewell, Katie. Thank you.' Then breathed her last.

Herne and Williams, sometimes with Guppy, practised mostly from a first-floor parlour at 61 Lamb's Conduit Street, Holborn. It was a simple venue: a bare room above a clothing shop, containing nothing but an oval table and ten chairs, packed tight around it. The advantage of the space was that the séance room was actually formed by closing two folding panel doors between it and a back room. Sitters were allowed to examine the space prior to the sittings but there was a plethora of hidden cubbyholes and secret panels, ideal for hiding the paraphernalia necessary for the meetings. What drew the crowds to these sittings every Friday, as well as to the fortnightly Monday and Wednesday night séances held by Herne and Williams at James Burns' Progressive Library and Spiritual Institute, was that, finally, London believers could see the faces of the spirits of John and Katie King.

It was an adapted form of the Davenport brothers' cabinet that made these new manifestations possible. On the nights when the meetings were due to take place, the table in the Holborn parlour was replaced by a moveable cabinet. As with the Davenports', it contained two benches to which the two mediums could be tied. The difference was that above each of the three panel doors at the front was an aperture, about a foot square and five feet from the ground, which was covered by a heavy black curtain. In an account for *The Spiritualist*, Emily Kislingbury reported:

> Through these three openings, after the mediums were entranced, the spirits first projected hands and afterwards

showed their faces for a few seconds at a time, raising and dropping the curtain as they required it. The gas here was lowered, but the light was sufficiently strong to allow even those who were furthest removed from the cabinet to see the faces quite distinctly.

Last night the face which presented itself was that of John King, with strong black beard and moustache, dark, piercing eyes, and white turban.

(This disguise was patently ridiculous and especially offended me because the physical appearance of John was so similar to that portrayed in Maskelyne's insulting 'music hall' show. I can understand the mediums' need to disguise them- selves, but to do so with a stupid white turban, just like that worn by the late James, and some false bushy facial hair, showed little intellectual rigour or creative thought.)

From time to time, the elderly Katie could be seen too. On these occasions Mrs Guppy, using her physical skills, would creep into the back room by coming up the narrow staircase concealed by one of the wall panels. Any noise that she made would easily be drowned out by the instrument playing of the spirits which preceded the physical manifestations. She could then join Herne and Williams in the cabinet by entering it through a concealed door to the rear.

With their physicality came a new aspect of their persona. John and Katie chatted to the audience and formed friend- ships, making appointments and promises to meet in the weeks following. They were amiable and helpful spiritual entertainers, but they were also reassuring and safe guides into a much darker, potentially frightening world, where one might meet the dead, and even communicate with them.

(This is possibly the only real contribution that these mediums brought to my development. They impersonated me and I was both horrified that anyone could imagine me looking as physically ugly as Guppy and intrigued by the idea that, with a different vehicle, I could be remembered as beautiful.)

One attendee at the séance wrote in a letter to *The Spiritualist*:

> I can never forget or mistake these faces, and if these manifestations are only the forerunner of what is to come – if we may, each and all, hope to recognise our own beloved friends from the spirit world, in living, breathing forms, like those with which I stood face to face last night – I can only say that, at present, the thought seems to me almost more than I can bear; and it is as well that we should first become familiarised with such sights through the introductory efforts of our kind, hard-working friends John and Katie King.

Imagining a physical representation of myself, one that was of a far more appealing kind than that offered by Guppy and her balding, middle-aged, pot-bellied confederates, naturally led me to a whole new arena of possibility, that of sexual desire. I was surprised that I was affected by the remarks about Guppy's girth. Of course, I despised the woman and was happy to see her mocked, but I did not like the idea that my personality was inextricably linked with the physical presence of a middle-aged drab. Instead, I thought, it would be good if the people who flocked to see me wanted me also in the physical sense, either as a charming and seductive John, or as an alluring Katie. Surely this would make them think of me more often. I did not have to look far to find the perfect vehicle for this endeavour.

Florence Eliza Cook was just sixteen. She lived with her parents, two sisters and a brother in a terraced house in Hackney's Eleanor Road. It was a slightly shabby street but in a quiet neighbourhood, with houses that were both affordable and large enough for the family to live in relative comfort, given Henry Cook's modest employment as a printer.

The neighbourhood was attractive to the family for another reason. At their previous home in Kent, Florence, their eldest, although still not quite ten years old at the time, had enjoyed some local success at helping friends and neighbours communicate with their lost loved ones. Eleanor Road was around the corner from Navarino Road, where the Dalston Association of Spiritualists was based. The association was a discreetly presented organisation, based in an unassuming semi-detached house with intricately whorled, white lace curtains, a brass plaque and midnight-blue door. Tiny Florence, with her natural pallor, tight dark curls falling past her shoulders, and her lithe, flexible body, had quite a few attributes to start with, but there was a checklist of skills to acquire if she was to retain anyone among her followers who was more than a curious and cursory thrill-seeker. The Dalston association could both nurture her and guarantee the kind of audience that she would need to attain any degree of success.

The Cook family attended meetings there from time to time. Henry was a keen spiritualist and more than a little proud of his daughter's shared interest. So, with her family's support,

Florence began to hold small invited meetings for local friends and neighbours who had suffered a bereavement, at which she presented them with messages, usually delicately handwritten notes, from the other side.

She was not only young and lovely but also intelligent. During the day she worked as a school teacher at Eliza Cliff's school on Richmond Road, conveniently situated between her home and the spiritualist headquarters. The advantages of an innocent appearance with a devious set of mind are manifold.

(Remember, in my other incarnations, physical beauty, beyond that of some rather graceful fingers, had never been on display. The mediums were seedy-looking men or, in the case of Mrs Guppy, an obese woman with bad skin and signs of early ageing. Here, however, was a chance for that haunting voice, those cold little hands, to find a body that might do them justice.)

Florence's ambition meant that I only had to bring a single dream, a brief night-time vision when she was in that halfway place between sleep and waking, for her to know what she should do.

Florence was a vain girl and immediately delighted in the idea that her looks might bring reward. However, she was also canny, and her first endeavour was for a small invited audience, all of whom were committed spiritualists. I recall it here in full because it marks the tentative beginnings of a new step in my development, and a concomitant, highly significant, growth in my influence.

The Dalston Association of Spiritualists was enjoying large audiences and financial rewards by impersonating a rather dull but learned version of the male me, John. This imposturous John King was the guide at séances hosted by Herne and

Williams. Florence's parents decided, wisely, that a good way to share their daughter's talent might be to align themselves with the Dalston group.

Thomas Blyton was invited to sit with them for Florence's display of her abilities. He was the secretary of the Dalston association, and a bachelor, and wrote immediately to his closest friend that he was very taken with Florence's 'tightly ringleted hair and creamy complexion'; he would become one of her best friends.

In a small, dark parlour within the Dalston Inquirers' meeting rooms at No. 74, he was seated with Florence, her mother and her father. The room was cosy, with hints of opulence in the heavily brocaded claret curtains which were enough to suggest prosperity but not so much as to detract from the homeliness and comfort of the space. The gas light was extinguished and Mr Blyton became aware of the chair beside him, on which Miss Cook was seated, being lifted high above his head. Florence was heard to gasp slightly at the shock of the movement.

(This was my doing; she had not prepared for a levitation of this kind and I frightened the poor girl. I was, however, absolutely determined that this séance would be a huge and unqualified success.)

When it was replaced on the floor, some ghostly, very faint illumination seemed to surround the seated medium, so that for a second she shined as if she herself were ethereal in nature. Then suddenly, much to the surprise of the onlookers, a large portion of her dress was whisked away.

(This was nothing to do with me; needless to say I cannot make things glow, but I thought it an enchanting display.)

She remained motionless as if completely unaware of the

immodest state she was in. This, given her obvious innocence and purity, was, for Blyton, incontrovertible proof that she was undeniably in a trance-like state. A cassock came flying from a corner of the room and landed on Mr Blyton's lap, where it was joined soon after by a vulcanite necklace that he had earlier seen around Florence's neck, which also appeared to rise up from the corner and came to rest on his upper thighs. Mr Blyton's hands went under the cassock as he tried to make himself more comfortable.

The loud raps that followed caused the table to rock alarmingly, although not enough to dislodge the cloth that covered Mr Blyton. When the gas was relit, the still partially clad Florence remained in a trance and wrote spirit messages, some in response to a question from Blyton about the necessity for darkness and dim lights during part of the séance, but also to stress that she was no longer human.

Je suis un esprit

The final message was followed by a translation into English:

I am a spirit

Florence Cook, the tender, uneducated girl, according to Blyton (he seemed to have forgotten her daytime occupation), could not conceivably know a word of French. The spirit who was possessing her was someone else entirely. Perhaps a little less modest, with a disregard for her clothing or lack of it, again in keeping with the possible foreign aspects of the spirit's background, but educated enough to speak both French and

English. This was a new figure in the séance room, and one which the spirit herself intimated in her writing would be good for the Dalston group, as well as for Florence. Her name too was Katie King, but she was a young spirit, clearly a very different entity from the others who shared her name. For my part, this was a far more interesting incarnation than those that had preceded it. The upwards trajectory that I saw for myself was not, however, to be as straightforward as this initial success had seemed to promise.

(Watching myself, I saw a new future before me. I, who had always thought of myself as somehow timeless, looked forward to what I might achieve with ambition.)

Just as poor dead Filenia had made Jonathan Koons open to the possibility of me, so the death of many a loved one brought those hoping for a message *from the other side* to Dalston and the intimate rooms where Florence Cook began to conduct her nightly meetings. Yet there was far more than the longing to communicate with someone who had passed away at work here, far more than the need to believe that the dead were in fact alive and well but living on some astral plain somewhere. Here was an opportunity, and let's be frank about this, to stare at a scantily clad, very pretty young girl, and still be perfectly respectable. Did all of those young – and not so young – men who came to follow, finance and support Florence Cook truly believe she was speaking to spirits of our dear departed? I doubt it. However, so long as every outward, public action presented firstly their conviction, and secondly their attestation, then they could enjoy their shabby encounters without impunity or moral censure.

(The thing I love most about Florence is that she made me a kind of self-fulfilling prophecy. And the more that the great and

the good came to believe in her talent and by extension in the existence of me, the more a kind of 'Emperor's new clothes' effect took over. But I am getting ahead of myself.)

Less than a week after that first manifestation in Dalston, a second meeting was arranged, this time at Wilkes' Library in Dalston Lane. Florence was already an excellent ventriloquist and there was a plan to include a spoken message from Katie prior to her appearance, and thus to develop her presence. The guests at this meeting included William Harrison, the editor of *The Spiritualist*, who would play a crucial part in publicising Florence if her career was to develop.

Using the same method that I had with William Davenport, I whispered to the small invited group through Florence, but the message was one that took both Florence and Mr Blyton by surprise. It urged that she meet with Frank Herne and Charles Williams, and be reunited with someone else from the spirit world who longed to see her again. John King wanted to meet Katie, and he wished to do so at a Herne and Williams séance.

Florence had very little to learn from these two charlatans, but they had much to gain from her. The one person who did not benefit from the new liaison at all was Agnes Guppy. Mrs King was now promoted, on the rare occasions that she appeared, as the mother of Katie, while John was her father.

(I was annoyed by these purported familial relationships. Yes, of course I can see how they might work to promote spirit reputation, but it was in no way logical. Obviously John and Katie were simply different aspects of the same idea; gender, intelligence, attractiveness, wit were all no more than traits that could be added or subtracted to my non-existent personality. My being was a nebulous, changeable thing, created and

*manipulated according to each time and place. Familial rela-
tionships seemed to me to be a very simplistic way of dealing
with my spiritual complexity.)*

Yet my dislike of Agnes was not the principal reason I saw the
collaboration as beneficial to my protégée. Herne, like Agnes,
was a private medium. He was not from a wealthy family and
his wife had no independent financial means, but he did have a
sponsor – a Manchester businessman, Charles Blackburn.

If Florence was to achieve credibility and substantive fame
rather than fleeting notoriety, it would be necessary for her to
have a similar benefactor. Blackburn was an obvious candidate.
He was a keen spiritualist and a very rich man, owning a large
area of land in Didsbury, Manchester, which would increase
even further in value with the extension of the railway. His
patronage would allow Florence's meetings to be free, with the
implication that they were philanthropic and that the medium
was sharing her gift so that the bereaved might find comfort
in a message from beyond. Invited guests, rather than paying
ones, could much better attest publicly to the genuineness
of a sitting. And finally, Florence, freed from the necessity of
teaching, would be able to devote herself wholeheartedly to
perfecting and refining the techniques of her profession, while
building a reliable and regular following. Competition between
mediums for followers and regular audiences was fierce, articles about exposure and disgrace far more common than those
attesting to real spiritual experience. A new approach – one that
would serve to expose Herne, encourage Blackburn to support
Florence, and be useful in preserving me for posterity – was
essential.

The Wallace quote is from a letter dated 8 May 1968 with the WCP Identifier: WCP147.1266, Wallace Letters Online. The letter to *The Spiritualist* appeared in the edition of 15 December 1872 on p. 46.

The reference to comparisons with Philip the Evangelist and Elijah is from Fritz's 1873 book, *Where are the Dead? Or Spiritualism Explained.* The account by Maskelyne is in his book, *Modern Spiritualism* (1876).

The Quarterly Review (1871) wryly commented on the dramatic events at Mrs Guppy's as follows:

If they [the spirits] can bring in any quantity of fruits, flowers and ices for a dessert, they must surely be able to furnish forth her breakfast and her dinner-tables. When she wishes to travel, they save her not merely the fatigue of the journey, but the cost of cabs and railway fares. What on earth, then, has Mrs Guppy got to do with 'household accounts'?

Florence Cook's abilities were immediately remarked upon as being exceptional. Here at the Magic Circle we have a letter from Blyton to a friend where he states, 'Today I have seen the most delicious piece of delicacy. Florence Cook is her name and she is the most delightful example of the female species, not just physically enchanting, but with mysterious powers that seem to overshadow all of the other mediumistic phenomena I have witnessed.' (U/D 1871, Navarino Road.)

In more recent accounts of Florence's career, much is made of the fact that she may have lied about her age; see, for example, Trevor Hall's *The Medium and the Scientist* (1984), Duckworth and Co. This is slightly odd, as the record of her birth is easily found and she was in fact born in September 1856. See Birth Certificate Florence Eliza Cook, Sept. 1856, North Aylesford, Vol. 2a, p. 247.

On the other hand, there is an excellent contemporary account of the difference in status between private and commercial mediums in Alex Owen's academic study *The Darkened Room*. She observes that 'public mediumship was associated not only with the working classes but also with middle-class assumptions about lower-class morality. The rationale that working-class mediums needed to earn a living and might therefore be tempted to resort to legerdemain if their gifts deserted them or failed to come up to scratch merely cloaked other class-based anxieties.'

My partner's sister, who used to live in Manchester, tells me that Blackburn Park, named after Charles Blackburn, still exists today. [AM 2007]

Nowadays the exploitation still exists, and it is two tiered. There is the obvious, well-publicised corruption and deception of entertainment mediums who profit from the bereaved. But there is too a much less recognised layer, that of young working-class boys and girls who are lured to the industry with promises of fame and money, and who pay every penny they can earn to dubious, scurrilous schools of mediumship, where they claim to teach a skill that cannot be learned. I saw it in my Scottish council estate when I was growing up: kids lured to mediumistic circles, handing over their wages because they were told they had 'the gift'. In my head I hear Katie's scorn fall on them like acid rain. I want her to chronicle the time that I am leaving, not just the one that is past.

Sex is not so much part of it now. I think of the most successful mediums, the ones who have television shows and West End appearances, and none of them that I can name could be said to be attractive in the popular sexual sense. Now we are beguiled by comforting familial camaraderie.

If I had time, I'd tell those kids there are better things to long for than celebrity and riches, not that they'd listen, but I'd feel better for having tried. Being remembered is so much more than being known and recognised by everyone for a heartbeat or two. [AM 2012]

SEVERAL SÉANCES IN LONDON

Alfred Russel Wallace was eager to try out the latest phenomena from the spirit world. Frederick Hudson's north London photographic studio was the first in England to offer the production of spirit photographs, usually taken in the company of their mediums. Occasionally the shadowy figures posed beside or behind their surviving loved ones, once again corporeal, thanks to the magic of photography.

(This was an interesting development. Generally it was people's lack of understanding of the photographic process that made them open to such belief. It seemed mysterious and magical that one might have a likeness of someone that out-lived the person. In Wallace's case, as with the other scientists who became involved with the fad, it is frankly baffling as to why they thought the exposure of light-sensitive paper might be conducive to a spiritual visit.)

Wallace's first attempt met with some success and the negative showed a male figure carrying a sword. Buoyed up by this, he returned again, duly paying another ten shillings to Hudson. This time, the shadowy white figure in the background was undoubtedly female. Clasping a bunch of flowers in her hands, she seemed to proffer them up to Wallace. At first he was puzzled. The spirit was dressed like his mother and carried roses, her favourite flowers, yet seemed somehow heavier.

'Ah, it's the aura,' Hudson explained to him. 'It will be your dear mama, but with blurred edges that make her appear to be greater in size than she was. It is a common phenomenon with this medium and the spirit form.'

On his third visit, all doubts vanished. The figure was now in a dark dress, with a more pensive expression than was her custom during life, but it seemed to Wallace that this could only be his mother, and he was very glad of it.

(The spirit photograph and the Victorian love of the post-mortem photograph are inextricably linked. The latter shows the preoccupation that the living have with the dead, while the former offers reassurance that the dead are still interested in the living. This latter point is at least an accurate assumption. I am indeed obsessed with the living. However, we spirits are not really dead in the sense that you understand it, although of course it is possible that we have been, and just don't remember.

It is important to note here that as we are non-corporeal, in fact these images are nothing like us at all, but rather how the living imagine we might be.)

Hudson had a network of casually paid helpers, who often worked as servants in the homes of his sitters. There they could acquire images of the dead beloved, and he would then copy the image onto a plate, so that the photograph that was taken subsequently would appear alongside a pre-existing image on a prepared plate. He was excellent at sleight of hand: even after showing the sitter that the plate he was using was new and unused, he was able to switch it deftly for another which he had prepared in advance.

Sometimes things went wrong – perhaps the servant failed to find an image. But as Hudson led all sitters to accept that spirit activity might not actually happen, this was easily covered by an explanation that the spirits had failed to materialise on that particular day.

(Spirit photography and scientific photography are analogous: both are concerned with how photographs can reveal things not visible to the human eye. Later that decade, in 1878, Eadweard Muybridge's motion study of a horse would show that at one point a galloping horse has all four hooves off the ground, something that couldn't be discerned by an observer. This was seen as further proof that photography could make the invisible visible. It is clearly a ridiculous idea. There is actually nothing to see. There exists the odd rare percipient person who is aware of me, but they can't actually visualise me unless I am inside a human body.)

Wallace shared his experience with Mr and Mrs Guppy, and, keen to enhance his wife's reputation as well as to create some record of her talents for posterity, Samuel contacted Hudson and arranged for a sitting. The results were very satisfactory, with both Agnes and a spirit form being shown together on the pictures. Herne and Williams, eager to share in the success of their colleague, also arranged for sittings. Enjoying the rewards of his spiritual foray, Hudson was able to charge exorbitant amounts for sittings with clients who were eager to have an image of someone they had lost but were bound by contract to accept that it might not happen.

At this point an alliance developed. Hudson, in cahoots with Herne, Williams and Agnes, arranged for a series of pictures where a white-clothed figure stood beside the medium. Frank Herne wrapped himself in sheets of muslin and posed beside Mrs Guppy, who in return did him the same favour. Although the double-exposure pictures had numerous tell-tale signs, such as the background still being partially visible through the main sitter, these photographs were much harder to doubt without specifically slandering their subjects and the photographer. Photos that were taken as a tableau with actors pretending to be spirits were infallible testaments of the success of spirit photography – or at least that was what Hudson and his group of mediums believed.

The spectre of doubt (a clever and appropriate phrase at this point, if I may say so) came from an unexpected quarter. William Harrison, founding editor of *The Spiritualist,* a periodical with a huge following of believers, directly accused Herne and Williams of fraud. It was especially surprising given that the primary sponsor of *The Spiritualist* was none other than Charles Blackburn, the financial supporter of Herne.

The reasons for this *volte face* were far more complicated than the various accounts might suggest. William Harrison was a devout spiritualist, which meant two things. Firstly, he would assume that the weird and wonderful presentations by Herne and Williams in Hudson's studio were genuine, corroboration of what he himself knew to be true. Secondly, he would be very susceptible to any kind of direct interference. If Harrison discredited Herne and Williams, there was every possibility that Blackburn would take on the management of Florence, who was showing great promise. Agnes Guppy, when faced with someone of Florence's talent and beauty, would fall very quickly into obscurity. My intent therefore was to first discredit Herne and Williams, using Hudson as a starting point. I could then doubly damn Agnes, by Florence's meteoric rise, both financially and in terms of publicity by way of support from Harrison, and by her previous association with the disgraced, publicly shamed fakes, Herne and Williams.

(I admit to some surprise at my own ingenuity; I had evolved, in eighty years or so, from being a displaced, floating spirit, an observer of limited influence, to this, a Machiavellian architect of downfalls.)

The Plan

Step One: Make Harrison aware of double exposures

Step Two: Use the ensuing row as a means to create a rift between Herne and Williams

Step Three: Harrison reports their fraud

Step Four: Blackburn stops sponsoring Herne

Step Five: Blackburn starts sponsoring Florence

Step Six: Guppy is forgotten in the wake of Florence's triumph

The first step was accomplished with relative ease. Harrison arranged to meet Herne and Williams at Hudson's studio one afternoon in the summer of 1872. The day was sunny and warm, the third consecutive hot day in a June that was promising to have much better weather than the previous year. Harrison was struck by the contrast between the brightness of the day and the shadowy supernatural phenomena they hoped to witness. He was already delighted by the results that Herne and Williams, as well as Agnes, had produced with Hudson's help, and had arranged to meet them that he might experience the process first-hand. Additionally, he would check for fraud so that he could testify to their authenticity in *The Spiritualist,* a move that would not only reassure his readers but also please his principal sponsor, Blackburn, especially as Blackburn was also financially supporting Herne.

For the photographs, Harrison had brought along four clean plates. This would ensure that there was no possibility of 'double exposure', that is, using a plate on which a figure, one that might be believed to be a spirit, had already been captured, and on which the portrait of the sitters would then be superimposed.

(For my purposes I wanted to discredit Herne when he was being photographed alone, so that Williams could deny all knowledge and thus create a breach between them. Needless to say, I am familiar with the expression 'divide and rule'.)

Hudson, already revelling in the publicity that might ensue from this visit, and calculating how he might further increase his already hefty fee for prospective clients, ushered in Harrison.

Herne and Williams were seated in a small anteroom leading into the studio, which was comfortably furnished with five armchairs upholstered in dark green silk, and a small dark wood table, on which lay some reading matter, including, of course, two copies of *The Spiritualist*. Harrison didn't join them, but instead was led straight through to the studio so that he might conduct an examination of the space. He was already largely convinced as to the authenticity of the phenomena and made no more than a cursory examination of the studio before handing over his clean plates. These were then placed very conspicuously on a large oak sideboard positioned against the wall, behind the screen that would be the backdrop to any pictures.

Harrison did look inside the sideboard when he examined the room but completely missed the false back on the left-hand side cupboard, behind which was stuffed several yards of very fine grey muslin. Conveniently, this was the part that was concealed by the screen.

Herne and Williams joined the other two men in the studio and, for the first two photographs, were posed together. For these, Hudson made a point of using the first pair of plates that Harrison had brought, dramatically flourishing them as he slid them into the camera.

'Gentlemen, you do know that we do not always meet with success in our endeavours?' Hudson spoke to the room but looked pointedly at Harrison.

'We can but hope for the favour of the spirits.' Herne smiled at both Harrison and Hudson, and Williams nodded his approval.

'Perhaps we should take a picture of each of the mediums alone?' Mr Harrison posited. 'Just in case one is more blessed than the other today.'

'Of course. Mr Herne, perhaps you might oblige us next.'

Harrison picked up the third plate from the sideboard and handed it to Hudson, while Herne took his position on a chair in front of the screen. Just as Hudson went to slide a plate into the camera, a tremendous gust of wind (me!) blew open the window and took him by surprise, causing him to drop not one but two plates, one of which bore a faint image of a young girl swathed in a white sheet of cloth. Three bewildered men turned as one to the window, to look out on the continuing calm sunshine they had enjoyed on their stroll to the studio less than an hour before. Hudson quickly went to collect the two plates, but not before Harrison caught sight of the offending second one, lying side by side with his own on the Turkey rug. Hudson then found himself possessed of a great and irresistible itch in his right leg (me again!), one that was so great it rendered him temporarily unable to bend down to the floor without first scratching vigorously. Harrison, thus unhindered, picked up the plates and wordlessly, but with an accusatory expression, presented them to Herne and Hudson.

It was Williams who broke the quiet, with a noise of disgust and shock. Harrison looked sympathetically at him; he had obviously been betrayed both by his partner and by the photographer. Herne did not help himself or the situation by retorting, 'How dare you! It was your suggestion in the first place!' Williams looked close to tears.

(His acting skill was actually far greater than his mediumistic abilities and he would have been better advised at an earlier stage in life to make his career in the theatre.)

Harrison moved to his side and put a steadying hand on his arm. 'I am a witness that you were no party to this, Mr Williams. I will not have you slandered by this obvious trickery.'

Hudson pleaded and cajoled. It was, he argued, the importance of the event. He did not feel he could rely on the vagaries of the spirit world when so much was at stake: his reputation and that of the mediums, in the greatest of spirit publications. While taking some pleasure in this description of his magazine, Harrison remained unconvinced.

The Spiritualist duly published a piece about the exposure. It signalled the end of the partnership. And, as I had hoped, Blackburn terminated his sponsorship.

(In case the reader is wondering, I had absolutely no compunction in destroying the reputation of Herne, Williams and Guppy. Herne and Williams had made no real attempt at a spiritual apprenticeship, which can take many years and a

great perfection of skill, and Guppy was a gold-digging adventuress, trying her hand at something new, without having the faintest idea of what she was getting into. In this instance, I was unequivocally on the side of the doubters.)

The next part of my plan was ready to be enacted.

It was easy for the most casual of onlookers to see that Blackburn was susceptible to pretty young women. While I pondered over how to progress my plan for Blackburn to sponsor Florence, the dear girl had already begun to exercise her feminine wiles on him. Although she was doing so not as herself, but as a new and sensational figure in her sittings.

Late in 1872, Florence wrote to Harrison that she had experienced a new development in her mediumship and that he and Blackburn should come immediately for a private séance which would be held at her parents' home. The letter recounted a spiritual event that had taken place the day before and had been witnessed by the whole of the Cook family as well as both of their servants. Harrison had been experimenting at various séances with different kinds of light, in an attempt to move beyond the secretive and easily corrupted nature of the dark séance. Most recently, at the Cooks', he had created a kind of spirit lamp by dissolving phosphorus in oil of cloves, using it to coat the inside of a warm glass bottle, then exposing it to the air so that it glowed. He left the remaining phosphorus oil with Florence. Katie, Florence claimed in her letter, had urged her to use the phosphorus so that she might better manifest herself.

(Actually, I had nothing to do with it; this was entirely a device of Florence's own making and an ingenious one at that.)

The Cooks' home did not have space for a dedicated séance room and so the effect of a cabinet was created by putting drapes over the kitchen door and the household gathered on the steps just outside it, to see what might transpire. Florence went into the enclosure, and after a few minutes, a fully formed hand and arm appeared, glowing in the light from the phosphorus bottle which it held. The arm moved upwards and, as it did so, gave light enough to show a head and shoulders, covered in a diaphanous white material. The hair beneath it was clearly not that of the medium for it was longer and much straighter, and everyone who witnessed the event marvelled at the beauty of the apparition, who spent but a few minutes in their presence. It was, Florence claimed in the letter, to be the beginning of a whole series of meetings with Katie, who, with the help of 'clever Mr Harrison's phosphorus' and the 'developing abilities of her humble medium', would present herself in public many times in the months to come.

Blackburn and Harrison, accompanied also by Thomas Blyton, arrived in Hackney the afternoon following receipt of the letter. Mr Cook had opened up the basement and made it into a less makeshift space than the kitchen and stairs arrangement. Heavy picture tapestries now hung on the white walls and the only natural light came from a window that was partly subterranean; the piano had been moved into this space too, positioned against the wall furthest from the window. There were four other sitters, including Mrs Cook, besides the gentlemen. A curtained cabinet was erected, in such a way that it blocked the window completely, leaving only the light from the very low gas lamps. The seven guests settled themselves in a semicircle of chairs that had been placed before the dark blue drapes. Mrs Cook addressed the small assembly from her chair, without standing, 'We'll need silence, so that my Florrie can speak to her spirit, please, gentlemen. Remember, whatever you do, please, please do not try to touch Katie when she is with us. To do so would be gravely dangerous for my girl.'

Within less than a minute the curtain had parted and the hand and arm appeared, carrying the phosphorescent light, although this time, rather than coating a bottle, the oil had been used on the inside of an oil lamp. As hoped, the head and shoulders followed, draped with the finest of cloth, so that features and hairstyle were entirely visible. 'My word!' Blackburn was unable to contain himself, but was immediately shushed by his companions. The face turned towards him and smiled sweetly. Then she spoke.

'Mr Blackburn, I think you know the German language, do you not?'

'Why yes, I do, having spent some time in that country for my business.'

'Then perhaps you would join me in the song "*Du bist die Ruh, der Friede mild*", and perhaps Mrs Cook might honour us with her playing?'

'Katie, you do mean that we should sing in English, I assume?'

'Why no! My medium is a poor ignorant girl but I know the language well.'

(*A slightly inaccurate version of this exchange was recounted in Epes Sargent's* Proof Palpable of Immortality. *She also conflated two séances into one event and exaggerated her own role to make it appear more interesting. My account is, needless to say, far more accurate.*)

Mrs Cook had already taken her place at the piano in the far corner of the room and began to hit the opening notes. Katie moved still closer towards the crowd so that not only were her head and neck visible beneath her veil, but her cleavage too. Her voice was lilting and clear; her German was flawless; Charles Blackburn was utterly enraptured. I found that my planned interventions, lifting Blackburn's chair perhaps, or moving some items around the room, all activities that tired me, were completely unnecessary.

Katie retired to the cabinet after the song and Mrs Cook played a short instrumental piece for five minutes or so to allow her daughter time to recover from the physically and mentally exhausting experience of mediumship. When a tired-looking Florence was led by her mama from the cabinet, Mr Blackburn rushed to her side. From now on she would be a private medium, with a regular stipend that would free her from teaching, thus allowing her the time and energy necessary for her to fully develop her exceptional natural talent for spirit communication.

The success of my venture delighted me, although my pleasure was brief because I had not reckoned on the spite and determination of Agnes Guppy. Agnes's revenge came in the shape of Mr William Volckman (a loathsome creature, and a hypocrite, something I despise even more than a doubter).

The ageing Samuel Guppy was not party to his wife's various peccadilloes. Volckman had started out as one of the opportunistic flirtations that she indulged in from time to time, but in this case it evolved into something more serious. This development happened largely at Volckman's insistence when he saw the precarious nature of her husband's health and his amassed riches and decided that there might be some future in the association.

(As it happens, he was entirely correct in this, and he married Agnes Guppy shortly after her husband's death.)

The initial sequence of events which transpired as a result of Agnes's resentment at her rival are documented in a very interesting letter sent from the celebrated medium D. D. Home to a fellow medium in the US:

In January 1873, Mrs Guppy called at our [that is Home's] residence, 16 Old Quebec St, London W., and endeavoured to enlist our co-operation in a plot whereby a certain Mr Clark, Mr Henderson and one Volckman were to be hired to attend a séance at Miss Cook's, and, watching their opportunity, at a favourable moment, while the manifestations were in progress, to throw vitriol [sic] in the face of the spirit, hoping to destroy for ever the handsome features of Miss Florrie Cook, and thus at one fell stroke to effectually remove from further use a medium who, Mrs Guppy claimed, had taken and was taking all her, Mrs Guppy's, friends away from her and upon whose patronage Mrs G. had long depended.

Home did not welcome the offer and was enraged both by what he called a 'horrible scheme' and by Agnes's obsessive hatred and bitter rancour at what she referred to as Florrie's 'doll face'. Home ordered her from his house and followed up by sending a note to Mr Guppy saying that his wife would never again be welcome there.

Volckman, who was *(to my utter bewilderment)* enamoured of Agnes, was less shocked by the plan. However, he did insist on modifying it so that rather than risk the legal and moral difficulties of scarring a young woman for life, he might only destroy her credibility and thus lose her the sponsorship and reputation so intrinsic to her success.

(I chose not to interfere very much in this attempt to thwart me because I wanted to see how Florence would handle herself. I was, of course, ready to intervene at any time if it became necessary. I also admit that Volckman's reluctance to throw the acid was in part, but only in part, my doing. He did have a conscience of sorts, prompted by a vivid dream about the harsh reality of life in a penal colony.)

It was not difficult for Volckman to engineer entry to Florence's circle. He was a member of the Dalston Association and well acquainted with Harrison. However, for the plan to be a success, it was essential that the sitting he attended was also one where Charles Blackburn was part of the audience.

His perfect opportunity arose at a séance to be conducted in the Cook family home, with not only Blackburn and Harrison as guests, but also the Earl of Caithness and Lady Caithness. It was, as Volckman himself would later relate, the foggiest night there had been 'for many a year' and, moreover, he had to walk more than four miles to reach the Cook home. Both Harrison and Blackburn were aggrieved by what they perceived to be Volckman's brusque manner when they greeted him in the lobby of the house.

The guests took their places in front of the usual blue curtained cabinet, all except Mrs Cook and Lady Caithness, who both went inside to testify that Florence was indeed tied up and that no clothing or fabric was hidden on her person that might later be used as a spirit veil.

Mrs Cook led Lady Caithness to her seat, then stood in front of the audience briefly to address them. 'Ladies and gentlemen, I must ask you that no matter what you see here tonight, no matter how much you may wish to, if Katie graces us with her spirit presence, you MUST NOT touch her under any circumstances. To do so would be injurious to my dear daughter, who could be caught between the spirit world and this. Katie has promised something special for us tonight, but I must ask you all to agree to this condition before we can begin our meeting.'

There was murmured assent from the audience and Mrs Cook dimmed the gas lamps, but did not extinguish them entirely, before taking her place with the assembled spectators.

In just a few minutes the veiled face of Katie appeared. But then, in a dramatic new phase of her public manifestations, she stepped out from the gap in the curtains and began to walk around the sitters.

(This took me as much by surprise as it did the audience, and had I known it was going to occur, I would have tried to engineer a better séance audience for this innovative display of Florence's enhanced mediumship.)

Everyone stared. Florence was truly magnificent. She wore a fine white robe, right to the ground, of a flimsy, almost transparent material, and a light auburn wig that was noticeably different from her usual dark hair, even under the muslin veil. The bottom edge of her skirt was of a more opaque but equally fine white fabric, principally so that the spectators could not see the very high shoes she was wearing, which added to the impression that Katie was several inches taller than her medium. Hours of practice had enabled Florence to glide on these as if they were no more difficult to move in than ballet slippers. The dress, carefully sewn in the finest of fine material, had been carefully hidden in her under-drawers so that, even when Lady Caithness examined her, it was not in evidence. The wig and shoes had been concealed behind a false panel in the cabinet.

I was delighted, absolutely certain that Volckman would now be thwarted in any plan that he had by Florrie's brilliance. She moved amongst the sitters, occasionally even running her very cold white hand across an outstretched hand, or deigning to rest it briefly on a bowed head. But the flawless, spellbinding performance did not entrance the entire audience. Volckman leaped up from his chair, so quickly that he caused it to fall backwards behind him with a crash, and grabbed Florence around the waist, crying, 'She is not a spirit! See! See! She is a fraud! This is just the medium in disguise!'

Two of the other men present, Blyton and a young, good-looking fellow called Elgie Corner, leaped to the spirit's defence, trying to pull him away from her. Mrs Cook cried out, 'The light! Turn off the light!' and someone obligingly did so.

In the darkness there was noise of a scuffle and Volckman cried out in some pain. Katie disappeared into the cabinet and Volckman was taken upstairs and forbidden to leave the house until it was ascertained that the medium had come to no harm through his intervention.

After several minutes, moans and sobs were heard to come from the cabinet, and Florence's voice called out faintly, 'Help me, oh please, please help me.'

Florence's little brother, who had been in the audience with his mother, started to bawl, 'Florrie is going to die!' and 'The bad man killed Florrie!', and while Lady Caithness soothed him, Mrs Cook opened the curtains on her daughter. She lay where she had been placed, dressed in her own black dress, her ringlets spread around her head on the floor, but with tears running down her cheeks. Mr Corner and Mr Blackburn immediately came to her assistance, untying her bindings and helping her to stand.

Volckman was told to leave, and did so, sporting two scratches on his nose that Florence had managed to bestow upon him in her bid to be free. His actions were condemned in the spiritual press and even the Earl and Lady Caithness added their signatures to blast his action as 'a gross outrage'. But he defended himself in *The Medium and Daybreak* against the various accusations levelled at him, claiming that he had not gone to deliberately disrupt the proceedings at the behest of a rival medium. He had, he stated, acquiesced at the outset not to touch the spirit if she appeared. However, the figure was obviously not a spirit, but rather Florence Cook, and so he had not broken any public promise. Moreover, the scratches he suffered testified to a very human struggle. He wryly remarked in his letter to the publication:

> But, reader, remember the poor ghost is a young, impulsive woman, and, although some three hundred years old, may not have *quite* forgotten the use of nails in an emergency.

(The idea that I was 300 years old was nonsense, but was a popular one at the time. It related to a ridiculous story circulated by some unknown idiot that I was the ghost of a dead pirate girl. Thankfully it was never adopted by any of my important mediums but did occasionally get mentioned in the press.)

The publicity that followed did nothing but increase the numbers trying to gain admittance to Florence's salon. However, the incident also led to uncertainty on the part of Blackburn. He wrote to Florence, informing her that if she were to continue to be his ward, she would need to be subjected to stringent tests that would dispel all doubts about her honesty.

Alfred Russel Wallace was one possibility I considered as a suitable witness, but I decided that his devotion to Agnes Guppy might be problematic. Instead I turned my attention, and more importantly, that of Florence, towards another learned man, one who had only recently been drawn towards spiritualism.

Spirit photography was already popular in America, having been pioneered by William Mumler. Most famously of all, Mumler photographed Lincoln's widow, Mary Todd Lincoln, with the spectre of her husband apparently standing behind her, his comforting hands placed on each shoulder. The photograph became an emblem of hope to many people suffering from the huge and terrible losses of the Civil War.

An interesting feature of this section is that the writer (unusually) does cite the Epes Sargent book, but only to tell us how the account there is inferior to her own. The letter from Home I found in the *Proceedings of the Society for Psychical Research*, 1964, Vol. 54, part 195, pp 58–9, and the amusing quote about Florence using her nails is from William Volckman's 'My Ghost Experiences' in *The Medium and Daybreak*, 16 Jan. 1874. However, Katie's voice, as presented by the writer, is even more in evidence than in earlier sections and her involvement with the events around her is evolving, as she herself notes. It's interesting that she takes a series of well-documented factual historical events – the falling out of Herne and Williams, the business with the acid, the growing success of Florence Cook and Blackburn's support of her and so on – and makes it seem as if she herself has orchestrated the events. As a literary device it follows that described in

David Rain's 2006 article in the *Creative Writing Review*, which considers how fact can be manipulated by a fictitious narrator. [AM 2007]

The key feature of this manuscript is Katie's own evolution. She is obviously delighted by her own interventions, but I wonder if, at the time, she even considered the possibility of her own demise, or did that seem like far too human a thing? How can something that has never lived die? Can she cease to exist or somehow, one day, just fall out of consciousness? [AM 2012]

Spirit Writing
Approximately 1878, Magic Circle Collection

WIDOWER

I have other worries too. In 1871, an unexpected sadness comes to test Robert's faith. Mary, his wife, twelve years his junior, dies suddenly in the United States, where they now live.

It has been a marriage of affection and sharing. The very first time she heard him speak, she confided to her sister that, although he might be the ugliest man in the world, she would marry him, or die a spinster. He wrote to a friend in similar ilk, that although Mary was neither pretty nor even interesting to look at, he had not before met a woman with so much to like in her. He argued for women to be financially independent; even before she met him, in defiance of her family, Mary was mastering a trade.

The strangest thing was that I did not resent her closeness to him, nor his to her. He told her before they wed that in the past he had loved another far more passionately than he did her, but that now he was happy with her and always would be. For her part, she seemed to recognise in him the same goodness that I had first observed.

Mary's death seems to make him vulnerable, lonely. At the funeral in New Harmony, Indiana, the hot August sunshine blazes down as a small group of musicians play merry music. It is an event more mindful of a parade than of a burial. There is no tolling bell to mark Mary's passing, for that is what the couple have agreed. When Robert steps forward to speak to the vast crowd of assembled mourners, his eyes are dry, his voice is steady, he even offers a sad half-smile to a woman who is sobbing in the front row. He says:

I do not believe more firmly in these trees that spread their shade over us, in this hill on which we stand, in those sepulchral monuments which we see around us here – than I do that human life, once granted, perishes never more.

His idea of marriage, the convictions that made this partnership what it was, are expressed best in a letter from Naples on 2 April 1856 to his daughter on the eve of her wedding:

I know of nothing more important to be remembered in wedded life than this, that each human being has his or her own peculiarities of character, and that, so long as these do not encroach on the rights or comforts of others, they should be carefully respected. I pray you not to imagine – for it is a dangerous error – that the intimate character of the relation in which you will hereafter stand to one another absolves you from this obligation. It but renders it the more important.

The secret of long-lasting, quiet, domestic love, perhaps even of what love is, as well as Robert's true worth, was shown in his added observation that 'Familiarity never breeds contempt unless familiarity forgets the respect which every human being owes to the individuality of another.'

This was donated to the Magic Circle by the same private owner as the 'Lanark' spirit writing. The style is similar, and bizarrely it too seems to dovetail precisely with the much later 'bookshop' pages. Scottish-Italian families are common in the area – perhaps some link between Cesenatico and Lanark? The quote that purports to be from Owen's letter to his daughter is apparently fictitious, as it does not seem to come from any of the letters in the various collections. [AM 2007]

On a last trip to New Lanark, I go to examine the new acquisitions in the archive collection. There was not much to see. In truth, most of the papers relating to the junior Owen were copies of letters stored elsewhere. However, in a box file, I did find one amazing thing. It was a letter that had been sent to New Lanark by a distant relative of Owen in the US just last year. The covering note said simply that the owner's mother had never wanted to share it outside of the family, but now, a year after her death, he wished that it be passed on to the archive so that it might benefit scholars or researchers. The letter was dated 2 April 1856, was from Owen to his daughter, and ended with a paragraph beginning 'I know of nothing more...'

It seems my previous note was arrogant now. I assumed that because I couldn't find, couldn't see something, it did not exist. Now I know that seeing does not mean belief, but believing means you can see. [AM 2012]

FROM HAVANA TO LONDON; HOW I LEARN TO UNRAVEL A MAN WITH A KISS

In Havana, a young Londoner called Philip turns twenty-one on 29 August 1867. He does not celebrate his birthday because he is overworked, so exhausted that he is barely able to stay awake to continue testing the telegraph cables that he has come to help to lay.

The Cuban climate is hotter and more humid than most of the crew were really prepared for, and he is homesick and impatient to be sailing back to London. He writes to his father and his elder brother, the scientist William Crookes, about his shifts; they are unbearably long – at one time he is on duty for eighteen hours without reprieve. There are days of weary dredging in a small open barge where tropical rain soaks him through at regular intervals. There is wading in bilge water where the mosquitoes swarm thick and buzzing in dense clouds and leave ugly, itchy lumps on even the smallest patch of uncovered skin. His face and neck are a mass of red marks, one or two of which have puffed up and are now circled with white. He applies calamine lotion when he has the chance, but he has little time to sleep between the long shifts and the constant urge to scratch.

His head aches constantly and he, along with everyone else who came on the ship, is continually battling with diarrhoea and vomiting. The water in the tanks where the cables are to be laid is stagnant, and the smell would be enough to turn a man's stomach under normal con-ditions. The water is pumped out and replaced but the insects linger, hovering, humming, biting, feeding.

Finally, the work is complete. Illness has got the best of many of the crew; yellow fever is mooted as a possibility. Despite the fact that the cables are laid, the ship does not sail, and Philip writes to his father and brother of his impatience at what seems to be a needless delay. Eleven people become so ill that they are sent to a hospital on shore. Nine days pass. No one understands the delay.

One of the men who was admitted to the hospital dies. In his possession he had a bag with some valuable instruments. Philip travels to the hospital in Havana to collect them; he is not allowed near the body for fear of contagion. No one is sure how yellow fever is caused or spreads. It is an unpleasant journey. He is drenched to the skin in a storm, and when he returns to the boat he has all of the symptoms of flu. He is shivering and aches all over, his legs seem unsteady and even the gentle swaying of the docked ship makes him nauseous. He returns to shore the following day, in part to escape the waves of sickness. The streets are lively and colourful, the women beautiful, and he feels restored. He finds a stall covered by striped canvas and buys a small pair of gold earrings for his sister. They are filigreed and deli-cate and he thinks with pleasure of how they will look against her ash-blonde ringlets, a touch of the exotic for her friends to admire at tea parties in Regent's Park. His happy mood fades when he returns to the boat; he takes to his bed and in the morning calls for the ship's physician.

His pulse is fast, but not alarmingly so; his tongue is coated with a fur the colour of mucus. His lower belly hurts because he has not had a bowel movement for two days and he feels queasy and bloated. The rhubarb pills which the doctor prescribes are efficient, but now even the thought of food disgusts him, makes him dry heave over the side of his bunk. A little brandy seems to settle him on the second day and he takes milky tea with a little bread, but then the vomiting begins and the surges of water from his back passage that catch him unawares and necessitate changes of sheets and awkwardness.

By the fourth day, his reason is lost. He sweats and jibbers and speaks to people who are not there, but thousands of miles away, in the cool rain that has settled over London. His vomit is dark brown water and even the doctor cannot understand why there is so much of it.

He starts to wander, will fight anyone who tries to stop him, but his weakness prevents him causing any harm to them. For twenty-four hours, his last whole day and night, he lies flat, his skin yellowing slowly, his pulse quickening, his mind in his bedroom at home in Camden, waiting for his mother to kiss him goodnight. In the early hours, at 2.20 a.m. and again at three, he vomits, and it is thick and black with blood. He falls out of consciousness, silent this time, and still, and after just ten minutes, he is dead.

William Crookes was poleaxed by his brother's death. He read and reread his last letter, wished that in the final days Philip had at least been coherent enough to write again. His effects arrived in brown paper and William wept over the delicate gold earrings he found there, wondering if Philip had a sweetheart he had yet to tell him about.

But he was a scientist, and he turned to the newest explorations and experiments of the scientific in this, his darkest time. Initial attempts to speak to his dead brother proved futile. On more than one occasion Crookes and his wife left a séance in disgust, appalled by the obvious trickery, the planned deceit. However, by 1871 he had come round to the idea that there were invisible, intelligent beings who were able to communicate with certain gifted mortals.

(I like the fact that he specifically used the word 'intelligent'; it was praise indeed from such an exceptional man.)

He did not have the philosophic brilliance of Robert Dale in considering our nature, questioning only whether such 'entities' were the spirits of the dead or 'an order of beings separate from the human race'. Nevertheless, he was a prominent and respected scientific man.

One blustery day, as Charles Blackburn strode briskly across a park in Didsbury, near Manchester, heading for the warmth of his home, an old newspaper page wrapped itself around his shoe. He tried to kick it off, but some combination of the wind and the movement seemed to make it wrap more tightly around his ankle. With a grunt of annoyance, he bent down and paused to pull it off and throw it away, but as he did so a headline caught his attention, and instead of crumpling the offending sheet into a ball, he found himself smoothing out the creases, walking to a nearby bench and sitting on it, despite the inclement weather, to read what was written there. The headline was an invitation to spiritualists to meet with the scientist William Crookes.

Crookes' eagerness to experiment scientifically with mediums seemed like a gift from the spirit world. Blackburn wasted no time in writing to Crookes to ask if he might test Florence and thus vindicate her character from its recent slur, suggesting that he could do so in the privacy and security of his own home.

Florence was less enthusiastic about this proposal, which Blackburn made without speaking to her, and which Crookes delightedly accepted. The main problem was that her manifestations depended on paraphernalia that would not be easily available to her inside Crookes' own home.

William Crookes and his wife Ellen lived with his five sons and one daughter in a large town house in Mornington Crescent in London. Their eldest son, Henry, shared his parents' interest in spiritualism and had started going to meetings when he was as young as twelve. Now fifteen, he was excited at the prospect of having a medium in his own home, especially one who was as celebrated in the spiritualist press as Florence, to say nothing of her oft-reported physical attributes. Henry was an emotionally immature teenager. Although among the brightest of his class at University College School in Gower Street, he regarded females, especially young, pretty ones, as a kind of mystical species akin to the spirits who created the activity at séances. This was not unusual for a Victorian teenage boy, but while some of his classmates were entirely uninterested in the female of the species, Henry found himself enthralled by them, as well as somewhat embarrassed by the physical effect that they had on him. Florence had arranged to sit at his father's house in the presence of an invited audience. Henry begged his parents to be allowed to go and was readily given permission. The event was set for January 1874, a matter of a few weeks after the Volckman incident, and as early as Blackburn had been able to travel to London, allowing for the Christmas and New Year festivities that he enjoyed with his family.

In the week before the meeting, Henry found himself troubled by vivid dreams. A figure that he somehow knew to be Florence appeared to him for three consecutive nights. Her bosom was bare, and all she wore was some white silk material loosely tied around her waist, transparent enough that the V shape of her dark pubic hair was just visible beneath it. It was, for Henry, a wonderful dream, and one that he often woke from in a state of some embarrassment, only dispelled by the no-nonsense approach of the chambermaid, Queenie, who quickly changed his bed linen and told him not to worry.

The troubling aspect to these dreams for Henry, something that made concentration on schoolwork impossible, was that he could not see the figure's face. He worried that the object of his night-time lusts was in fact a hideous creature and that when he finally saw Florence he would be disgusted by the fantasies he had entertained of her unquestionably lovely body. After the third night of sensual fulfilment, he did not go to school but instead walked the four miles out to Eleanor Road, where he knew the Cook family lived.

Henry arrived in east London with no idea of what he was going to do once he had found the Cook family home, which he did with the greatest of ease, using the address given in an account of a recent séance in *The Medium and Daybreak* periodical. He slowed his step as he approached Bruce Villas, the four town houses that were grouped together, wondering what he should do. It was obvious that I would need to intervene further if some kind of meeting was to be effected, but I struggled to find a means by which I might engineer it. However, it had been a long walk on a cold day, and prior to his departure from the house, I had watched Henry, a somewhat greedy young man, guzzle food and drink in a very unappealing manner. I focused on this and on the fact that the liquid had now made its way through his body and into his bladder, from whence it most urgently started to request evacuation. As he approached the Cook house, the urge to urinate became almost irresistible, and he found himself at the front door, introducing himself as his father's son, and, with some embarrassment, asking if he might make use of a pot. Mrs Cook welcomed him in and showed him proudly to the new Twyford water closet they had just had installed, thanks to Mr Blackburn's generosity and his concern for their guests, in a small room at the back of the house. After he had relieved himself, Mrs Cook invited Henry to join her for some tea and Henry readily agreed, taking a seat in the comfortable armchair by the fire in the front room.

'Good morning, Master Crookes. Mama tells me that you were passing by and decided to visit us. It is a pleasure to meet you.' Surprised by the voice, Henry turned towards the door and saw the most beautiful woman he had ever beheld. 'I'm Florence Cook,' the vision continued.

He stumbled quickly to his feet and made a little bow. 'Forgive me, I am forgetting my manners.'

'Not at all, there's no need to stand on ceremony. We'll soon be seeing a lot of each other. I'd like us to be friends.'

The maid of all work arrived with some tea and Mrs Cook stood suddenly. 'I have lots to be getting on with. Florrie, perhaps you might entertain Master Crookes.'

Afterwards, Henry couldn't recall everything they spoke about, but late-morning tea became lunch, and it was three in the afternoon before he left the Cooks' home. In fact, he spoke very little, but tried to concentrate on what Florence told him, feeling very grown up that he was being entrusted with her confidence. After lunch, they sat again in the front parlour for what would be the last hour of his visit. He had never met anyone who was quite so – well, so captivating, that was the word. She giggled and talked and smiled and rearranged her dress from time to time so that the creamy breasts he had seen in his dream were easily imagined, just a few inches beneath the frilled edge of her simple black dress. However, as the afternoon drew on, she grew more subdued somehow, and Henry ventured, 'Miss Florrie, have I offended you somehow?'

'Oh no, dear Master Henry. It is just that I realise you will leave soon and I have so few true friends in this world that it saddens me.'

Henry blushed and paused to collect himself before speaking in a sudden rush of emotion. 'That cannot be true, Miss Florrie, but I am pleased that you think I am a true friend and want you to know that I will always be so, as long as I live. If ever I can help you, please call on me.'

'Ah, Master Henry, your friendship is kindness enough. And anyway, I will see you soon at your home. I am very afraid of it, though, so it seems our next meeting will be something for me to dread, however much I might look forward to seeing you again.'

'Are the spirits so very frightening?'

'They can be, but it's not so much that. Katie King – you have heard of her, have you not?' Henry nodded. 'She is capricious and can be cruel. I have known her to deliberately leave things so it looks as though I am cheating when in fact I am not. Sometimes she makes a wig or some clothing appear, even once a music box, so that the audience think that I have used artifice to create her. I am afraid she might do something like this in your papa's house. He is such a great man. I could not bear it if he thought ill of me.'

(I am neither capricious nor cruel but concede that this was a necessary ruse and so took no offence.)

'I'm sure Papa would understand if you explained it to him, as you have to me.'

'Oh, dear Henry, would that it were so, but your papa is a very scientific gentleman. I'm sure he would not see it like that.'

'Well, perhaps I can help.' Henry leaned towards Florence in a conspiratorial manner.

'That is so kind of you. What a dear boy you are – a young man, really, not a boy at all – but I do not know what you could possibly do.'

'Well, Miss Florrie, I could look for the objects after you've finished your séance, and if Katie has misbehaved then I could easily remove them before Papa or Mama have a chance to see them.'

'What a clever chap you are too! I would never have thought of it – and you would really do that for me?' Florence leaned towards Henry and placed her hand on top of his.

'Of course, I am your friend and would be happy to.'

'You have no idea what relief you have brought me. I have been so worried and so afraid, and now I find that I need not have been so. How fortunate that you found your way to me today.'

They conversed a little longer, then Henry announced he would have to leave. He would already find it difficult to be home at the time that tallied with his usual school day. Florence looked stricken at first, but brightened when Henry reiterated that he would see her very soon, in just four days' time. They stood together at the parlour door. Florence was about to call her mother so that she too might wish their guest good after-noon, but then she appeared to hesitate. 'I should like to do something very much, Master Henry, but I fear you would think me a very forward girl, and not be my friend any more.'

'I could never think ill of you, Miss Florrie. What is it you would like?' Henry was convinced that she could see him trembling with anticipation and the words did not come out quite as strongly as he would have liked.

'Why, I should like to kiss you goodbye,' and as she opened her mouth on the last syllable she rose up on tiptoes, for Henry was a good few inches taller than her, and kissed his forehead very gently.

(Kisses carry more power than anything, because they bear promise but not fulfilment, and so may offer more than might ever be realised. The lightest of kisses bear more still because the receiver will always want and wish for more. This much I learned abstractly from watching little Florrie Cook.)

I watched Henry, his jaunty walk along Eleanor Road as he headed for home, and marvelled at the girl I had chosen for a medium. Perhaps I would need to intervene at some point, not so much to make her convincing, for her guile was truly remarkable, but to keep her under control. Florence Cook might have created a persona for her Katie spirit, but I was interested in seeing how I could exploit it.

The evening of the séance came. It was to commence at seven thirty but Florence arrived at the Crookes' house just after five, with her mother. There was to be no cabinet but rather the back portion of the long drawing room had been partitioned off with dark red curtains. It was a much grander environment than the basement space the Cooks could offer for their own meetings.

Ellen Crookes, who shared her husband's belief and passion for all things ghostly, had endeavoured to create an atmosphere conducive to spirits in the room. Wooden chairs were draped with elaborate fringed shawls in various deep hues ranging from charcoal to purple, and a Turkey rug in burgundy and gold had been purchased the day before and given pride of place at the entrance to the room. In the twenty minutes before the meeting was scheduled to commence, the various guests arrived. Edward Elgie Corner, a sea captain and frequent attendee at Florence's séances, Blackburn and Cromwell Varley all took their places in the customary semicircle of chairs, alongside Florence's parents, Henry and his mother.

Ellen Crookes and Florence's mother examined Florence in one of the upstairs bedrooms. She was stripped to her underwear to make sure that she had no means of disguise or deceit on her person, and then clad in a black cotton dress of Ellen's, to avoid the possibility of hidden pockets in her own clothing.

Victorian modesty meant that Florence's under-drawers

were not removed at any time. They concealed the small piece of very fine white fabric that hung from her vagina, and which she would pull out, once she was safely behind the curtain, revealing a tightly wrapped piece of larger material which would make Katie's veil. Wrapped in this was a tiny wooden box filled with fine white powder which she would use to dust her hair so that it appeared much lighter than her own. It was not ideal, but without hiding spaces for the light wig and high shoes, it was the best she could do. She had decided that Henry would need to see at least one or two manifestations without any discarded paraphernalia so that in the future he would believe absolutely that any such items were of Katie's placing.

Behind the curtain, Crookes and Harrison tied her wrists together with a ribbon which was then passed through a piece of brass, affixed by two screws to the floor. Crookes had even gone so far as to have the head of the screws sealed so that a screwdriver, were there one to be found, would be useless. The ribbon was then knotted and sealed with melted wax and Crookes and Harrison left Florence alone behind the curtain. At Florence's insistence that it was a new venue for Katie and she would not be able to draw on past spirit energy accrued from other manifestations, the room was kept dark.

There was no music, so the small group waited in a silence broken only by occasional shuffling or rearranging of shawls for almost fifteen minutes before the – by now familiar – white veiled figure appeared. The delay was due to the fact that Florence's usual trick, which was like that of the Davenports, had gone slightly awry. It involved creating tension in the ribbon by small movements that made it appear tighter than it actually was. Once she was alone and relaxed her hands it was usually a simple matter of wriggling out of her bindings. This time, however, possibly because of slight nerves at the importance of the occasion, she had misjudged the tension and found it difficult to escape. I found that by concentrating on her hands I was able to help her to elongate them in such a way that she could take them from the loops. She seemed aware that some presence was acting on her and became quite afraid, at one point even sobbing quietly.

Katie stood in front of the curtain and announced, 'My medium is very upset tonight. I shall not be with you long.' The assembled group could hear sounds coming from behind the curtain, which they all took as yet further confirmation that Katie and Florence were separate beings. Once she had recovered from her upset, Florence had decided that a small crying sound coming from behind the curtain, produced by ventriloquism, might be helpful while Katie was with her audience. Obviously it would add to the effect that Katie was distinct from her medium, but it could also emotionally involve young Henry more fully in the proceedings, because she was sure he would be very worried about his Miss Florrie.

Katie stopped beside Ellen Crookes and invited her to run her hands over her body to show that she was not wearing anything other than the veil, that her modesty was protected only by the fact that there was light from a solitary gas lamp turned low. Henry was seated beside his mother and Katie lifted his hand and clasped it to her breast, whispering, so that only he could hear, although everyone else in the room strained hard to listen, that he was a true friend of Florrie and that Katie would always love him for that.

Charles Blackburn was invited to open a phosphorus lamp

to the air so that it gave its unearthly glow, and then to look at her hair closely, although she asked that, on this occasion, he didn't touch it, because she felt it was very sensitive and that it would hurt if he did so.

Just before she retreated behind the curtain, she asked if they might sing for her, just so she could hear their voices as she was called back to the other world. 'They will cheer me greatly,' she added, 'and make me feel less alone.'

Mrs Cook led the sitters in a popular hymn and by the time it was over, Florence was heard calling out to them, asking for someone to come and release her.

The unmitigated success of the meeting filled Crookes with excitement. Here, at last, was the chance to scientifically investigate some spiritual phenomena in a controlled environment, that of his own home. Florence, realising both the advantage and the limitations of such a programme of investigation, decided to make some ground rules of her own.

She returned alone to the Crookes' home the following evening and settled in the parlour, in front of a welcoming fire, to speak to Crookes, Varley and Henry, who had invited himself to join the adults.

'I'd be happy to do the tests, sir. There's only one thing.'

'Yes, my dear. Whatever you need.'

'It's the room, well, the cabinet and the room. It doesn't feel right somehow. Katie says she can't get her energy up properly and she is using so much of mine that I fear I may get ill.'

'Is that why you were moaning, Miss Florence?' Henry looked concerned.

'Indeed it is, Master Henry. I felt she was draining my life force away from me.'

Henry gasped and looked upset.

'Well, we do need to have some controlled space . . . If the experiments are to be conclusive, that is.' Crookes drummed his fingers on the arm of his chair, something he always did when he was vexed.

'It could still be here, sir. Just maybe in another room?'

The four made a tour of the house shortly after. It was not of a great size, but there was, on the first floor, a large study where Crookes' working apparatus and project materials, as well as his desk, were kept. Just off it, a smaller room was entirely lined with heavy oak bookshelves crammed with volumes, journals, and even some of the novels that Mrs Crookes and the girls enjoyed. Florence looked delighted. 'It's perfect!' she exclaimed.

'Isn't it too small for the cabinet?' Varley looked at the tiny, crowded room with puzzlement.

But Crookes understood immediately. 'Ah, she means to have the meetings in my study and to use the library instead of the cabinet! What an excellent idea, Miss Florence!'

'Do call me Florrie, sir. If we are to spend so much time together, it seems much more homely. I am not a very formal girl.'

'And you must call me William.' Crookes beamed at her. He bustled around the room, muttering about curtains to close off the archway that separated the two spaces, and matching drapes for the small stained-glass library window, which appropriately depicted some mythical angelic creature. 'Ellen, Ellen,' he called as he headed back downstairs, leaving his guests in his wake, 'we need your fair hand.'

The library offered a myriad of hiding places. Its clutter meant that disarray could easily obfuscate any manner of paraphernalia, which meant that the only remaining difficulty was how to get it into the house, and up to the room, without being seen. Help came in the form of Ellen Crookes. It was, she told her husband, *unconscionable* that Florrie would have to return home across London in the evening after his various experiments. It was not just the matter of safety – of course they could get a carriage – but the poor girl would be run ragged. She would have to stay, there was nothing else for it, at least for a week or two. She then might go home for a break and return again for a second run of investigation, *if she so wished*. At these last words, Ellen Crookes smiled conspiratorially at Florence before giving her husband a warning glance.

Florence arrived with a small bag two days later. She offered it up to be searched, and it was. Neither Ellen nor William discovered the false bottom, beneath which nestled one fair wig, one pair of heeled shoes, two different veils, and a small purse containing phosphorus and perfumed oil.

The first test was an electrical one, devised by Varley, using a very new piece of technology: the Galvanometer. William Thomson had designed the Mirror Galvanometer to be an instrument that could sense any variations in current over a long cable. It was far more sensitive than any of its predecessors and consisted of a coil of copper wire covered with silk. Within the coil was a mirror with minute magnets attached to its non-reflective side. A light would shine onto the mirror, which would reflect it back onto a scale. When no current was passing through the coil the mirror would remain at rest, but the application of current would cause the magnets to twist out of position, moving the reflected light to one end of the scale or the other, depending on whether it was a negative or positive current.

The idea was to create a circuit that would include Florence as human resistance. The Galvanometer would remain outside the library cabinet, in full view of an assembled audience, and act as proof that she did not loosen her bonds to impersonate Katie.

Varley and Crookes did some practice exercises to ascertain how much deflection might be caused by any natural movement that Florence made while falling into a trance state. She was contained within the circuit by means of wires fixed to her wrists with blotting paper that had been soaked in a conducting solution.

Varley was convinced that it was 'simply impossible for even a thoroughly experienced electrician to escape from the electric circuit without producing such an alteration or resistance as would claim the fact instantly'. I admit that I was worried. I had had no practice in focusing on currents and had no idea if I would be able to influence them enough to allow Florence sufficient time to become Katie.

During the rehearsals, I found that I could hold the light in place for a few seconds only; the rest depended on Florence's speed and skill. Her plan was very simple. When in the safe privacy of her library cabinet, she would remove the wires from her wrists and attach them to her ankles, which were hidden by long skirts. She could then present herself as Katie at the curtains and display her bare wrists, while the audience would be in full sight of a Galvanometer that showed no fluctuation in current. The speed with which she moved the wires from wrists to ankles was, she thought, crucial in preventing a huge deflection of the light that would betray her deception. In fact, the instrument was delicate, and without my intervention, the test would have quickly exposed Florence for the ingenious little trickster she was.

Once again Blackburn, Harrison, Varley, the Crookes family and Florence's parents assembled in William's study for the display. His scientific gadgetry had been placed to one side and the kitchen chairs placed tightly together so that everyone might be accommodated. The only light, at Florence's express request, was the lamp used for the Galvanometer, and a phosphorus lamp placed at the opposite side of the curtains.

Varley observed the Galvanometer, while Harrison recorded the measurements he read out. Varley wrote an account of the meeting, which appeared in a very nice volume in the Crookes' library, some years later (a very fitting end, I thought).

Varley's Account

Time	Deflection	Account of Proceedings
7.38	155–7	Katie appeared from behind the curtain. She showed both of her wrists.
7.38	157	No movement.
7.39	158	Katie placed her hand on Mr Crookes' head. He remarked that it was cold. No movement. EXCELLENT TEST.
7.40	156	
7.41	155	Katie reached out towards Master Henry and asked, softly, if he might come close to her. We heard the sound of moaning coming from Miss Cook, behind the curtain. No movement of Galvanometer.
7.42	156	Katie took Master Henry's head in her hands.
	157	She kissed his forehead. She then asked if he had a handkerchief she might borrow.

7.43	157, 158	Master Henry looked very awkward and Mrs Cook obliged with a clean, cotton square. Katie then seemed to wave it in the air. There was a very little deflection in the Galvanometer. Truly Astounding (note).
7.45	156	Katie handed back the handkerchief to Master Henry. Some words had appeared, faintly written on it. He read them out to us: 'I am lonely'.
		The Galvanometer did not move at all. Excellent Test.
7.46	157	Katie stood before the company with her wrists and hands outstretched. She opened and closed her fingers several times. The Galvanometer light remained almost completely still. Had it been Miss Cook's hand the deflection would have been more than ten degrees. Again, we all heard a mournful, almost pained sound coming from Miss Cook in the library. Master Henry asked if perhaps we should end the proceedings as 'Florrie was in such distress'. Katie thanked him for being kind to her medium and said, yes, he was right, that she would have to leave them.
7.49	149	Katie retired behind the curtain and there was a deflection in both directions. We assume this was caused by the entity's power leaving the medium and Miss Cook's consequent movements.

When Florence asked for her audience to be admitted to the library cabinet, they found her lying on a chaise with the wires still attached to her wrists. Varley noted that she looked 'very tired', and despite the earliness of the hour, she retired to her bedroom soon after. He also found the strain of the evening was too much for him. Stunned by the phenomena he had observed, he ceased his examination of mediums thereafter. He wrote in his account that physical séances 'very much exhausted' him and that rather than continue he would pass his equipment to Crookes, who was not similarly affected.

Florence was well aware of the ephemeral nature of fame. She had seen countless contemporaries' reputations rise and fall, and while Master Henry's friendship might help prolong the success of her manifestations, he was neither old nor established enough to present any kind of long-term security. She had initially alighted on Charles Blackburn as a perfect target for her affections, but while in thrall to her mediumship, he seemed entirely unmoved, and even uninterested, in her more human flirtation. Edward Corner, the sea captain, was proving to be a much more steadfast and willing suitor. When, days after the Galvanometer test, he proposed, Florence accepted with alacrity. She did however ask that their betrothal remain secret until such time as her mediumistic testing was complete. Corner agreed but stipulated that there would be no more séances after their marriage.

(The vagaries of human interaction are impossible to comprehend. Blackburn clearly liked the female, rather than the male sex, but seemed sexually immune to Florence. Corner, with his stipulations and authoritarianism, was a very poor second choice. While I appreciated Florence's dilemma – the brevity of the financial security offered by her success, as well as the public's discarding of old idols in its fascination with the new – I was disappointed when she settled on her sea captain.)

At the next public testing, to which Crookes invited a small group of witnesses, Katie appeared, despite the complicated bonds that were fastened both to her medium and to part of the floor which was in full view of the audience. She curtseyed to the assembly and made an announcement. She was tiring of this interaction with the living, and her medium was no longer able to sustain her for very much longer. Katie would appear for only another few months, after which time she would say a fond farewell to her followers and her friends.

Crookes channelled his energy into trying to capture some lasting memento of Katie before she vanished forever. Hudson had overcome his association with Herne and Williams and was again enjoying unparalleled success as a spirit photographer, so it was to him that Crookes turned in the first instance. The news that Katie King would soon return to another realm dominated the spiritualist press; Hudson was eager to benefit from the unprecedented level of publicity and warmly welcomed the opportunity to collaborate with Crookes.

For my part, this joint project heralded something I can only describe as a new desire. After all these decades of watching human activity, I wanted to see if I could find a trace of myself in any of these images. Obviously, I can't see myself, nor can anyone else. However, I wondered if I might inhabit someone, just for that brief moment of exposure, and in the image that was produced, perceive somehow that I had done so. Perhaps it was conceit, a very natural emotion, but Florence, with her tight ringlets and soft curves, was how I would have liked to see myself. I wished her no harm, although I did wonder if my occupying her body might leave her disorientated, but I convinced myself that anyone who spent so much time thinking about the spirit world would be well prepared for a little ghostly activity when it happened to occur. I thought she might even welcome it as a vindication of her talents.

Hudson was someone I mistrusted, even disliked, given his

friendship with the fraudulent and lazy Guppy, so I had to convince Crookes that he should undertake the photography on his own. The collaboration resulted in just one photograph. It is still in circulation today, and you can find it on the web or reprinted in some old books. Katie King did not appear at the sitting. Florence laid her head on a chair, in a trance, while some white mass appeared to float in the background. It was clearly double exposure and Crookes thought that perhaps he would have better results if he attempted to photograph the spirit by himself. What he hoped was that the materialised Katie would appear in sufficient light that he might capture her likeness.

He spoke to Florence and asked if she thought it might be possible. She said that yes it might, but that it would require a great deal of care lest she be disturbed during the manifestation. Her powers were low now; she felt constantly drained and tired. A disruption during trance might even prove fatal. Crookes agreed that only he and his son Henry would be present during the attempt. Towards the end of March, Katie made a public declaration that she would appear only three more times with Florence. The week following her announcement, Crookes and Henry dedicated themselves totally to trying to capture an image. In total they took forty-four photographs, although of these only thirteen survive today.

Florence would be enclosed in the library behind her curtain, fastened to a chaise where she reclined. The two men would leave her there with no light except a gas lamp turned to its lowest setting. They waited in the study in similar light conditions. Only when the curtain moved and Katie presented herself could they, with her agreement, then light the room so that photographs might be taken.

Crookes left nothing to chance. Five different cameras were set up: one that would take whole plates, one half, one quarter and two binocular stereoscopic cameras. Numerous plates were prepared in advance and five sanitising and fixing baths set up. The electric light, a new device and one that Crookes believed would allow a more distinct and detailed image, was lit only when Katie acquiesced. The first session was unsuccessful from my point of view. I was not able to imagine myself inside Florence's body, or at least not in such a way as to make anything actually happen. Several images were taken, about twelve in all, but they were so obviously Florence in disguise that Crookes' consideration of them as 'interesting' shocked even me.

For the next session Florence, aware of the anticlimactic nature of the first attempt, was far more cunning. This time her false-bottomed bag contained not one but two wigs, one of which was a copy of her own hair. With the fair wig on her head and the white muslin dress around her, she quickly and expertly applied a white foundation. The second wig, the auburn, tightly curled one, was placed so that it just peeped out from underneath a blanket. This blanket also completely covered some books and objects sequestered from around the library, piled into a lumpen form, which in very dim light suggested an entranced Florence.

When Katie entered the study where Henry and Crookes awaited her, she invited them to go back into the library before they illuminated the room for their photographs, so that they might 'see my sleeping medium'.

They returned, convinced anew by the apparition, and prepared to photograph her. Once again I tried to imagine myself inside Florence, and this time I found that, with great concentration, and for only the briefest of times, I was able to inhabit her physical body. I fixed my attention on the rise and fall of her breathing, and then, as if I had been inhaled, I felt myself to be the air that entered her. Once there, I did not become her in any sense, rather I was as a moth that had accidentally flown into a mouth and rested within, fluttering, delicate, vulnerable, only to be expelled seconds later.

I did affect her positioning, by my thoughts alone, although it was not in any way different from what I could have done had I not been inside her. By my will she crossed her arms, thus accentuating her little cleavage. Without Florence being phys- ically aware of anything, except a slightly annoying humming noise inside her ear that I learned of much later, she and I were photographed many times in the days and nights that followed. There is a picture of us, arm in arm with William Crookes; another where he holds the light up towards us that he might better see our form, or rather Florence's form. I am there, in those old photographs. My essence is there. And I know that something is visible, some fleeting change in Florence's expres- sion, whether caused by the humming noise that so irritated her, or by whatever feelings I engendered but do not know of. In the albumen silver print, where Florence, dressed as Katie, leans on Crookes, her eyes are closed, her face serene. But the way that her hand touches the side of her head, the little finger that curls at her temple, is a reaction to the low buzz of my intervention. I think that Crookes recognised it. In fact I am sure he did. Some of the photographs looked so like Florence in disguise that he destroyed them, lest they detract credibil- ity from those that were true. My proof is that all of those that survive – the ones you can still find anywhere and everywhere that the heyday of séances is remembered or debated – were taken when I was with Florence, every single one of them.

At the end of the sessions, Crookes wrote in his journal:

Photography may be inadequate to depict the perfect beauty of Katie's face, as words are powerless to describe her charms of manner. But there is a glimpse of mysticism afforded by even the vaguest of these plates that vindicates my championing of spiritualism. It shows that if the time is not now, for our kind, the lucky few who have been privileged to share intimate space with one from the spirit world, to be treated with respect, then it will be soon, and history will bear testament to our early understanding.

In Crookes' 1871 letter to *The Spiritualist*, he stated his considered belief that 'historical testimony is overwhelming as to the fact of communications having been made to mortals from invisible intelligent beings distinct from the human race: and contemporary evidence to similar occurrences is accumulating daily.'

The narrator makes an error here in saying that thirteen photos survive; in fact there are only twelve, as documented in various places, including *The Perfect Medium: Photography and the Occult* (2005), Yale University Press.

The use of the vagina as a means of concealing props is well documented in spiritualism trickery. The most publicised case is actually a relatively recent one. Helen Duncan, the mid-twentieth-century Scottish medium and the last person to be prosecuted under the witchcraft act of 1735, was reported as having a light dress, a cheesecloth sheet (which she used to replicate ectoplasm) and a phial of phosphorus hidden inside her, all at the same time.

Given that high-heeled shoes were very much in fashion in the 1860s and 1870s, it is all the more surprising that no one thought of attributing the difference in height between Katie and her medium to her wearing them! [AM 2007]

There are thirteen! Just this year another plate was discovered. Crookes' home in Mornington Crescent was bombed during the war, but two houses from the period remain on the street. On the death of the elderly owner of one of them, her attic was cleared out and there they found a final plate. Florence stands alone. She looks, and I can think of no other word, serene. It is as if she is in prayer with the spirit that inhabits her. How can anyone doubt now that she is real?

In the past months, since the discovery of the last plate, the photographs have become an obsession with me. Again and again I return to them, looking for some glint, some expression that betrays the inner difference. The most obvious is in the photograph she describes; the one where Florence, possessed by Katie, stands beside Crookes, with that telling hand raised to her temple, an outward sign of the soft buzzing that the spirit brings to her.

I think of that sound, what it might be like to have Katie's spirit inside me, to loan her my body, even if it is broken. Men found me pretty enough once. Would she arrange me? Control me? Speak to me?

Oscar Wilde wrote in *De Profundis*, a piece I never tire of returning to, that 'Behind all this beauty...there is some spirit hidden of which the painted forms and shapes are but modes of manifestation, and it is with this spirit I desire to become in harmony.'

I close my eyes and focus on a solitary wish, that Katie might inhabit me for a second, that she might be in the air that I breathe, so unnoticed, yet so necessary. [AM 2012]

THE LAST LONDON SÉANCE OF KATIE KING
AND FLORENCE COOK

I was disappointed by Florence's easy acquiescence that I should so soon retire from celebrity but was also determined that my last appearance should be a memorable one. On 21 May 1874, just after 7 p.m., there gathered Mr Harrison, Henry, Mrs Ross-Church – a regular attendee at Florence's meetings who would subsequently document much of what she saw – Mr and Mrs Cook and their other daughter and the Crookes' servant girl, Mary.

Mr Harrison's account appeared just one year later:

Mr Crookes, 7.25 p.m., conducted Miss Cook into the dark room used as a cabinet, where she laid herself down upon the floor, with her head resting upon a pillow; at 7.28 Katie first spoke and at 7.30 came outside the curtain in full form. She was dressed in pure white, with low neck and short sleeves. She had long hair, of a light auburn or golden colour, which hung in ringlets down her back, and on each side of her head, reaching nearly to her waist. She wore a long white veil . . .

During the séance Katie drew the curtain back from time to time so that all assembled could see the shape of her sleeping medium, covered with a red shawl, but with her dark curls showing through its widely spaced fringes. The only light in the cabinet was from a small oil lamp, covered in a globe of dark red glass, placed on the ledge of the stained-glass window.

Katie spoke of her imminent departure, and Crookes, so moved that I could see a solitary tear run down his cheek, presented her with a bouquet of lilies. In the relatively bright light of the study, Katie sat cross-legged on the floor and proceeded to divide the flowers up between her sitters, adding to each small bunch a handwritten note. To every one of these gifts she also attached a lock of her beautiful hair, cut with scissors by her own hand.

Mrs Ross-Church, who would publish her own books under her maiden name, Florence Marryat, also had an account in the same publication as Harrison.

On the 21st, however, the occasion of Katie's last appearance amongst us, she was good enough to give me what I consider a still more infallible proof (if one could be needed) of the distinction of her identity from that of her medium. She summoned me to say a few words to her behind the curtain, I again saw and touched the warm, breathing body of Florence Cook lying on the floor, and then stood upright by the side of Katie, who desired me to place my hands inside the loose single garment which she wore, and feel her nude body. I did so, thoroughly.

(The warmth from Florence was my doing, of course, the breathing movement entirely in the Ross-Church imagination. The search was far more intrusive and extensive than was

warranted by the circumstances, and made me ponder the true
sexual proclivities of this supposedly happily married matron.)

Finally there was Crookes' own account. Katie imparted
instructions for the care of her medium, saying:

> Mr Crookes has done very well throughout, and I leave
> Florence with the greatest confidence in his hands, feeling
> perfectly sure he will not abuse the trust I place in him. He
> can act in an emergency better than I can myself, for he has
> more strength.

Katie returned to the soft red glow of the library cabinet and
after just a few minutes, Crookes was called in to look upon the
sleeping medium. At first he could hear Katie but not see her, a
disembodied voice that said,

'Wake up, Florrie! Wake up! I must leave you now.'

'Please, please stay, just a little longer.' Florrie sounded disorientated and Crookes, even in the dimly lit room, could see
the distress on her face which had now appeared from under
the shawl.

It was then that I took the boldest step of all. The veil had
been hastily stuffed behind a row of books and I willed those
books to fall and the fabric to rise. A white shape, reminiscent of
a girl spirit, hovered beside Crookes and the reclining Florence
for more than a minute. It was absolute proof that the spirit and
her medium were distinct. Crookes went on to describe how
he 'came forward to support Miss Cook, who was falling on
the floor, sobbing hysterically'. When he looked round, all that
remained was a piece of fine white fabric lying on the floor, inert,
discarded, with no sign of the life form that had inhabited it.

Florence wrote to Blackburn, anxious that he should share in her final night of glory.

Dear Mr Blackburn

Katie has gone!

I need not tell you how grieved we all are. Some people cried last night. I am told she was lovely. She cut off pieces of her hair for everyone present and sent you a piece.

I am so sorry she has gone. I am dreadfully lonely without her. My only consolation is that we have some splendid photos.

I am not at all well. I have had too many séances and am very much used up and nervous. After a rest I shall be better.

Mama sends her kind regards. With best love I am ever yours affectionately

Florence E. Cook

I will write more fully soon but at present I do not feel equal to it. Katie sends a piece of her dress.

From Crookes' point of view, it was the justification he had searched for. He had witnessed both medium and spirit in the same room. There was no possibility that a second person had been involved; there was no other door to the library and the window was two storeys above a busy road.

He wrote, '... to imagine, I say, the Katie King of the last three years to be the result of imposture does more violence to one's reason and common sense than to believe her to be what she herself affirms'.

The faith I gave Crookes with this demonstration carried him through the years of ridicule that followed, before Queen Victoria's favour redeemed him in the public eye. Florence, however, was less fortunate. She was no longer the devious, sceptical girl that I had so admired. She did give séances still, but only occasionally. Her husband was often away at sea, but when he was home, he was enraged by Florence's refusal to sleep in the dark. A spiritual investigator spoke to her not long before her death, at the age of just forty-two. He recounted:

> ...she did so [slept with the light on] because she had so often impersonated spirits and pretended these manifestations at séances that she became afraid that possibly there might have been such things, which might have a spite against her for her deceptions, and she had consequently a dislike of being in the dark.

(I did often visit her in those later years, but never, ever through spite. I worried a little that there might be consequences from my interventions, and I observed her sympathetically.

If they were spirits that she perceived, and not just her own imaginings, they were far darker than me. Her terror was not feigned and I still regret that I was never able to find a way to impart some reassurance to her.)

The farewell appearances of Katie King and the new surge of publicity surrounding Florence was of particular interest to two successful American mediums, Nelson and Jennie Holmes. They had met Florence in 1871 when they gave a short series of guest séances at the Dalston association and currently had a successful act featuring a rather awkward ghost who, as far as I could ascertain, had no substance at all in the spirit world. The cachet of Katie King was too important to ignore. Furthermore, her anticipated departure from the London scene, the Holmeses reasoned, might herald an American debut of considerable significance. With Florence's marriage and decision to follow her husband's wish that she no longer pursue her career, I was pleased and relieved to hear in *The Spiritualist* of the 'new American Katie King'. I would go to North America; I would be close to Robert Dale once more.

The American Katie made her first appearance at the Holmeses' Philadelphia salon, nine days before the London Katie made her last. There was, for the short time that the two manifestations overlapped, competition between the American and British spiritualist press as to which ghost was prettier. The celebrity surrounding Katie was so great that even the mainstream press took up the debate, with the *Atlantic Monthly* reporting:

> Our Katie's nose is short rather than long, while the London Katie's is very long and aquiline. Our Katie looks about eighteen, and is very pretty, while the London Katie is quite plain, and might pass for thirty. Our Katie's head has but a slight covering, while the London Katie's is heavily bandaged. The London Katie's hair is described as coarse, and of a light auburn. Our Katie's is dark brown (darker than the medium's) and of a silky texture.

A regular attendee at the Holmeses' séances was Dr Henry T. Child, a practising physician in Philadelphia. Dr Child was a distant friend of my Robert, and an easy conduit by which I might bring him to me. In London, I thought of how we might converge and sent Dr Child a dream of my making.

In his book *Touching Visitants from a Higher Life*, Robert Dale recalls:

> On May 29th I received a letter from my friend, Dr Child – a well-known Philadelphia physician – stating that a spirit, purporting to be the same which had appeared to Mr Crookes and usually known as 'Katie King', had shown herself ... had conversed with him in audible tones, and had requested him, on her behalf, to write and ask that I would come and see her in Philadelphia. A startling summons, surely, if in very deed from a spirit! Was such an invitation ever before extended by a denizen of the next world to a mortal in this?

I had known of Robert Dale since 1812. Now he knew of my existence too. I would have to see how close I could be to him; much would depend upon the actress who was pretending to be me. And it *was* an actress this time; both Mrs Holmes and her husband remained in plain sight during the sittings. Her name was Eliza White.

This is an unusual section in that so many different accounts by various people of the same event are presented. It is as if Katie is daring us to disbelieve something that has been so often attested. But of course she is also highlighting the importance and celebrity of the event.

Mr Harrison and Florence Marryat's accounts cited here are taken from *The Proof Palpable of Immortality* by Epes Sargent. I had some difficulty finding the source for the letter from Florence to Blackburn and thought it was a fiction. However, I finally traced it to the SNU archive at Arthur Findlay College: BP12 of The Blackburn Papers. It is handwritten in ink with the address 6 Bruce Villas, Eleanor Road, Richmond Road, Hackney, and dated 22 May.

The source for the remarks about Florence's later years was also a little obscure. It is in the files of the Society for Psychical Research, 23 Nov. 1949, Statement by Mr Anderson to K. M. Goldney.

The narrator's comment about Florence's examination affects me. There is something deeply unsavoury in the way the wealthy Marryat relishes the opportunity to touch the medium. I am disquieted by that word 'thoroughly'. Although, of course, selling sex was part of a medium's stock in trade. Strangely, I had naively only considered the old men who flocked for a glimpse of leg or cleavage, when of course complicity in sexual activities of any kind might be excellent currency to secure an eye-witness account of something that never happened at all. [AM 2007]

Katie felt some responsibility for her actions, a conscience. It is as if the development of her abilities (that she could now enter into a body) were complemented by an emotional evolution too. Did the new, closer physical proximity to humankind awaken some kind of empathy? Before, only Robert Dale Owen, with whom she had such profound contact, seems to have been a recipient of her care. She is watching me die; does that move her? [AM 2012]

A SÉANCE IN A CARNIVAL

Eliza White had been a married woman, working a carnival psychic act in the Midwestern states, travelling with an alcoholic husband named Joe and a dog called Bluey. It was a stock-in-trade code-working act. Joe would sit on the stage, blindfolded, while Eliza went round the audience holding personal items that belonged to them, the idea being that the spirits would tell Joe what the items were, as well as, sometimes, a story associated with them. The ruse worked by means of an elaborate code, carefully written in a small moleskin notebook and memorised by the couple. If Eliza was holding a fan, the code word for fan would appear in her preamble. If in the hours before the show opened she had gleaned something about the mark while wandering round the carnival site, the code would be enhanced to hint at that too. The act was baffling and wondrous but depended absolutely on the ability of both performers to remember the code, something that became increasingly difficult with Joe's heavy drinking.

Eliza was eighteen, ambitious and pretty. As well as the psychic act, she sang for the heavenly tableau acrobats, with a voice they advertised as evocative of the angels. While audience applause turned to derision as, night after night, Joe forgot how to read the messages his wife passed to him, Eliza sequestered tips from her singing act in a purse hidden under Bluey's bed.

A week before the end of the season, she took Bluey, the code book and a small case that contained everything in the world she had ever owned – from a childhood doll to the silk negligee she wore on her wedding night – and caught a train to Philadelphia. Psychic acts did well there and she thought that she might find some work in the world of spooks, or even as a singer if her luck was in.

At first she worked as a singer in a restaurant, where Mrs Holmes saw her when a client took her to dine there one evening. Eliza's voice, sweet but not screechy, as Jennie Holmes told her husband, could work beautifully in a séance. She was thin, not much more than some bones wrapped up in pale skin really, almost a ghost already – it wouldn't take much. They found out where she lived and visited her rooming house. The Holmeses were chary, afraid of giving away their deception but eager to see if she might join them. Eliza, a carny girl since she was thirteen, understood before they even had to tell her. She knew her letters, but not well enough to read much. In those first weeks with the Holmeses, she read more than she ever had in the whole of her life. They paid for her to learn about me. Spiritualist papers, magazine articles, accounts in pamphlets – Eliza's Katie King would be informed by them all, but she would also be better.

When I joined them, the day before I expected Robert Dale, they were all living together. Nelson and Jennie, Eliza and her dog, all squeezed into a two-room apartment above a music shop on Ninth Street, near Arch. There was a bedroom and a parlour, the latter furnished with a huge walnut spirit cabinet. It was seven feet wide and eight feet high, with two curtained apertures, and a door that led into the parlour. Inside the cabinet was a low upholstered couch which by night was Eliza's bed, and during a séance was where Mrs Holmes would be tied.

The cabinet also had a second compartment, hidden behind a false back. It was narrow, claustrophobically so, but big enough to hide Eliza, skinny as she was, and the phosphorescent limbs, fine gauze drapery and bunches of flowers that she needed to create her illusion. The dog had been a problem at the start. He followed Eliza from room to room, and when she went into the hiding space refused to move from the cabinet back. In the end, they locked him in the bedroom, although Jennie Holmes, despairing of dog hair on her pillows, argued constantly that they should get rid of him. Eliza was insistent. Where she went, the dog went. He had been hers since she was nine and they were all each other had in the world. If Jennie wanted her to be Katie, she'd learn to live with him.

Robert Dale arrived in Philadelphia on the fifth day of June. I couldn't go to see him. I wanted to watch him get off the train, but as usual, I was tied to Eliza and the Holmeses, the believers who had brought me to them. I was impatient that I had to wait for Robert Dale to attend a séance before I could see him as a living, breathing man again.

It was not long; he came that same evening, just after seven. There was the sound of his footsteps echoing in the close stairwell that led up the side of the shop to the flat and it could have been any of the other two visitors we expected, but I knew it was him, my Robert. He was older than I thought (bodily ageing often takes me by surprise). But apart from that he was singularly unchanged. Only a small difference, then, a superficial thing, and with him came the warmth. It was a hot day, especially for early summer, sweltering and humid, an atmosphere the Holmeses used to great effect in the stuffy atmosphere of their meetings. But it made no difference to me. I am cold, not in an uncomfortable way, but I don't register temperature like skin and blood capillaries do. Yet, when he came through the door, and even for those seconds before, when I heard the soft shuffle of his old-man walk across the landing and the intermittent tap of his cane, a gentle heat suffused me, making me feel much more part of a world where I usually seemed to be on the sidelines.

He was early but he was welcomed in. The parlour with the spirit cabinet was well lit and he was invited to examine its interior. Robert Dale asked to see the bedroom too, and excused himself when Eliza, in the clothes of a respectable widow woman, answered his gentle tap at the door. She ignored his apologies and ushered him in, asking that he pardon Bluey. In truth, there was nothing to pardon: that usually ebullient, noisy animal was as affected by him as I was, and trotted up to him, expectant of the patting that was immediately bestowed. I caught myself then in jealousy of that careless caress. Puzzled over what it was that I wanted, I decided that it was curiosity to know what his touch might give to me, and wondered all evening how I might bring it to pass.

Eliza, the Holmses informed him, was a widowed friend, living with them for the time being. Of course he might check the room for any hidden door or means to enter the parlour. She had to leave to visit an ill friend, so if he would kindly close the door behind him when he was satisfied and leave Bluey inside, she would be very pleased.

While Robert Dale checked the walls of the room and the bookcases, Eliza walked into the parlour and hid in the compartment behind the false back of the cabinet.

Dr Child, accompanied by a well-dressed woman, arrived as Robert Dale re-entered the parlour, and the three guests were invited to see Mrs Holmes, tied to the couch in the spirit cabinet, before they were seated. Mr Holmes dimmed the lights so that only shadows could be seen, before taking his place next to Dr Child's companion.

I thought of a hundred things I could do to convince him, and then was afraid that all or any of them might make the Holmeses so afraid that they would give up spiritualism. At one aperture of the cabinet, the curtain drew back and a thin, pale face appeared. At the other, a ghostly white hand peeked between the still-closed drapes.

'Hello, Robert Dale Owen,' said the head, 'and welcome. I am Katie King and it is a pleasure to meet you.' Eliza's voice had a slight quiver; she was nervous, something I had never seen in her before. His early arrival had caught her off kilter, I thought, and her language seemed stilted, unnatural. Unless her performance improved, I would have to intervene, if only to be sure that he would come and come again.

'Hello, Katie.' Robert Dale smiled in the darkness.

'Perhaps you might sing for Mr Owen.' Mr Holmes, sensing Eliza's insecurity, intervened. And so she did. Although instead of the practised hymn, she sang something I sent to her, a Scottish song by Robert Burns. 'Ae Fond Kiss' brought the Clyde and the hills and the mills of New Lanark into the Philadelphia parlour. The Scots words came flawlessly; her voice was a beautiful, ethereal, sweet sound that was just how I would wish to sing if I could. Robert Dale was moved and sceptical in equal measure, but it was enough.

When the lights were turned on and Mrs Holmes, so obviously

not the youthful beauty who had greeted him from the cabinet, was wakened from her trance, he made arrangements to return the following evening. To Dr Child, he confided, 'The possibility of a confederate and staging presents itself, of course, but there is enough beauty in it all to warrant a return. Indeed I think I must, because I am on the verge of believing in a wonder.'

After he had left, Mrs Holmes had new respect for Eliza, who shrugged it off.

'You know, I've sung a hundred, no, a thousand songs, in every kind of place you could think of, but I don't remember that one at all. No idea where it came from. Funny how old songs come back to haunt you sometimes, isn't it? My grandmother was Scots, perhaps she sang it to me.'

'Well, all I can say is, bless your grandmother's ghost. He left a ten-dollar donation and he's coming back tomorrow.'

The next night Robert Dale arrived and removed from his coat pocket a small chain made of human hair, a dark, tangled thing that carried memories of its own ghost. It was, he said, a talisman from Scotland, and the song had made him think of it again, after many, many years, although it had always been with him. I concentrated hard and saw, with perfect clarity, the little girl Hyacinth who had accompanied him to the mill with his father. I saw again Robert Dale, the boy, rally from his sickness and call for water, while Hyacinth's mother tried in vain to wake her from a sleep she had thought would only last a night.

'Perhaps Katie can speak to her for me.' Robert Dale passed his coat to Jennie, who hung it on an oak portmanteau. Two of the other guests were already seated in the parlour and an elderly couple came in just after Robert Dale.

Eliza waited in the blackness of the walnut cabinet, with only the glow from a phosphorescent hand to see by. She was dressed more conservatively than she often was for their clients, but Owen was a respectable man, had been a senator. The Holmeses had thought him far too intelligent and honourable to be impressed by semi-nakedness and the musky smell of sex. She wore a heavy white dress, of cotton, not silk. Silk was expensive and in any case would make too much noise if it rustled behind the curtain when she took her place at the aperture. The neck was cut to show only the powdered skin of her neck and throat and there were sleeves as far as the elbow. Her hair hung loose, and the white powder on her face and lower arms and hands seemed to accentuate her thinness somehow, so that she looked barely there, an insubstantial thing, not flesh at all. (This, of course, was the idea but rarely had I seen it so convincing.) She did not move, and during the long minutes that Robert Dale supervised the tying up of Mrs Holmes in the cabinet, she focused on her breathing, to try to make it as inaudible as possible, because in that dark, silent space, it seemed as loud as the wind.

I had already decided on my intervention and it was a simple one. To Eliza in her upright walnut coffin, I brought the scent of hyacinths, sweetly powerful and all-pervasive, so that Eliza imagined the wood itself oozed the fragrance from its pores. When, after her face had appeared briefly at the lifted curtain, she stepped out of the cabinet and joined the sitters in the expectant gloom, when Owen stood to pass her the lock of woven hair, she said but one word to him. 'Hyacinth.'

His face turned ashen, and Eliza, in momentary pity, for he was an old man, offered him her arm, which he took gladly.

'She's happy, sir. Don't fret. She wants you to know she has lots of children to play with now.'

'My dear.' He was close to tears. 'Hyacinth was my childhood friend, my best friend until she was cruelly taken. Her mother gave me this when I recovered from an illness that no one expected me to survive.'

'Yes, sir, I know, but she's happy now.' Eliza struggled to deal with the outpouring of conversation and still retain her ghostly demeanour. Singing and the odd word or two was fine, but this was difficult to sustain.

Rescue came in the shape of Mr Holmes. 'Come now, sir, we mustn't tire Katie. Remember my wife is channelling her and we wouldn't want Mrs Holmes to be ill, would we?'

Katie retreated back into the cabinet and Robert Dale looked after her wistfully. 'Perhaps tomorrow . . .' he ventured, but she was gone.

Nelson Holmes pulled him a little too firmly back into his chair, before standing himself. 'I think we should sing a hymn together,' he announced. 'Katie has had a lot of interaction tonight, and I know it soothes her.'

(In fact there are few things in this world that irritate me more than a rousing chorus. However, I do appreciate that it is an excellent way of drowning out any tell-tale noise.)

There was no séance the following night. The Holmeses were far too experienced not to know the value of expectation and impatience. Robert Dale waited and watched the clock. I felt like smashing the crinoline china ornaments on the mantelpiece, reducing the crystal candelabra to a million smithereens, but instead made do with breaking an oil lamp on Mrs Holmes' best dress. She blamed Bluey, so the rows about him began anew, but Eliza had leverage now. If Bluey went, so did she, and then what would Robert Dale think? I would have gladly got rid of the dog; I hated how it sniffed around whatever part of the room I was watching from, as if it sensed me somehow. But Eliza was opening new possibilities to me too and I did not want them to end precipitously. I would have to be more careful. If I was going to break something in a fit of temper, it would have to be somewhere that the dog was not.

At the next séance, Robert brought a gift for Katie, a mother-of-pearl cross on a fine, thread-like silver chain, with a note. It was an almost private meeting, the only other guest being the Swedish minister to the States, a longstanding friend and supporter of Robert Dale's. This time Eliza touched his face after he had presented his gift.

(For days afterwards, I thought constantly about that small movement, wanted to feel the sensation of it, wondered what it was like to feel his bodily warmth as a solid thing.)

She fastened the necklace around her own neck and went into the cabinet with the note. There, in the darkness, while Mrs Holmes dozed in her fastenings, I sent her a soft glowing light to read it by. The paper itself was luminous, but briefly. Eliza looked perplexed at first but then seemed to shrug it off. When she returned to the parlour, she thanked him for his message:

I offer you this because it is as beautiful
and pure as you are.

(Pure!? My derision briefly overcame my affection. Robert Dale's kindness was not matched by his ability to recognise corruption, but perhaps the two qualities are incompatible.)

He later marvelled that she could read it in the pitch blackness of the cabinet. Katie was always viewed with the cross from then on. Encouraged by this reception of his gift, Robert brought presents to almost every séance – gold bracelets and rings and a brooch set with stones.

He also found himself defending her honour. When an unknown sitter requested a kiss and Katie, apparently insulted, promptly vanished, Robert rushed to her defence, remonstrating with the man for his rudeness and lack of respect. When Katie next appeared to him he was moved almost to tears, because her 'pale and beautiful face' wore 'such a look of weary sorrow and deep depression'. She sought his protection and his reassurance and asked him to promise that he would protect her from unwanted overtures as he had shown he could, adding that 'when you touch me, it gives me strength; but when others, with whom I have no sympathy, are suffered to approach indiscriminately, it wearies and exhausts me'.

Mrs Holmes was less understanding. Robert Dale Owen might be important, but he wasn't the only sitter. Some of the men liked a bit of a fondle and Eliza shouldn't get ideas that she was too good to oblige. Eliza did not argue, but the following evening, her Katie entreated Robert Dale, 'Tell my medium not to urge me to communion; it hurts me to refuse her but I must.'

Eliza did agree, though, to a gradual change in costume. The neckline of a new dress sat low on her breasts, the material fine, semi-transparent, and beneath it she wore only a white cotton slip. My Robert looked at these new manifestations of Katie with something more than kindness; I caught him fixedly staring, looking for a glimpse of darkened oriole, perhaps, through the thinness of the fabric. He desired the person who was being me and I longed for her body, her being, so that I could feel his need.

Forty times he came in all, forty visits, and in thirty of those he touched, or was touched by, Eliza being me. He testified publicly to my existence, and to the abilities of the Holmeses.

In August he travelled on business and did not return until mid-October. At times I was afraid he might not come again. Yet really I knew the lure was too strong and that he would be drawn, over and over, to the Philadelphia parlour where Eliza played out her tableaux, and a dog barked, and a solitary spirit waited and watched close by, while he poured out love on an unreal thing, a facsimile of me. In some way I hated this deception of him; it seemed ignoble to taunt his greatness with fallibility. And yet I thrived on it too. I absolutely needed his belief in me, in Katie King, even if the spirit he had set his heart on was not me at all. Above all, I wanted to see him, to feel that warmth that did not diminish with familiarity, to imagine, with hope, how I might experience more.

Others came, often drawn by his public attestation of our wondrousness, but the idea of how I might sense his physical humanity obsessed me in his absence. Yet, in the way of such things, I have no idea why it suddenly happened, what change in me made it finally realisable. All I know is that, by concentrating, something I had tried and failed to do countless times in the past became possible one late October evening, when the paths outside were strewn with early fallen leaves that rustled with his coming, and a chill wind blew in from the Schuylkill River.

The direct quotes here come from Owen (1875), *Footfalls on the Boundary of Another World*. As this work is so often referred to in the texts, it is clearly being used to corroborate the account of the writer; a continuation of the literary device whereby the account will seem more real by being in keeping with contemporary descriptions. [AM 2007]

Despite the way her abilities have developed, Katie is still unable to move freely of her own volition here. She is tied to the Holmeses in the same way that she was unable to leave the Davenports. Reading the manuscripts again, I can see her progression much more clearly, especially from this section to the next. Where once I saw flaws that were confirmation of a fiction, I can now see the evolution of a different kind of organism, with a developing awareness and knowledge of how to interact with something other than itself. [AM 2012]

Spirit Writing, etched on metal plate
(very rare and unique)
Approximately 1874, Private Collection, New York.
Copy in the Magic Circle Collection.

WE ARE BOTH UNDONE BY A KISS

As usual, I watch, silent and unnoticed from the corner. There is only the dimmest of light; the lamps flicker and are turned to their lowest setting so that there are shapes rather than identifiable figures huddled around a circular table.

The seating is a haphazard affair; at least two people are on armchairs that are far too low for the table height and the others sit bolt upright on uncomfortable wooden seats, placed so close together that in some cases, fabric-clad thighs have overspilled the sides and now touch those of their neighbours.

There is a rich smell of perspiration, for although it is a chilly autumn evening, the room's windows and doors have been shut against the elements all day and this is an unusually large crowd for a séance here, eight people in all. There is the swish of three fans, waved restlessly, incessantly by the three ladies present in the group.

Even in this darkest of spaces I am aware of him. He sits right next to Mrs Holmes, the medium, and while he is very old, with his wrinkled face and his hunched body, I feel the brightness of his mind, his utter kindness, as if it were a light in the room. This is a different setting from our usual one, where the audience watches from a row in front of a cabinet. For now we all look

215

towards the centre of the wooden table and the cabinet seems almost a forgotten object behind us. It is a new format to celebrate his return, something they hope will bind him still further to this dingy flat above a shop.

Mrs Holmes grows stiff and the atmosphere changes. The fans miss a beat and one even stops altogether. A wailing noise escapes from her, an inhuman, almost feral sound that reminds me of foxes in their wild coupling in the springtime.

Mrs Holmes slumps forward and from the corner opposite to mine, Eliza appears from the cabinet. Everyone looks up from the table towards her. A thin white cheesecloth dress is edged with phosphorus and glows as it trails, bringing a ghastly green light to the community. She has never looked lovelier. Some kind of white powder has taken all the rosiness from her cheeks but instead of looking ill, she looks ageless and ethereal, and I am in awe as well as more than a little envious. Beneath what is the flimsiest of garments, she is naked, and I glimpse the carefully shaped dark triangle that marks her sex, the most blatant display of her musky, warm-blooded humanity, yet not perceived here as such. He looks at her and I see his face open up and I am saddened, if only briefly, that he might be so easily deceived.

The other men gawp, their eyes fixed unashamedly downwards, but he does not, seems instead to look at her features, the skeletal cheekbones, the slightly mussed, curling hair, then glances at his pearly cross nestling on her skin. She glides around the table to stand just behind him. Her movement, the fluidity of it, is the result of hours of repetition and practice, the rehearsal of a dancer preparing a role, but for a sequence that will be over in seconds.

I would hold my breath if I could. She is close to him now, surely he can smell her scent, know that she is as real as he is, but even as I think this, the scent of hyacinth permeates the room, although the season for them is long, long past. I am creating an atmosphere with almost no effort at all, and I am astonished that it is so.

'Hyacinth.' He speaks, and is barely audible, afraid to break the spell that brings her to him.

'Aye, it is, sir, I'm bringing your Katie to see you.'

The voice comes not from her staged apparition, but from a corner of the room, as if there are indeed two spirits here, and the guests again crane their necks and turn towards it, moths to a candle flame. I marvel, because the voice has a gentle Scottish lilt without even a hint of any of the Lower East Side characteristics that so often fill this flat, this very room. This is not of my doing. I am discomfited and curious. Involuntarily, I think suddenly of hyacinth flowers, tiny, six-petal pointed stars, gathered together on stalks that so often bend with the weight of their mass.

And before his face three, then four, then half a dozen tiny lavender-coloured flowers from a hyacinth bloom fall onto his breeches. He turns around a little in his chair, better to see Eliza, his Katie as he thinks her to be. A Katie that I would truly be, if I could. A foolish old man, but such a kind and good person who has done so much for a world that has given him scant recompense and will give him even less now that he has fallen under our spell.

Eliza reaches forward and places her hand on his cheek. Mrs Holmes seems to murmur in her slumber but remains with her head still on the table before her.

He lifts his hand and places it on top of hers but at that she glides again to another chair. This time a lock of blonde hair fastened with a pink ribbon falls onto the lap of one of the fanning ladies so that she begins to weep, but quietly, with simpering sobs and unchecked tears.

Even I am mesmerised by this artifice, curious as to how Eliza has managed to conceal these objects somewhere about herself when her dress seems to show there is nothing beneath it. I think that this part of the show is about to be over, that she will vanish again, back through the curtain, take her place in the narrow darkness that conceals her trickery. But it is not, and she does not.

Instead she moves back to him, to Robert, who has his hands cupped and filled with hyacinth flowers, and this time he stands. It is unexpected, this break from the assembled group, and there is an unvoiced disapproval from the circle, but Mrs Holmes does not stir and he does not take his seat again.

His hands fall to his sides at the nearness of her and the precious petals float to the floor. I am between them; I look into her face and see only innocence, despite the guile I know she carries; I look into his and see that it is imbued with sentiment. I think I know what hurting is.

And then it happens.

I become her. For no more than a few seconds, but I do. I concentrate hard, wish with all my will and then I find I am touching his sleeve, its stiff fabric. The heaviness of a human body imprisons me and I do not know how long it can be this way, how many seconds or minutes I can be within a living thing. Once more I feel like a flying, fluttering thing, but unexpectedly, and despite the discomfort of the strangeness of

218

the sensation, delightedly, I share the experience of the skin that I inhabit.

And so I take my chance. Bending forward, I feel the slight roughness of his parched lips against my own softly powdered ones. He pushes, just the tiniest pressure in return, the asking for something further, and I reciprocate in a kiss that has passion despite its fleetingness. Softest of mouths. We touch with the places where words are made. I am communicating silently and Eliza is nothing more than the means. It is more than I thought it could be, yet it is the simplest, silliest thing. I am overwhelmed that these physical interactions happen every day to everyone, yet I never have been part of them. I have missed more than I knew. I am undone in his unravelling.

It is over in the briefest of moments. Once again, I am but an onlooker, apart from life, but moved by it. Eliza draws back and vanishes behind the curtain; Mrs Holmes begins to stir. I look at my Robert, and see only the line of wetness that settles in the crags and crevices of his long lived-in face. I watch and know that he is all but lost to the world. My realisation becomes regret that I have wished for this, that I should have been so unaware of the consequences.

This suffers a little from the floridity of the very early papers, but given its topic, it is perhaps understandable. [AM 2007]

Of all the spirit papers this one haunts me. Her evolution is almost complete. It is not just the physical aspect, the fact that she is inside one person and able to kiss another, but also the emotional one. She is realising, too late, that actions have consequences that should be considered. She acknowledges responsibility for her actions. It is a very human evolution and it makes me long for her more. It is so limiting to try and understand a spirit by rational thought. As a student I had to read the Christian mystics. I have a battered old copy of *The Cloud of Unknowing* still and in it there is a line I keep returning to:

By love he can be grasped and held, but by thought, neither grasped nor held.

So I think it is with my ghost. The Victorians who wrote on spirit nature had a much clearer understanding than we do now. We embrace a pick-and-mix philosophy these days. We applaud Crookes' discovery of thallium, which we did not know existed until he found it, while disregarding and scorning his belief in a dimension that our physical senses do not allow us to easily perceive. We are so rational that we have forgotten how to feel for what is true. I know that I cannot logically argue for the veracity of the knowledge that I now have, but losing an argument does not mean that I am wrong, only that I am as limited in my ability to explain as my listener is in his ability to accept the possibility of anything that cannot be proven by scientific means.

I have dreams of this scene, words etched in copper, stored in a drawer on the seventy-first floor of a building in uptown New York; the kiss in a crowded place, both seen yet not seen at all. A consequence of my illness perhaps, or something with which Katie has graced me. [AM 2012]

A SÉANCE TO END ALL

The first kiss was not the only kiss; there were three in total. Three nights, one after the other, because Robert Dale could not stay away, and begged the Holmeses to let him visit.

Robert Dale finished an article for *Atlantic Monthly*, a glorious public declaration of my reality, and sent it off to Boston after our first kiss. He came to the apartment early and left late and I counted each second between his visits. It seemed I could only stay in Eliza for moments at a time, and, bizarrely, only during a séance.

It was the dog that precipitated the catastrophe. Somehow it escaped from the bedroom during the meeting of the third night. It barked at Eliza who was dressed as Katie, before it was hastily taken from the room by an irate Mr Holmes. Eliza shrugged it off afterwards as an accident averted. Mr and Mrs Holmes, treasuring the constant flow of gifts and dollar bills, were less nonchalant. They waited until Eliza was out buying some groceries. Bluey, thinking he was having an extra walk, bounced down the stairwell and onto the sidewalk, all along Ninth Street, wondering briefly, in his dog's way, why Mr Holmes wasn't heading for the park. The new veterinary practice on the corner charged twenty dollars to put him to sleep and Mr Holmes handed over the money, left him there in the bright white room with the brown glass apothecary bottles and the needle that brought death.

When Eliza returned, the Holmeses confessed all, reasoning that they had no choice. But she didn't even take her outdoor clothes off, just turned and walked out of the flat, leaving the Holmeses to worry if she'd return in time for that night's meeting. I went with her. Because, yes, I found that I could follow now. Perhaps then it was not the séance room I was chained to but rather to the emotion it engendered.

Eliza surprised Dr Child at his home across town. The servant who answered asked who she might say was calling, and she replied, 'Katie King.' He came to the door and recognised her at once. Not a spirit, then, but a young woman with a darker complexion than her ghostly pretence.

'I can't do it any longer, sir. You and that nice Mr Owen, and him an old man, getting all worked up. I wouldn't be able to live with myself if something happened because of it.' A tear ran down Eliza's face. Child's anger redirected itself to the Holmeses; he even felt pity for this girl who had been caught in their snare.

'I have a plan, though, sir. Something to make it right. With your help, if you please.'

When Eliza returned that evening, half an hour before the séance was due to begin, she left Dr Child loitering on the corner, so she might arrive first. She said nothing to the Holmeses, who assumed her love of trinkets had overcome her love for the dog and that all would be as before. Eliza took her usual place, in her customary garb, in the thin walnut space of the cabinet.

There were again eight guests. Eliza had a plan, but I had one too. Exposure would have meant the end of my nightly visits, my precious kisses. Tonight there would truly be supernatural activity; I would confound the deceivers with the reality of me.

They sat in two rows this time; the chairs had been arranged that way. Robert Dale had the middle seat in the front row and looked eagerly at the curtain in the minutes leading up to the spirit's appearance. She stepped out, and there was a collective gasp from four of the sitters who were new to this particular meeting. She walked, or more accurately, glided, up to Owen. The hem of her dress had been dipped in phosphorus and a pale green shimmer illuminated her bare feet showing beneath it.

Now.

Now was when I needed to do something to distract her from her purpose. I looked around. The dim red bowl of the table lamp glowed. I thought of it rising high into the air and then smashing, raining tiny shards of glass around them. Nothing happened.

I tried again. This time I thought of a chair rising high into the air and taking a corpulent man with it; I imagined his shock, but his delight too, at having such a good story to tell over dinner with port and a cigar. Nothing happened.

I watched, unable, it seemed, to do anything at all, while Eliza removed her wig, spat on her hands and rubbed the powder from her face, all the while standing directly in front of my Robert Dale. He looked stunned, unable to move, caught in the shock of it. Mr Holmes dithered, unsure whether to try to stop the exposure or to see what unfolded, then deny all knowledge. Every person in the room stared at Eliza as she bent down and slowly, as if she had no care at all of being disturbed, lifted her gossamer-fine white spirit dress high above her waist, so that the dark triangle that marked her sex was almost level with my Robert's face.

'I have a cunt, sir. Not a spirit at all, really. You can touch it if you like, you wouldn't be the first.'

Her voice was clear and distinct, an actress's voice, entertaining an audience.

Child, in a rage, acted first. This wasn't the plan he'd agreed to, discussed over lunch with a penitent Eliza. This was cruel and debased. He stood up abruptly. 'Cheats! Imposters!' Someone else, as if woken suddenly from a trance, jumped to their feet and turned up the lights. All I could see was Robert Dale, staring, not moving. His mouth turned down, saying nothing.

And then, too late, too late for anything at all, the lamp rose up.

It went unnoticed. Everyone now, except my Robert, was in a commotion. Two men held Eliza; Mr Holmes made for the door but his way was barred by two genteel women, who surprised me with the joy of their fury. There were shouts and curses and Eliza screaming. Mrs Holmes had emerged from her slumber in the cabinet to find her parlour in chaos and lost all composure, cursing Eliza with one breath and with another denouncing the sitters as gullible fools and dirty old men.

The red lamp hovered there above the scene for almost a minute, as if it was undecided, then it shattered into a thousand pieces. A shower of ruby splinters fell upon the room. Robert Dale alone looked up from his chair at my fragmented benediction. Still oblivious to the uproar, he felt the shards fall upon his face, and only then, began to weep.

He left for his home in Indiana the next morning, but not before he had cabled Boston to try to stop the article that would publicly show him to be a fool. Eliza, thrown out by the Holmeses, sold off her jewellery, even the mother-of-pearl cross, and for a hundred dollars, told her story to the press. On the same day that my Robert's testimony to the genuineness of his spiritual experience was printed, Eliza's exposure made the headlines in three different publications.

I left the Holmeses, discovering that I was freed of them and of the claustrophobic squabbling of their home, and followed Robert Dale to Indiana. I did not know whether to reassure him with my presence or just to observe him, lest it prove too much.

In New Harmony, Indiana, I was at last able to view his life's work. Robert Dale had transformed an experiment in communal living into a kind of idyllic community, or so it seemed to me. I looked forward to seeing him, settled at home, with at least two of his children close by. But it did not happen. The agitation that was the result of the encounter in the Holmeses' remained and, if anything, worsened. He was ill, almost feverish, and spent long hours alone in his home with only his two servants for company. When the servants had left in the late evening, he lay in bed, fitfully leafing through books. His daughter, Rosamund Dale, came every day and pleaded with him to move into her house that he might be better cared for. He refused, stubbornly clinging to a possibility I did not grasp, but hoped might be that of seeing me again.

I tried to comfort him but found that I had no way of communicating with him. It was as if I wasn't there. When he slept, he called for Katie in the night-time, cried out for her and could not see the sad spirit by his bed. I tried to enter a servant girl that I might reach him that way, but it was impossible; perhaps there was some kind of mediumistic gift after all. Or perhaps it was the atmosphere of collective belief engendered by the séance, with its palpable atmosphere of mourning and death, a heavy thing that hung about even the most light-hearted of spirit meetings. For whatever reason, I could not be inside someone just because I wanted to, that much was apparent. I sent him dreams that he never dreamt, thought of words that never reached his mind, a constant stream of muttering, of love, of reassurance, of the mundane, of the life that is written here, of questions, suggestions, of everything and nothing.

I was invisible and unperceived and questioned my own existence in the utter solitude that resulted.

In the end I did the only thing I was able to. As he lay with a book, just before midnight, a bedside lamp on the small chest beside his pillow, I lifted up the photograph of his dead wife that he kept there. It hovered, unmissable, just before him, then went back to its usual place. I expected wonder, perhaps even joy at this new vindication. Instead he wept, how he wept, with huge sobs, the likes of which I had never heard. Still crying, he got up and dressed himself and went out to the stables where he saddled up a small grey roan.

When he arrived at his daughter's home, in a state of partial collapse, his eyes were red and swollen and his shirt was fastened incorrectly. She came to the door at the beckoning of a maidservant, still dressed in a white cambric nightgown, and took her father in.

The next day Robert Dale was committed to the Indiana State Hospital for the insane.

The newspapers that had lauded his political and humanitarian successes now publicised his demise. 'A dispatch of this morning tells a sorrowful story. Robert Dale Owen has become insane' headlined the *Chicago Tribune* on 2 July. The *New York Times* recognised his true nature, calling him a 'kindly, genial, whole-souled man' who had met a fate worse than death at the hands of 'a trio of swindlers'. The *Sacramento Daily Union* commiserated, finding it a 'sad, painful ending for a man who was honest, noble-minded, pure as a child' but thought him now 'done to death – or worse'. The descriptions of his person, despite the circumstances, showed me that I had not been alone in recognising the kindness of his spirit.

(I felt a new emotion for me: guilt. I was consumed with sorrow that I had done a terrible thing, however unwittingly.)

His room at the asylum was not as bad as some; his daughter had been solicitous and arranged and paid for a private room. Sparsely furnished, with only a narrow bed, a table and chair, it was a dark cell, the only natural light coming from a small square window with thick bars, set high up in the wall.

But there were other wards in that place, long corridor rooms where row upon row of the mad raved and shouted and sang and screamed incessantly. This, the unholy choir of insanity, was audible in Robert Dale's room, but at least he was spared the sight of its obscenity and its heartbreak.

He did not lie on his bed during the first few nights but sat bolt upright, as if afraid to be caught off guard, by dream-filled sleep or by some waking nightmare. At times his tiredness overcame him and he slumped to one side. I looked on. I wished that I could catch him, let him rest against me, send him dreams of pleasant things.

His brief slumbers never lasted; the hellish din always interrupted. There was a woman who sang music-hall songs; she sang them well but repetitively, even as her voice grew hoarse and broken. Robert Dale endured. During the daytime he walked out among his fellow patients and tried to strike up conversations with those who were least afflicted. He even played chess once, for almost an hour, before the stench of his partner's incontinence brought two orderlies with restraints and chloroform.

I was disorientated too. I replayed the events that had brought me there yet still could not understand why I was there when I seemed to be able to do nothing at all.

Many of the poor souls spoke to unseen figures and I could not be sure if they were delusional or if they conversed with spirits that I was unaware of. There was a man called Charles, stocky and ruddy, with a gap-filled grin on good days, and a private room, who befriended Robert Dale. But on his bad days he thought himself Christ and dispensed blessings to the other inmates. On these days only, he sensed me. I knew for sure from the focusing of his eyes, the way he would turn to follow me if I moved from one place to another. He asked me a barrage of questions, challenged me with a sanity that made him seem more mad to anyone who saw it. But when I replied, the chaotic distortions of his mind could not disentangle the messages I sent him. At least at first. After many weeks, finally, he was able to understand the simplest of messages. I was perceived again. Robert Dale was worsening in this place as if the madness around him was contagious, but with Charles came the hope that I might reach him.

Charles slept, a drug-induced heavy thing, but his eyes moved restlessly beneath his lids and I dreamt of a voice of my own that said:

'Tell Robert that Katie is here with him, will stay with him till he is well.'

Mad Charles banged on Robert Dale's door as soon as lockdown was over, his flaccid penis poking out of his breeches because, in haste, he had not fastened them. He was grinning and when there was a slight delay whilst Robert Dale made himself respectable, he shouted and hit the door with his fist. 'I have a message from Katie. Let me in!'

'Charles.' The door opened, Robert Dale peeked out. 'What's wrong? Hold your horses, man, I'm just getting dressed. Look at the state of you. Let's see if we can get you a nurse.'

Too late, I knew what I had done.

'Robert, I've a message for you, good news, from Katie. She says she's here and will be here until you're better.'

Robert Dale reminded himself that his friend of sorts was mad, not bad, and tried to reply with a kindness he did not really feel.

'The fact that you think such a thing only means you're even sicker than I am, Charles. When I can realise she never existed I will be cured. You've been stealing the newspapers from the orderlies again, haven't you?'

He waved to a nurse at the end of the corridor, who took Charles away. In his room, he sat on the bed with his head on his hands.

I could have wept too. He thought his sanity depended on disbelieving what was real. He wished to deny me. I was an aspect of the depth of his madness and nothing else.

I veered hopelessly in the hours that followed between my usual wish to convince him of my presence, and the realisation that to do so would have taken him further from the world that had so engaged and delighted him.

The horrors of his new home enacted themselves before

me that day. Charles was restrained in a linen jacket with long sleeves and taken off to some wing of new hellishness. I saw cruelties inflicted on the afflicted. I watched a young boy have his face pushed into a pail of urine because he wet the bed at night. He came up gagging, gasping, only to be ducked again. A woman who cradled a doll in her arms and walked from ward to ward, lamenting over a lost child, had her bundle taken from her and looked on as it was kicked by nurses, like a ball, so they could show her it wasn't a real baby. Of course, the effect was something else, and what she saw was her four-week-old son die another death. I was disgusted by the utter inhumanity of the people who were supposed to care, but I was also sickened by the ceaseless demands of the mad, their constant need for delusion to be acknowledged as truth. I saw that by staying I could do nothing except condemn Robert Dale to years of this, because truth was a nebulous thing, controlled by a majority.

In the asylum I learned how to hate. But it was love that made me leave it.

That night, he lay on his bed, naked, but covered by a dingy sheet. He slept fitfully, a troubled sleep of his own imagining. I wished him forgetfulness, although it was the worst thing I could envisage, and then I said goodbye. I thought of darkened rooms and people summoning me in hushed expectation. Instead of the music or the nervous cough of the séance, I was surprised by a cacophony of street noise; over this I distinctly heard the name John King, in an accent that I could not at first place.

A SÉANCE IN A NEAPOLITAN SLUM

It was the narrowest street I had ever encountered, long and winding, with washing on every balcony, and the smell of sewage in the air. There were a few seconds when I was disorientated by the sheer chaos that seemed to surround me. Women called out across the *vicoli* from their balconies; horses with laden carts trotted past at speed, causing the almost exclusively male pedestrians to flatten themselves against the walls. At one point a group of children of different ages and sizes, but with the same tattered clothes and sun-browned skin, refused to move, and a cart driver pulled his horse up to a stop, cursing the ragamuffins as he did so, '*Vaffanculo...*'

Italy, then, a newly formed country that wasn't really a country at all. A place I had never been to but one that I knew Robert Dale had lived in for many years. It was March 1876, the same month and year that I had left the asylum, according to the newspapers piled high on the back of one of the vehicles.

A man who looked out of place both in terms of his dress and his demeanour turned into the alley. This, then, was why I was here. I watched as he moved like a local, skilfully dodging the traffic and a bucket of water poured out from above. Clearly he was familiar with the ways of the streets, and somehow I knew that his smart hat and black coat belied his origins.

'*Ah, Damiani, come va la mamma?*' The questioner, peeping over one of the balconies, had a tiny head wrapped in a head-scarf, and a most impressive bosom.

'She's well, thanks, Signora Battista.'

Damiani continued almost to the end of the alley and then turned into another, even more impossibly narrow. A thin sliver of sky ribboned above him. He passed one door, then another, and stopped at the third. This one, with no number to differ-entiate it from the others, had peeling navy paintwork and a round doorknob that was covered in verdigris and only par-tially attached to the door.

He rapped the knocker loudly. The woman who came to the door was apologetic, although she had taken only minutes to arrive. The flat was nicely furnished and quite expansive despite its modest façade, and Giovanni Damiani looked around approvingly, before asking, 'Where is she?'

The owner of the house responded by leading him through a large, high-ceilinged sitting room into the kitchen. At the sink, a woman of around twenty-one stood peeling tomato skins from a huge pile of fruit in a crate beside her. It was clear from her expression that this activity did not give her any pleasure at all. 'This is Eusapia. Eusapia, Signor Damiani is here to speak to you about what happened last week.' The woman turned abruptly and retraced her steps. Damiani stood awkwardly for a second then extended a hand towards Eusapia. She put a newly peeled tomato in the pot, wiped her hands on a cotton towel that hung from a nail on the wall, and grasped his hand warmly.

Damiani was a little taken aback by the firmness and strength of her grip – there was something almost masculine about it – but he smiled anyway. 'Eusapia, my wife says that she saw you at a séance in the neighbourhood of the Palazzo Reale.'

'Yes, Signor Damiani. I was accompanying Signorina Riccarda. Her papa does not like her to go out unchaperoned.'

'Understandably so.'

'Perhaps, but she is not exactly attractive, so I have no idea what kind of harm he thinks might befall her. She would probably be pleased to have a man.' The expression on her face was one of utter bedevilment.

Damiani looked bewildered. I wanted to laugh or smile or make some other gesture of appreciation towards this, the liveliest of human females.

'I'm sure the young lady is lovely and has more than her share of suitors. But in any case, I am not here to discuss the merits of Gianna Riccarda.'

'Just as well. You wouldn't be here long if you were – she doesn't have enough to keep a conversation going.'

(This was both preposterous and wholly inappropriate; I was enjoying myself immensely.)

Damiani cleared his throat. 'My wife says that you are a very gifted medium, that she saw phenomena at the meeting last Tuesday she has never witnessed before.'

Eusapia stopped sneering and smiled a little. Really, her appearance was most odd. She had black hair, like most people of the region, and very dark eyes, but there was a small dent on one side of her forehead, and the hair growing directly above it was a tuft of stark white. Her body was rounded, curved but with a waist that was too thick to be fashionable, made worse by the fact that she was clearly not wearing any kind of undergarment to shape it more becomingly. The overall effect was of a half-mad, half-wild woman, one who would not have looked at all incongruous in the Indiana ward I had just left.

(Yet, despite that, she was compelling, beautiful even, although that word seems inappropriate to me, because it is more often used for physical forms that are merely pretty or well designed, like Florence or Eliza.)

'You mean the levitations, signor.'

'I do indeed. And I've come to ask if you might join us for a meeting tomorrow evening. That is, if Signora Pacitti can spare you.'

'Oh, she'll spare me all right. She doesn't pay me above room and board so she won't be getting much of a say. Will you be paying me to attend your circle?'

'Why, yes.' Damiani looked momentarily discomfited. He obviously had not even considered the question of money. 'I'm sure we can agree something.'

'How much, then? Don't want to say yes until I know what you're paying me, do I?'

'Shall we call it a lira?' Eusapia nodded. 'Let me write down the address for you.'

'Don't read or write, sir. Can do my own mark, but that's about it. You just tell me it. I'll remember. I've got a good memory.'

He said the address slowly and went to repeat it, but before he could do so, Eusapia had already recited it back to him.

He made a brisk farewell and headed back the way he had come. I assumed that I was to stay with Eusapia, but to my surprise found that I could not, and that I was to accompany Damiani. Eusapia intrigued and delighted me, but it seemed my interaction with her would come through Damiani for the present.

Damiani's home was in a much more prosperous neighbour-hood of Naples, as I discovered the city to be. His origins were in the backstreets where he had visited Eusapia, but a combination of showmanship and trickery had granted him considerable success as a performing psychic. He was also known to act as a medium from time to time, but privately, and for gifts rather than money.

Maria Damiani had been deeply impressed by Eusapia's talents. It was not trickery, Maria had insisted, but something else, some truly strange, inexplicable ability that allowed the young woman to communicate with spirits. Damiani had been initially sceptical but open to the possibility that this young woman might have something he could use vicariously, per-haps by managing her. Now that he had met her, he thought she would be nothing but trouble and said so.

I watched Damiani and his wife sleep that night, touched by the way their bodies spooned against each other. Of course I thought of my Robert in the Hell that I had abandoned him to, but again I reassured myself that he could only find his way out of what society deemed insanity by forgetting me.

Maria Damiani snored gently. She was the opposite of Eusapia in so many ways – refined, with thin, almost skeletal fingers, and her hair, even while she slept at night, was tidily fas-tened in some kind of plait. She could have been a sophisticated Katie, I thought, but it was the male me that had been called to this place – not Katie but John – and perhaps, in Eusapia's strength and lack of feminine propriety, I could find a place for him.

As she tumbled into sleep, Maria Damiani dreamed, and in her dream:

A message came to her from the spirit world, and this message was that John King desired to incarnate himself in the body of the medium called Eusapia, if she was willing.

Eusapia arrived at the Damiani house the next night. There was no cabinet, only a table with a white cloth and five chairs around it. A couple, Maria's sister and her husband, joined them and the five joined hands in a circle. I watched, curious to know how Eusapia would be able to effect her trickery with no preparation, and was prepared to be impressed if she managed to do so. The sitters closed their eyes. I watched. Eusapia began to hum, tunelessly, on a low note, one that did not sound like a woman's voice at all. Then it happened. A voice said very clearly to me, in quite an authoritative way:

'Lift the table.'

I was so taken aback that I did nothing, and after no more than a minute, the voice insisted:

'Lift the table.'

Eusapia had not spoken aloud; she was still humming, yet she had managed to communicate with me. I lifted the table, to the usual gasps and exclamations of surprise.

'Are you John King?'

the voice asked, but in tandem I heard another voice below it, giving a commentary in Eusapia's usual tones: 'That silly Damiani woman has no idea, but if she wants John King, the least I can do is ask. As if a spirit is going to have a name. It's all made up, this John and Katie King rubbish, a way to get an audience. I want to be unique, I don't want the same bloody ghost as everyone else.'

At this point, I intervened. I looked at Eusapia and imagined saying, 'Yes, I am John King.'

Eusapia stopped humming and opened her eyes. She looked slightly panicked; the table still floated a foot or so above the floor. I decided to drop it and it crashed to the ground. The sitters looked at Eusapia expectantly. Her eyes remained open but now she stared glassily as if in a trance. 'Are you John King?' she asked the room. Maria Damiani smiled and nodded.

'Yes, I already told you I was.' It was obvious that only Eusapia could hear me, but in order to entertain the others I opened and closed the large sideboard door twice.

'Do you have a message for anyone here?'

Now, of course, I thought it would be nice to give a message, but rapping was so tedious – all that tapping out of yes and no to each question, which also presupposed that any question you did want to ask could be answered by yes or no. Eusapia had already said she couldn't write, which meant I couldn't dictate something to her. I looked at her, thought about how I had won my kisses, focused on going inside her, and it happened. I was sitting at the table, a link in a circle of hands. And this time, it was easier, as I imagined it might be to don a new suit of clothes. It was as if I had somehow become more used to the weight of humanity. 'I am John King,' I thought, and a male voice came from Eusapia's mouth, introducing itself to the gathering.

I cogitated. Maria Damiani had lost a baby girl the year before; I saw the moisture welling up in her eyes, the hopeful desperation of this house, this room, this meeting.

'Baby Carlo is here, and well.'

(Of course I had no idea where baby Carlo was, but it seemed only a kindness to the woman.)

'He is playing with angels,' I added hastily.

Eusapia's voice came in my head: 'God, this is awful, I finally get a spirit to come into me and the best they can do is offer some sentimental twaddle about angels.'

So I was the first spirit to be inside her.

(Again, I made my usual assumption that there were others like me, which seemed the only real possibility.)

'John King, be gone now, I am tired,' Eusapia said.

I didn't leave her, but instead thought of floating above them. Suddenly I was looking down from the ceiling onto the upturned faces of the sitters, their circle now broken – something that was believed to be an ominous portent during a séance – because Eusapia was floating a few feet above them. 'John King, put me down!' Eusapia was annoyed. I lowered her body to the floor, unwilling to push her too far, although I had contemplated dropping her.

A strong wind – although that's a metaphoric image because I find the sensation difficult to describe – caught me then and seemed to blow me out of Eusapia's body. I was back in the spot where I had first viewed the five, and Eusapia was lying on the floor. Her body twitched and contorted uncontrollably, beating spasmodically against the tiles, her tongue protruded, and a damp patch spread onto her skirts. Maria Damiani was kneeling beside her but looked as if she was too afraid to touch her. The thrashing slowed down and finally ceased altogether. Maria and her sister helped Eusapia to her feet and ushered her out of the parlour to find a clean set of clothes.

Eusapia claimed to remember nothing of what had occurred.

Maria insisted she spend the night, and sent the neighbour's boy with a message to that effect. Eusapia lay in the guest room in the darkness, finally alone after they had stopped fussing, and spoke directly to me. It seemed to me that Italian had a wide variety of very colourful curse words, and that Eusapia knew how to use them to effect.

'*Porco dio bastardo* (roughly translated, God's a pig and a bastard), who are you?' she spoke aloud, or rather muttered. Even in extremity, Eusapia was worried about holding onto her newfound opportunity; the last thing she wanted was for them to dismiss her as mad.

'I've said this several times now. I'm John King.'

'So you're not going to speak to me, is that it? Why the silence?'

She could not hear me again; it was as if I did not exist.

'This is ridiculous. We all know the whole séance get-up is a lot of bollocks of God, so why are you not communicating with me any more?'

I persisted, but it was clearly pointless. I found myself dismayed at the return of my isolation. She must acknowledge me somehow. I thought of the covers on the bed lifting up and away from her, and they did so.

'It's freezing in here,' she said in a matter-of-fact way. 'Anyway, you're obviously a very sleazy ghost if you're trying to see me in Signora Damiani's nightie, not that it's exactly revealing.'

This was something I had not even considered. As a male spirit, or rather a spirit that was to be perceived as masculine, I would have to observe certain proprieties with women – or not, which would of course be much more engaging. Eusapia was evidently well able to deal with anything I could do, although her epilepsy troubled me.

As if she had heard me, she pulled the covers back up over herself. 'I have no idea why I had a fit like that. It's the first time since I was a child, maybe ten years old or so. I hope that wasn't you too.'

Even in her sleep, Eusapia was restless. She tossed and turned, fought with her coverlet, and at one point even threw one of the pillows to the ground. Her constant motion and relentless energy were incongruous for her size and shape; people I had seen with that nervous propulsion were generally thin to the point of emaciation. She was contradiction personified and I was both intrigued by and admiring of the traits that seemed to coincide in her. This foul-mouthed, argumentative woman was also the demure, uneducated one who had so graciously greeted Maria Damiani and thanked her for her hospitality. Yet with her husband she had shown not even a veneer of nicety. What was it, then, that allowed her to distinguish so quickly and to adapt accordingly to whatever persona was best suited to the person she was addressing? It was a skilful artifice akin to artistic creation, but Eusapia Palladino was manufacturing herself rather than a piece of sculpture, so seamlessly that my only concern was that she herself might not know who she was.

She returned to her former home only once; long enough to collect her two other dresses and some undergarments and stockings. The Damianis invited her to live with them; Giovanni claimed his motivation was care for her well-being. He would, he said, be a father to her. They were alone at the time, walking back to the Damiani house with Eusapia's possessions, and she snorted in a disbelieving way. Yet later, when they joined Maria, she thanked both of them for the protection they had offered her.

Undoubtedly Damiani, with his years of experience in entertainment, could provide Eusapia with the kind of publicity and reputation she needed. But it was equally true that the lull in his popularity meant that she offered him an opportunity to rekindle his success, albeit vicariously. Eusapia was wily, though, and when he drew up a contract, which she could not read, about any earnings that she might accrue, she asked Maria to look over it, somehow knowing intuitively that she was honest enough not to ally herself with her husband in any deception.

Initially Eusapia sat only for small circles of invited guests. They were not charged for the privilege but instead were invited to make donations, which they did with unfailing generosity. Eusapia did have a repertoire of trickery, like any other medium. This included the usual ventriloquism, as well as a few small contraptions for table lifting. I was intrigued by a set of slates that arrived with her, wrapped in her underwear to prevent them breaking. She had said she was illiterate and had even been unable to read the contract that Damiani presented her with, yet she carried apparatus that was only used for spirit writing. I found out later that night. In preparation for the second séance, Eusapia had asked only that she be left alone to rest for an hour or so beforehand. In the privacy of her room I watched her chalk an ornate message, ostensibly from a dead man called Gianni Carini. This was then slipped between two blank slates, ready to be introduced, using a quick sleight of hand, during the meeting. So, even her illiteracy was part of an elaborate act.

A spirit cabinet had been set up at Eusapia's request, by curtaining off one corner of the parlour to create a small triangular room, hidden from view. Within it was placed a table, on which were laid the slates, a prayer book and a doll. Eusapia sat at a second table, with the audience, and in full view of them, until the lights were turned off and the room was plunged into blackness. The idea was that the objects from the makeshift cabinet would fly across onto the table in front of Eusapia. The blank slate, which had been shown to the audience, would have a message on it when it appeared.

The doll and the prayer book made their way across with little ceremony but with a good reaction from the eight assembled guests; the slate, rather than coming over the curtain, was heard to slide across the floor and up the table leg. Eusapia asked for the lights to be turned on and read out the message.

Dearest Angela,

Do not grieve for me. I am with our dear family on the other side. Pray for us and know that we are waiting for you.

Your Gianni

Angela, who was an elderly woman in a brown velvet dress, started crying loudly, and her companion put his arm around her to comfort her.

'Is John King with me tonight?' Eusapia's question took me by surprise.

'Yes, can you hear me?'

'Yes, John, we are pleased to have you with us.' I wondered if she really did hear me or if this was pretence for the assembly. She closed her eyes and began to hum.

'I am John King,' I announced to the room. Eusapia had

slumped onto the table but it was clear to the audience that my voice came from her.

'What manner of trickery is this?' The man who had comforted Angela Carini stood up from his chair. 'We did not come here to see ventriloquism and fakery.'

Eusapia remained with her head on the table, and Angela pulled her companion back to his seat. The others shushed him and tutted with disapproval.

(I was struck by the irony of my situation. It was obvious that no ventriloquist, no matter how skilled, could create the deep bass voice I was using to greet them.)

I began again.

'I am John King. The same who has entertained séances in America.'

The audience looked perplexed. The culture of the séance here was apparently quite different to what I had become accustomed to. I continued.

'I am here to help you communicate with your recently dead.'

The whole room seemed to relax a little; this was obviously far more familiar territory.

'I see a little boy. He has dark hair.' Child mortality was high in Naples and the locals are usually dark, so this was as good a place to start as any. A gasp from the crowd and a young woman in a very shiny lilac dress swayed to one side. 'It's Raffaele!'

'He says his name is Raffaele and he is being looked after by an angel of the same name. I want to read you some words to take with you after the meeting.'

Eusapia opened her eyes, sat up gradually and took the Catholic prayer book that had earlier landed miraculously in front of her. I reckoned that with the general belief in Eusapia's illiteracy, this might be a memorable way to close the proceedings.

> Come, Holy Spirit, fill the hearts of Your faithful
> And kindle in them the fire of Your love
> Let us Pray:

(I paused here, anticipating that they would join me and they did so.)

> O God, Who instructed the hearts of the faithful by the light
> of the Holy Spirit, Grant us in the same Spirit to be truly
> wise and ever rejoice in His consolation. Through Christ,
> our Lord. Amen

Damiani stood as if to mark the end of the séance and Eusapia looked dazed. I had left her as soon as the reading was over and now watched warily to see if she would have an epileptic seizure. Apart from tiredness, which could have been feigned or real, there were no signs of any discomfort, although a small furrow in her brow denoted some consternation that I assumed was annoyance rather than fear or worry.

In her room, after the visitors had left and the Damianis were asleep, she upbraided me.

'I don't know if you can hear me ... but you must never, ever do that again. It's far too risky. What if they think it's fake and that I can really read and write? Everything will be lost. Do you have any idea how hard it is to keep up a pretence like that, every day, for years? No, of course, you don't. I don't give a fuck how advanced your intelligence is, you WILL NOT do that to me again.' Her voice was a loud hiss and I was taken aback by its venom. 'This whole thing only works because they believe I'm ignorant as well as common. How can someone as stupid as me possibly fool them? Don't you realise that? You idiotic phantasm, you. Yes, the voice is great, far more male than I could ever manage, but please, reading the Catholic litany? You'll have the priests here complaining. Things have to go MY WAY. I will not have you jeopardising everything when it's all so close at last.'

She could not hear my response, which was perhaps just as well. I did appreciate her worry about the church – any established church would have been equally problematic – and I was furious with myself for not thinking about it. However, I was also appalled by her utter lack of gratitude for what I thought was a brilliant display of psychic communication. While Eusapia Palladino was by far the most interesting medium I had had to deal with, as well as the first who showed any signs of being able to understand me, she was going to have to learn that I was not a plaything to be controlled at her whim. I thought back to Florence and her clever lie to Henry Crookes that sometimes the spirits set things up to make it seem as if trickery was involved. I probably wouldn't even have to go that far. I could just as easily expose her trickery as enhance it and it was important she realised this early on in any collaboration we might have.

Eusapia's regular meetings at the Damianis' drew huge crowds. Entry was meant to be by invitation only, but chains of friends and acquaintances, by word of mouth, obtained the small, neatly printed blue card that was necessary to secure a welcome into the parlour. We worked together in an uneasy truce for several months. Eusapia did not reprimand me again and I was a reliable presence at her meetings. There was a certain deviousness in my decision not to be flighty; I wanted Eusapia to become reliant on me. When she stopped practising her mediumistic trickery, her carefully choreographed sleight of hand would become less effective. If, after that, I decided to absent myself, she would learn who was in control. But Eusapia was wily too and so, while always contacting me and involving me in her meetings, she also continued to develop innovative ways of beguiling her audience. There was the added consideration that culturally I had a lot to learn about séances in Italy, which, with their almost exclusive focus on death, were quite different from those in Britain and North America, where psychic contact was neither more nor less important than entertainment. There was too a heavy sexual element, at odds with the focus of the meetings, something which I perceived as far more dark and brooding than the flirtatious advances of Katie King. It was as if Eusapia's earthy qualities, the way in which the majority of her audience regarded her as an ignorant peasant who had been granted this one gift, coupled with her unusually open attitude to sex, had changed the pale and brittle longing of the séance room. Whereas this taut desire had been embodied by Philadelphia Katie and shattered by the exposure of a woman's vagina, Eusapia's mediumship seemed to combine both the physicality of sex and the notion of spirituality.

After several months, I was unsurprised when the tests upon her became more and more focused on her clothes. She was stripped naked by women who would normally blush and look away from their own nakedness, let alone look upon that of someone else. It was reminiscent of Mrs Marryat's wandering hands on the naked Florence Cook, but even less subtle, and more invasive, because the process often involved three or four women at one time. Eusapia was dressed in garments of their devising, with the pretext that they avoided any possibility of concealment. She questioned me in her room after the séance was over, asking if I was capable of sexual longing, if I found her attractive. If she had been able to hear my reply, and if I had wanted her to know, she would have learned that her humanity both attracted and repelled me. The fluids and smells that her body oozed and emanated disgusted me, but I envied the rush of heat to her skin, the swollen flesh of her own needs, the calm that came from her self-satisfaction.

I was addressing the small group of six who sat around the table. There were the usual requests for communication from dead relatives, but I had begun to elaborate on my presentation, creating a whole spirit world with enmities and friendships that would nowadays be likened to a serialised soap opera. On this occasion I was troubled, without quite knowing why. Now that we had our routine established, Eusapia usually spent my deliberations passively, with only the occasional thought running counter to my activities. The physical sensations of her body bewildered me less and less. My occupations were brief, but over time I learned to recognise some bodily states: a full bladder, the cramps of menstruation, the slight urgency of mild thirst or hunger. My publicly male persona dominated gatherings, and occasionally the curious or puritanical whispered about the *propriety* of such an obviously male spirit being inside a woman medium.

Now my feeling of unease turned to alarm when Eusapia closed her eyes and started to drool. I went on speaking through her; in fact, if anything, the showmanship of my performance became more intent so that I could distract the guests, and her discomfort might pass for a normal part of the evening. The saliva was unsightly and copious, though, and I watched the guests recoil. I did not want to wipe it away with my hand because to do so would destroy the illusion of Eusapia's trance. Instead I focused on it to see if I could somehow make it move away or disappear. What happened was that it levitated and flattened into a fine mist of spit, so thin that it was almost half a foot in diameter. The circle gasped and began to point at it for the half minute or so that it floated there, before falling to the ground as a glob once again.

Eusapia came around suddenly and I was back in the corner of the room, looking on at the proceedings. Mrs Damiani led Eusapia away but I lingered, listening.

'It was ectoplasm, I'm sure of it,' a young man declared to two women, who tittered at his proclamation.

'Nonsense, that's all fakery,' said another male voice.

'Some of the newer manifestations in New York are quite convincing.' Damiani smiled at his visitors. 'We've never actually had it here before.'

'Did you see the face, Fredo?' One of the tittering women leaned over towards the young man standing beside her.

'I did indeed, Rosa. Did the rest of you see it too?'

There was general assent around the room and Alfie nodded. 'It was just like the face of Christ on the veil of Saint Veronica.'

'I thought it was more like the Madonna.' Rosa looked towards Fredo for his support, but Damiani interjected.

'No, it was definitely male. I thought it might have been your father, Alfredo.'

'Good God, now that you say it–' Alfredo looked excited-

'I think you are right! I didn't think of it at the time. I was too pre-occupied with working out if it was a trick. As I said, I've always thought of this ectoplasm business as fakery, but perhaps . . .'

Damiani smiled broadly and started to usher the group towards the portmanteau in the hallway. He had been impressed by our latest display, but he was also tired.

In her room, Eusapia had not undressed. Instead she was pacing restlessly, pausing only to look out of the window at the gas-lit street below. I did not sense anger in her disquiet, but rather an abject bewilderment that made her seem unusually vulnerable.

She was whispering when I came in, a monologue directed at me. 'I just don't understand it. It doesn't seem possible. They saw a face. If spirits are non-corporeal, how can they see a face? They think I'm ignorant, but I know how you come inside me to do things, to *communicate*, and if you had a physical form of your own there just wouldn't be a point. Whose face is it? Is it Jesus? All those years of doubting priests . . .'

It was ludicrous that a woman so brilliant at creating illusion should fall victim to the most common figment of all, pareidolia, the creation of a recognisable image from chaos, the brain's attempt to recognise and categorise gone wrong. She had been fooled by her own audience. This was how doubt was born. Yet I was discontented; much as I had hoped for her to be uneasy, to be less secure, I did not want her to question my nature in this way.

The phenomenon classified as ectoplasm brought visitors from further afield. Men of learning from other countries requested a sitting in carefully worded letters in Italian, which were either archaic in their attempts at formality or flawless, perhaps written with the help of a native speaker. Damiani read the letters and researched each prospective guest. The testing was inevitable, but if someone was already a believer and well disposed to the possibilities of the spirit world, then their findings were much more likely to be favourable. Eusapia's standing in the house grew and the large study upstairs was converted into her bedroom so that she might better recover from the rigours of a meeting.

In the interesting nineteenth-century book *Gendered Voices* by Rev. P. Scott there is a discussion of the different focuses of male and female ghost presentations at séances of the time. The King character is unique in that the two different vocal aspects are being associated with a single spirit entity. Perhaps it is a device to account for the multiple authorship. [AM 2007]

Now that I have read the whole thing several times, I find I have no doubt about the authorship and wonder why I questioned it before. It is inconceivable that more than one author could have achieved the consistency of style and narrative, and as the spirit writings together with the Cesenatico scripts span two centuries, they could obviously not have been written by a mortal.

I wish she had written even more about what she thought of those sensations she was able to feel and understand. What is it like for a spirit to 'read' (for want of a better word) someone's body?

The sexuality question still concerns me. It changes, and indeed my ideas about it fluctuate too. Eusapia hears the spirit voice as unquestionably masculine. It is as a male personality that Katie first experiences period cramps. Gender seems to be a nebulous, fluctuating thing, whose fluidity intrigues me. [AM 2012]

Spirit Writing
1880, Magic Circle Collection
Acquired at auction from a private
collection in Naples in 2009

WHEN IT IS LEAST EXPECTED

I remained there, in that Neapolitan house. I had no wish to move, was pleased to be distracted from my concerns about Robert Dale by such new developments in communication. Whenever I was tempted to look for him, I made myself think of the madness I had engendered. I thought that by now he would be recovered, returned to his family and his life, and I scanned Italian newspapers and journals for word of him. But despite his long residency in Naples decades before, he was forgotten in this part of the world, and so I learned nothing. A year passed, two, and I promised myself that in time I would go to see him if I was able to will it so, but still, I reasoned, he was an old man, and perhaps the shock of even a simple dream intervention could tip him into senility, or, worse, death. I learned patience in those months that became years, both from handling my difficult medium, and from my heartfelt belief in the necessity of absence.

One night while Eusapia slept, her usual fitful, restless slumber, I looked at the books in Damiani's study – mostly recent Italian history, but also some classics (it was there, for example, I first read the Commedia *of Dante). It was June, a month when the heat is still bearable, and people do not seem to complain constantly about its insidiousness. There was a late-blooming white hyacinth plant on the window and the heavy scent permeated even the pages of the old books, bringing a chaos of memories with it.*

Suddenly, without warning, I was in a garden. The smell of hyacinth persisted but now it came from china-blue blossoms, densely packed together. They grew in a raised bed with white stones encircling it, a lovely juxtaposition of colours that seemed to presage good things for this unexpected transition. There was a summer house, wooden, with high windows, although all the curtains were drawn. The sun was bright, relentless, and I thought perhaps the drapes afforded shade against it.

Inside there was a sitting room with plain deal wood furniture, well made but unornamented. The sounds of grieving were audible there and I followed them to a downstairs bedroom. An elegantly dressed woman in her middle years cried by a bedside where a white sheet covered a newly dead corpse. The room was unfamiliar, the woman a stranger to me, but through her tears, I heard a name repeated, sobbed, choked back, then spoken again.

'Robert,' she wept, 'Robert, my Robert, why did we have so little time together? Why did I find you so late?'

A common name, but I knew, suddenly and surely, that it was him.

The thing I had both dreaded and wished for had happened without my knowing at all. I had been so certain that there would have been a sign, a warning, a realisation. I imagined that he might call for me before he died and that I would know of it. But he was dead and this woman I had never seen before cried over him as a lover. So little time had passed. Just under two years since the kiss and the madness it brought. Where was his spirit? I had wished, imagined, hoped, even believed that his death would bring his spirit to me, but there was nothing, only the noise of the living. Was it too soon? Did months, years, decades have to pass? I remembered nothing of any life I might have had before this consciousness. I had wanted to take him over to whatever lay afterwards, ease his passage with my presence. I remembered Mrs Marshall and how I had comforted her last hours and my sadness gave way to rage that I had not been able to do even this much for him. There was some conspiracy against me. I had thought it was against us both, but this woman's grief showed he had found a late, last love in those final months. I did not resent his happiness but I was envious of the woman who had brought it to him. Meanwhile, it seemed my youthful, ill-thought impulse to save his life as a child still caused me harm. Yet I would do it again. I wondered if it ended here, if this was my final punishment, or if that was what I knew would remain, the longing and endeavour to find him again: the irony of a ghost desperate to make contact with someone who was no longer living.

It was after seeing this piece in Naples that I first came to Cesenatico. Peter and I took a break from the tumult of the city, and instead of going to busy and popular Capri or Ravello, went further afield to Cesenatico, a place that Peter's friends had said was lovely, filled with Italian tourists rather than British people, and quiet out of season. Since then, really

without cessation, I have had a feeling of being watched.
Perhaps just the ghost of my imagination, a trick of my illness,
but one that seems no less real to me than if it were not.
[AM 2010]

THE CAMBRIDGE SÉANCES

Among the many letters that came asking for sittings with Eusapia, there was an elegantly composed request in purple ink on lavender paper. The postmark said Cambridge and no attempt whatsoever had been made to write it in anything but English. Damiani knew English well and was more than a little impressed by the summons to give a séance at Cambridge University, where some learned and respected men wished to see the phenomena displayed by Eusapia Palladino under the strictest test conditions of their own devising.

Eusapia too was thrilled. England seemed a romantic destination, one of fogs and soft landscapes, streets that in wintertime might have little or no daylight at all. In short, it was the perfect setting for someone who claimed to commune with ghosts. At any other time, I might have shared their enthusiasm, but I felt heavy, distracted; I was in mourning, and not of a mood to play at ghost communication with Eusapia.

By the time the trip was arranged, the summer was over. The months of preparation had passed uneventfully. There had been no major sittings and only occasional meetings with some loyal followers during the months since Robert's death, and I had remained within myself, not willing to banter or bicker with any humankind. Eusapia spoke to me during those scattered meetings, but whether to entertain her crowd with the presence of a familiar spirit or because she genuinely hoped I would hear, I do not know. I did not reply to her directly. In the weeks that passed, Eusapia seemed content enough; she still spoke to me late at night, although as she had never known that I could hear her - it was really more like speaking to herself or to some imaginary man that she could flirt with and chide in turn.

Cambridge did not disappoint Eusapia, with its meandering river and damp fog that hung around the historic buildings like a shroud of finest grey silk chiffon. For my part the sadness that I carried was multiplied a hundredfold by being so close to the country of Robert Dale's birth.

(*I would have left her there, gone wandering to other mediums, other séances, had I been able. I might have filled the days with variety in an attempt to lift my stupor, but I was tied to Eusapia, and, no matter how I conjured other scenes, was unable to leave.*)

With the new wave of fatigue came a lethargy I had never experienced before. I was numb and felt divorced from all that transpired about me. We stayed in an old coaching inn by the Cam for two nights before our appointed meeting and, as if she sensed that something was wrong, Eusapia lost her usual hectoring tone and spoke gently, almost pleadingly.

'John, do you hear me? I used to be so sure and now I'm not. Perhaps you're tired of me? Don't abandon me now.'

This vulnerability and honesty was entirely new and I was moved. I watched her as she paced the room; it was the early hours of the morning and a long day of testing lay ahead. Even if she had been able to hear me, I was not certain I would be able to reassure her. The torpor that infected my thoughts, the heaviness of my being, precluded any guarantee that I might be able to intervene in even the smallest way.

The meeting was to be held at the house of Frederic William Henry Myers, a classicist and poet who had founded the Society for Psychical Research and was a respected academic at Trinity College. There were two other people there when we arrived, one of whom was the well-known psychic investigator Frank Podmore; the other, much to my dismay, was John Nevil Maskelyne. Eusapia had withdrawn into herself. This was more than a pretence for the observers that she was preparing for spirit communion, rather I could sense that she was on edge. We were led into Myers' library and Eusapia, Damiani and the three men all sat round a circular table. I scanned the room, wondering if Eusapia or Damiani had managed to bribe servants to hide some devices or if there would only be what Eusapia could conceal in her voluminous skirts. But I was caught in my perusal, stopped by the sight of a small shelf on which stood not two, but three books by Robert Dale. On the spine of the third book was written a gift of words: *Threading My Way: Twenty-seven Years of Autobiography*. I focused on the volume and found inside the key to the lost years: Robert Dale's story from his birth until his residency in the United States was laid out in those pages. My intervention in his childhood illness was there, a miraculous, inexplicable thing. I consumed the words of the book as if there was no one else in that room. It was as if the years I had lost were being given back to me in some consoling grace.

The sitting and the testing were forgotten; it was as if I was transported with the devouring of pages. And so Eusapia came to grief.

Damiani had agreed to a simple display, a table levitation, some rapping where questions would be answered by a certain number of raps signifying yes or no. Had I been involved I could have made the table rise to a height that would have precluded the usual under-the-sleeve devices, but I was not and I did not. Maskelyne looked on with derision at what he identified as a series of badly performed conjuring tricks. He consulted with the other sitters and their report was conclusive. Eusapia Palladino was a fraud. The British mainstream press as well as the spiritualist newspapers lambasted her attempts at deception. She was lampooned as a grubby Italian woman who would have failed to find a job in an English circus, let alone be given any credibility as a medium. Satirical cartoons showed her wearing a beard with the words 'John King' written above her head. I became an object of ridicule. Crucially, the *Journal of the Society for Psychical Research* stated that it had no further interest in Eusapia's fraudulent mediumship and would no longer support any attempts to investigate it.

The distraction had cost me much in terms of my reputation, but it had cost Eusapia far more. I had hoped that she might grow dependent on me so that she would cease berating me and show some gratitude. Instead I had a woman terrified that she had already come to the end of what might have been a successful career, fearful of the threat of poverty in the Neapolitan slums that awaited her. She dreamt of cholera and malaria, the twin curses of the city, and I was powerless to circumvent those dreams. When she spoke to me, and it was rarely, she was apologetic and wheedling; her monologues were full of doubt as to whether she was mad and speaking to herself, or whether I had ever existed at all.

We returned to Naples. The storm of vitriol that we left behind us had blown away my passivity. In Damiani's house, I listened as Eusapia entreated me to help her.

'I'm here,' I said. 'I was away but I've come back.'

Her monologue continued; she was oblivious. 'You have no reason to help me, I know. I'm a worthless Neapolitan girl, nothing but dirt beneath your wings.'

(I usually found these ridiculous displays of fanciful language and exaggeration irksome, but for once, I was anxious to reach her, to try to make amends. It was laughable that the only person I had ever met who could communicate with me was the one who was being publicly denounced as a charlatan.)

'I'm here.' Again, I projected a huge concentration of will, normally enough to take me inside a body.

Eusapia turned her head towards me and smiled. '*Grazie.*' To my surprise, she began to weep.

I continued, 'Enough of that, woman. Pull yourself together. We need to try to rebuild some faith after our little fall from grace.'

I saw a flicker of the old Eusapia then in the light scorn that showed in her eyes, but it was gone in a moment and I could not catch what she was thinking.

'We'll work together again. John King is not a spirit to be so easily dismissed as imaginary.'

(I was starting to enjoy this. My John King persona had a touch of pomposity; I thought of smitten women, filled with adoration.)

Eusapia was less impressed. 'The most important thing is for them to believe in my abilities.' She was firm. 'Without that, you don't exist at all, do you? Why is it that we can communicate like this now? I've been speaking to you for years. I thought it was only during a séance I could hear you.'

I told her the truth, simply that I didn't know, and she accepted it graciously.

'I was afraid, you know. Of being a middle-aged woman with no husband, no talent, no money. Damiani would put me on the street if he thought I was of no use to him, and while Signora Damiani is kind, she and her husband wouldn't keep me as a house guest indefinitely. I'm not sure they could even afford to. You're the first spirit I've ever been able to hear, but all my life I've been aware of them. They come, they go. Ever since I was a child. You know the family that took me in when my mother died asked a priest to exorcise me?'

'You are aware of other spirits?' I did not know whether to believe her or if deceit was so much part of her that she was trying to exaggerate whatever ability I already knew she had.

'Of course. But you're the first who has actually answered me. For years I used to speak to a ghost I named Theresa. Of course, I have no idea what her name was. I just knew she was there and I thought that perhaps she might hear me even if I couldn't understand her. I prefer you, though. When I was aware of her I dreamt of terrible, evil things. I am not easily frightened but even remembering that time makes me scared.' There was a pause. I didn't interrupt and ask for more details, despite my curiosity, because her apprehension was almost a palpable thing filling the room around us.

'I imagine you as a rather dashing man in his thirties, you know.' Eusapia had recovered quickly and was now adjusting the low tied neckline of her white nightdress, pulling it down slightly and at the same time smoothing the fabric over her generous breasts. It was an attractive image but did not distract me from what she had just said.

'Have you ever been aware of another spirit while I was with you?'

'Not while you're there. You must frighten any others away.'

(I did not persist. But I thought that one day I might ask her to call a name out for me, to say the words Robert Dale Owen, like a charm. Not yet. I did not want to share that part of myself with her; it seemed like something too human to be part of the spirit she believed me to be.)

We spoke for some hours that night and became allies of a kind. It took time. But working together, we were *good*, without peers. After a few years of gatherings for generous donors, the incredulous rumours that spread about my appearances reached the most exalted circles, even if in the most hushed of voices. A Russian prince, a French minister, even a Chinese merchant – a believer in the hungry ghosts of his own culture – found their way down the alleyway to the Damiani parlour. And their wondrous conviction brought letters again, from Russia, from France, from America and eventually from Britain too – the country where we had lost all credibility was curious again.

We travelled to other European cities and were feted, but when the request from the son of an English earl arrived, Damiani was adamant. This time, the British would come to Naples and judge us on our own terms.

I find myself very envious of the relationship between John and Eusapia. But the mention of Eusapia's fear unnerves me, the unspecified threat of dark spirits. Of course, I cannot know what awaits me afterwards. [AM 2012]

(Cesenatico Bookshop Printout Number 5
incorporating spirit writing about the death of John King
through Eusapia Palladino from a private collection in Naples,
copy in the Magic Circle Archive)

THE SCIENTIFIC SÉANCES

Everard Feilding, the son of an earl, learns to sing Italian songs from the family cook, while his sister Clare accompanies him on the piano. His little brother Basil makes everyone laugh with his attempts to mimic his brother, the way he tries to pronounce the strange words in a foreign language.

But in no time at all, they are grown. Everard catches influenza and Clare, unmarried, as devoted to her brother as he is to her, nurses him through the worst of it until she herself falls sick. The fever becomes pneumonia and her heart fails not once, for that first time stimulants are able to bring her back to the family who sit around her bedside, but twice, and it is the second time that her hand drops from Basil's and Everard embraces his brother so they can mourn together.

Yet it is not this that marks the break from his church. Everard doubts privately but keeps faith with the Roman Catholicism he had shared with his sister, in part as a testament to her. He wonders if he will hear her again, attends séances but believes nothing that he sees, investigates mediums, learns the intricacies of their trickery and is elected an associate of the Society for Psychical Research.

Ten years later, almost to the day, he goes on holiday with Basil. They have boated together since childhood and they take a canoe onto the rivers of Germany. On the Rhine, just over the border from Switzerland, they weave amid the fast currents of lower Rheinfelden, laughing as their speed picks up, then concentrating to navigate a rock in shallower water. They move out deeper, hoping to avoid the patches of shallow and the currents that threaten to ram them into unseen obstacles. Around them mountains slope and fall, and wispy clouds, feathers in a summer sky, hover on the edge of the skyline, sometimes hiding summits with their tendrils. In the deep water the going is smoother, faster, and the brothers set a rhythm with their paddles. The current that finds them is unexpected. Suddenly they are upturned and in the water and swimming hard to reach the shore. Everard gets there first and hauls himself up onto a cluster of jagged rocks. He panics momentarily when he cannot pull himself up, keeps slipping back, but finally gets a firm hold and with a sudden angular movement lies across the rocks that spike into him uncomfortably. He sits upright and looks back, thinks he sees Basil still some way out, waves to him. Looks again, realises it is not. There is nothing for it but to wait; the rocky bank is too high for easy ascent and he hopes the current that has brought him there will guide his brother too. Together, he thinks, they will scramble up, laughing, and write home later to share their scrape. Time passes, although he will never really be sure how much, and then he sees again what he thought was Basil brought closer, and then much closer still. It is his brother, or rather his body, lifeless, floating towards him, carried by the water that killed him. He is face down; his shoulder-length hair has come untied and spreads out around his head, a floating halo of dark, entangled strands.

Everard's investigations change; he is impelled by an unfinished conversation, a life too suddenly lost, rather than by scientific curiosity. His Roman Catholic faith falls away from him utterly, a discarded, meaningless thing that does not offer the possibility he needs.

Then, in the bar of the Society for Psychical Research, he hears of Eusapia from the psychical researcher Hereward Carrington, who lives in America. Carrington does not know Italian and asks Everard to write for him, to request if he may be permitted to attend a séance in Naples. Carrington is well known for his work exposing fraudulent mediums, and in him Everard sees someone who might offer protection against his own desire to believe, a longing he realises will make him vulnerable to every form of deceit. They plan to go together, if at all, and the American SPR offers to fund them if they are successful in their petition for a series of sittings. They post the letter, the Italian language bringing fleetingly to mind his baby brother's attempts at a long forgotten song, and then they wait for news from Naples.

*

They left for Italy as soon as a wire in the affirmative reached them. Feilding and Carrington took adjoining rooms in the Hotel Victoria and arranged that the sittings would be held in Feilding's room, the larger of the two. A series of five sittings was agreed and an English shorthand writer engaged to keep a record of the events for Carrington.

Eusapia asked them to supply a black curtain and a table or alternatively to allow her to bring her own. Carrington readily agreed to her bringing her own paraphernalia, reasoning that if she tried to introduce a trick table they would be well advised against her from the beginning.

But the curtains that she brought to them were of finest black cashmere with no pockets or seams for concealment, and the table was a simple round wooden one. Eusapia asked for the fabric to be stretched across one corner of the hotel room to produce a triangular cabinet of sorts, and it was fastened there on a wire affixed to the wall by nails. Additionally she presented Feilding with a list of items to procure, including a tambourine, a guitar, a prayer book and a blank slate.

I watched carefully, my heightened attention in marked contrast to my previous distraction when faced with British investigators. This would be a masterpiece, a perfect marriage of Damiani's research, Eusapia's skill and my interventions. The men waited for the expected physical phenomena, the ghostly instrumentals in the pitch-black room, the writing on the slate, and were impressed but retained some scepticism. Then, surprisingly, Eusapia asked them to turn on the lights. They were electric, bright and new, and Feilding and Carrington even showed reluctance lest they end the activity altogether. Eusapia persisted. They watched as I entered into her, without knowing what they really saw. My voice was matter of fact. I had decided that neither of these men would be impressed by charm and wit, and that their assumption would be that I was no more than Eusapia's thrown voice if I were to recite some amusing anecdote. Instead, I sang, in a basso profundo, an old Italian song, and watched as Feilding's eyes welled up, then, speaking in English – although with a slightly Scottish accent that I had recently adopted in homage to Robert – I spoke of familiar things.

'Basil doesn't blame you.'

Feilding was too moved even to speak. Carrington was less caught up and asked, 'Who are you? Where do you come from?'

'I am John King. I come from the spirit world. Basil is here and tells me that he never thought his brother was at fault.' Eusapia's head turned to look at Feilding. 'You could not have saved him. You did the right thing to swim to shore.'

'And our sister?' Feilding's words were almost inaudible. I thought quickly.

'She is in her Catholic Heaven. She watches you with love, and Basil often visits her there but enjoys the freedom of spirit life.'

'He always was a free spirit, dear Basil.'

'You say a Catholic Heaven?' Carrington was preparing for an interrogation. 'Does that mean there is more than one spiritual afterlife?'

'I have no time for debate,' I said. 'It's only important that Everard knows this message from his brother. He says to tell you that the gentlest thing he has ever seen was the way you disentangled the hair of his corpse while you waited for someone to come.'

'How can you know that?' Feilding was unashamedly weeping.

'I know only what Basil told me.' And with that sentence I began to hum their cook's song once again, although fainter and fainter, as if I was receding into the distance.

Eusapia looked genuinely tired when I left her, although the amazement of the men more than compensated for it. When they returned to England her reputation was restored, and we prepared for further investigations and more international travel.

The early success of our accidental ectoplasm still remained with me. When we received an invitation to Paris, we knew that shock value was almost as important as psychic phenomena, and so, in 1905, we prepared for something that would combine both. One problem was that I was still unable to enter into Eusapia outside of the séance room, so practising was impossible, and we were both often unsure how things would turn out, no matter how much we discussed them beforehand.

Part of our appeal to the Parisian séance crowds lay in the scandalous idea that I was a male spirit entering a female medium. Eusapia's character as a medium had come to be that of a fairly demure middle-aged woman, so the idea that she might welcome a male phantasm into her shocked men with its impropriety but made her a huge success with women of a similar age, who seemed to revel in the heavy sexual metaphor made respectable within the setting of a séance. In reality, Eusapia was as bawdy as ever. She had fewer lovers than some of her critics suggested but that was largely through lack of opportunity, because Signora Damiani would have disapproved. On the occasions when it did happen, I discreetly absented myself and whiled away the time in the library or parlour. Any sense of decorum – and there had never been much – had vanished in the years of our partnership, and now she was frequently naked in her room while we conversed, and no longer made coy attempts at flirtation. I was curiously drawn to this intimate knowledge of a woman's body. One night, after our conversation, when she presumably thought I had gone to another room and she was settled in bed as if to fall asleep, I saw her push the covers down to her feet. It was July and sweltering and I had seen her nude body before so thought nothing of it. But her hand moved down to lie on her pubis, cupping it with her fingers. I was enthralled. I watched as she began a gentle pulsing press with her middle finger and her hand slid further between her legs. It continued for some time until the movements eventually quickened and Eusapia's body arched tensely towards the hand it was so focused on. She gave a little cry, a muffled, barely audible thing, and her body relaxed again. A few seconds later, she drew the sheet up over her and seemed to fall quickly asleep.

(*A passing doubt as to whether or not she was aware of my presence did flit across my thoughts, largely because the way she had uncovered herself before the act, and then recovered herself afterwards, had something of the finality of a theatrical curtain.*)

It was a difficult subject to broach. I did not want Eusapia to think I was spying on her. It had, after all, been an accidental observation, but the reports of the ectoplasmic meetings in Paris, a city for which we would soon be bound, offered an opportunity to bring up the topic of sex. Eusapia was not coy at all; her oft proclaimed desire to embrace the changing attitudes towards her sex was more than an attempt to be fashionable. I pretended more ignorance of the female form than I had and asked about the production of the ectoplasm in the French meetings. She explained, quite graphically, I thought, how the effect would best be achieved by tightly rolling fine fabric that had been treated with phosphorus and then concealing it in the passage through which women bore children and had inter-course. She added further, a little unnecessarily, I thought, that it would be an impossible feat to accomplish when it was the 'time of the month'.

Later I realised that, far from being surplus information, the last part of her lesson was what had most import. Eusapia still bled, although it was a far more erratic event than it had been when I first was inside her. To be honest, the effects of cramping and hot stickiness were unpleasant even for the brief time that I felt them; I was glad that it happened with less regularity.

(Occupying human bodies can be both an enjoyable and a deeply unpleasant experience. Enjoyable in that one is much better able to communicate, and human vision is so much more vivid than the way I usually observe things, which is more akin to a dream. But unpleasant in that every human discomfort, from indigestion to a hangover, is magnified because I am just so unused to it.)

I was also aware that Eusapia did not see the end of her courses in the same way and that she seemed to mourn the diminishing of what she saw as a mark of her youthfulness, perhaps because she was childless, but I never really knew for certain. It was an unfathomably physical concern and beyond even my imagining. However, by concentration I had changed Eusapia's drool into some kind of spirit form. Would it then

271

also be possible to do the same with menstrual fluid? I posed the question delicately. Eusapia looked more bemused than shocked.

'So you want to focus on my fanny, then?' she said. 'More man than spirit, you are at times.'

If I had been able to I would have made one of those awkward throat-clearing noises then.

'I don't see why we might not try it. We could have a kind of spirit birth on stage. That would give them something to talk about. Do it in partial light and make it rise up from the floor, so they'd know we weren't up to the old cheesecloth and phosphorus trick. Could you do that?'

'As usual, I can't be sure. I could try. I'd be respectful.' I was trying to find the right words, but it was difficult. I tried to think of medical men I had observed over the years and adopted the language of someone approaching a patient.

'Not sure I want you to be too respectful. Getting fucked by a ghost might be enjoyable. I'd rather it wasn't during my courses, though. Firstly, they are far too unpredictable now to guarantee that they'd be there on a specific day; secondly, it's not the time of month when I'm at my best. Couldn't it work with the normal secretions?'

Obviously I had no idea, but I agreed to try. We had, of course, several other manifestations planned so that if this experiment didn't work we would not diminish our reputation.

An article in the *Annals of Psychical Science* which mentioned Eusapia's 'erotic tendencies' as well as the concept that she somehow 'glamoured' her male sitters – a term used to describe the bewitching of men so that they were unable to think in a critical or analytical way, but were rather hypnotised by sexual magnetism – did much to prepare the way for our Parisian excursion.

The guests included both scientists and believers. Among the former were Marie and Pierre Curie. The scientific part of the tests was stringent. Immediately beforehand Eusapia was asked to urinate into a metal pot and her pee was analysed thus:

Quantity: 200gr
Sugar: 40%
Phosphates: 1.2%
Chloride: 3598 with slight traces of albumen
Nitrogen: 9.53%
Albumen: 1.25%

She was also stripped and examined, and, with a candour that surprised even Madame Curie, she suggested that they carry out an internal vaginal inspection to satisfy themselves that she did not have anything secreted there. Mme Curie and the two other women who would attend the sitting dressed her in a simple aubergine-coloured dress which they provided, and offered her some cotton drawers which she declined.

The venue was a grand one: a town house in the Marais that was owned by a former member of the French nobility. He had reinvented himself as François Perrault and was proud of his reputation as an expert of séances and spirit events. François was the only one of those present who had witnessed ectoplasm at a sitting and asked the ladies for precise details of the precautions they had taken against fraud. There was no cabinet; instead a heavy walnut table sat in the centre of a lavish front room, with eight matching chairs placed around it. Eusapia could not physically lift the table by herself so any levitation would be a guarantee of some inexplicable aid.

The séance began in the way of a theatrical entertainment, with a professional pianist playing the first of Satie's *Gymno-pédies*. Eusapia entered in an unnecessarily dramatic fashion with Mme Curie and took her place at the table. As the last note faded, Damiani initiated the séance by asking the assembled guests to hold hands and form a perfect circle. This could only be broken at the instigation of the medium; to do so prematurely might be injurious to her health. As soon as the circle was made and the lights had been dimmed by a servant, I focused on Eusapia.

I looked around me. Holding my right hand was Pierre Curie, who seemed far more involved with the proceedings than his wife, who had an air of boredom about her. On my left was Damiani, a necessary precaution, because if anything were to go wrong with my intervention, it was he who carried the paraphernalia necessary to create some spirit illusion.

Eusapia was nervous. I felt a fluttering in her stomach and, as if reminding me of our intent, she moved her legs slightly further apart. Her labia were swollen. It was warm in the room and her lack of undergarments heightened my awareness of her whole genital region. She may have been nervous, but from the moisture I felt in her vagina, it was evident that the prospect of my endeavour was far from unwelcome. She tensed her muscles, in the way she did when she was holding in urine. It was very pleasurable and I concentrated on the sticky discharge that was now copious enough to leave a mark on the skirt beneath.

We broke the circle, or more precisely Eusapia did. We seemed to share control of her body. She pushed her chair back and slid onto the floor. I was now lying on an Aubusson carpet; Eusapia's upper body was supported by her elbows and her legs were only slightly bent but apart. The skirt covered them with a certain amount of modesty so that only her ankles were visible. I felt Eusapia rock slightly and arch her back so she could press her vulva onto the floor. She was so wet now that the fabric of her dress was sticking to her. I concentrated. Eusapia hoisted her skirt high up on her thighs and spread her legs wide as if in preparation for sex. One man looked away, embarrassed; the others stared at the black curly hair of her pubis and her obvious display of sexual excitement. The discharge that stuck to her pubic hairs began to come together, tiny, gradual movements, so slow that they were not perceptible even to the fixated onlookers at first, but then ever more obvious as there seemed to be a mass, a thin, semi-transparent, veil-like substance exuding from her vagina. Eusapia moaned as if she was in the first throes of labour and Mme Curie, rolling up the sleeves of her dress, left her chair to kneel beside her. '*Mon dieu! C'est pas possible!* I examined her myself. For Christ's sake, let's help the woman.' She indicated to one of the other women at the table who came forward reluctantly, 'You, hold her shoulders!'

Mme Curie knelt in front of Eusapia's wide-open legs and gently began to pull the ectoplasm that was coming forth. I looked at Curie, waiting before us, but still thought about the vaginal fluid which was starting to form a much more recognisable shape. I thought of a real birth, the outline of a human child, curled in the shape of the egg that made it, and the substance rose away from Mme Curie and took form in the air. But I could not hold it there for long because the sensations were overwhelming. Eusapia's labia felt hot and swollen; the rhythmic motion against the carpet excited her clitoris but not quite enough to bring relief. It was as if some residue of the substance remained inside the tunnel of her vagina and was gently wrapping itself around each contour. Then tiny tremors began and increased, came together as a tensely vibrating thing that played until it broke and made me cry out through Eusapia's mouth, just as it made her do the same, so that of all the miracles witnessed there that night, there was that of a shared climax and two simultaneous but distinct voices, one male and one female, from the solitary ecstatic figure, legs spread as a common whore, lying on an expensive carpet, while seven incredulous sitters looked on.

Afterwards the Curies were professional and detached. Once again, Eusapia squatted and pissed into a metal receptacle and the readings were taken.

Quantity: 100gr
Sugar decreased by 20%
Phosphates: 1.8%
Chloride: 3598 with marked increase in albumen
Albumen: 2%
Nitrogen: 11.28%

The changes, while not astounding, were marked enough to be of interest, and the Curies were gratified that at least some physical scientific measurements could be given to substantiate what they had witnessed.

It was this, the endorsement of the Curies in particular, that led to the longevity of – and debate over – Eusapia's reputation, one that is unsurpassed to the present day.

(I find it wonderful that, as recently as the 1990s, Professor Richard Wiseman felt the need to write academic papers disputing her genuineness.)

For me, the delicious sensation had been a revelation. It was not an emotionally obsessive thing like my attachment to Robert Dale, but rather a pleasure that, even after I had left Eusapia's body, seemed to resonate in my awareness. The shared experience did not immediately lead to the intimacy of confidence and confession, though; Eusapia seemed uncharacteristically coy. I did wish for a repetition, but it proved impossible because I was only able to enter her under séance conditions, and neither Italy nor the United States, where we were next bound, was open to the titillation of such a display just yet. Eusapia might even have been prosecuted under one of the numerous obscenity acts that were current at the time.

Her testing continued, right on through that first decade of the twentieth century. The results were not always as we hoped. Even after a dramatic manifestation, in which I played a large part, not only levitating some inordinately heavy furniture but also speaking through Eusapia in five different languages, Eric Dingwall, the celebrated British psychic investigator, described Eusapia as 'vital, vulgar, amorous and a cheat'.

In her final years, Eusapia married. He was pleasant enough, a wine merchant from Treviso, but it meant that she lived with him, in a Roman town house on the Sestrieri, and we rarely spoke together as we had been used to do. Eusapia was old by then in any case, easily confused. I could come into a room and hear her chatting away, mid conversation, completely unaware of the fact that I had been in the library or the downstairs parlour for several hours previously. With her death, in 1916, a peaceful, uneventful passing, in bed with her husband by her side, I found that I missed her. I had got used to having someone acknowledge me, and in the years that followed I had to learn to turn inwards again, to remind myself that consciousness was proof enough of my own existence.

I was also free of the ties I had always known before, those that called me to one person or another.

Or perhaps there were so many people looking for spirits that it was impossible for me to focus on where I should be.

There is much documentation relating to similar episodes where a medium apparently gives birth to ectoplasm; see for example Loomis (1996) in *The Psychic Exposed* or John Cavanagh's account (2001) of the French medium Hélène Bertault and her use of music during such an event in his *Music of the Spirits*. But while it is well testified that Curie did attend and indeed was impressed by Palladino's séances, there is no account of such an event happening in her presence. This is clearly a fabrication of the narrator to accentuate the sexual content of Palladino's performances (which was undeniable). Wiseman has published several recent papers showing the tricks that Palladino employed. Here is a suggested list for anyone who might be interested:

- Wiseman, R. (1993), 'Barrington and Palladino: Ten major errors', *Journal of the Society for Psychical Research*, 59 (830), 16–34.
- Wiseman, R. (1993), 'Fontana and Palladino: Nine major errors', *Journal of the Society for Psychical Research*, 59 (830), 35–47.

- Wiseman, R. (1993), 'The Feilding Report: All things considered', *Journal of the Society for Psychical Research*, 59 (832), 210–17.
- Wiseman, R. (1992), 'The Feilding Report: A reconsideration', *Journal of the Society for Psychical Research*, 58 (826), 129–52. [AM 2007]

She writes of how her experience of human sensation is heightened because everything is new. I ponder on her orgasm, a first climax, and on her loss of control, so overpowering that she was no longer able to suspend vapour in air. Yet before I was only concerned with tedious articles of refutation. I return again to an incontrovertible fact: to prove trickery is possible, or even has been used, does not negate the possibility, the fact, of genuine phenomena. [AM 2012]

Spirit Writing
Approximately 1917, Stadhuis Museum, Amsterdam
Discovered in an attic of La Chaloupe d'Or Café
in Brussels' Grand Place 1937

All I know is that the people of Europe call for spirits, but no one calls for me.

With the Great War, the séances mushroom out of the dark, bloody chaos, but these are grief-filled, desperate rooms. No one wants a witty ghost, a glimpse of thigh, an ectoplasmic birth from a medium's vagina. Instead the palpability of loss weighs down each weary sitter as they come to the meetings, their hope a fragile, precious thing, glowing dimly but hidden from the others who congregate around them.

I flit through these darkened spaces but find I cannot intervene even if I had wanted to. I am not invoked but watch on as a plethora of mediums stumble through tricks learned lately, opportunistically, but not well at all. A year passes. I fear this twentieth century will not be kind, and then a blind man sees me.

The Great War marked an increased interest in spiritualism but it was significantly different from the entertainment-centred activity of the preceding decades. John and Katie King were ghost compères as well as guides. Like television hosts, their modern-day equivalent, they could draw an audience to a show and guarantee its commercial success. The death toll and immediacy of the war meant that people turned to mediums in desperation, and the spirit's role was much more like that of a religious figure than of a show-business personality. Saucy Katie and erudite John were not appropriate figures through which one might speak to one's dead teenage boy. There are numerous studies and creative works that consider this phenomenon; worthy of note is James Charlton's 2002 play *Speaking to the Dead*. One little known Dutch medium, Claartje Van Heuven, actually claimed to channel a dead priest who then communicated with the spirits of the fallen. Any hint of sexuality or salaciousness was seen as disrespectful, and indeed just two months after war was declared, London medium Sarah Banks had her house vandalised because she presented the kind of flirtatious spirit that would have guaranteed crowds just one year previously. The nature of spiritualism was very much guided by fashion and this writing is simply expressing a phenomenon of the time. [AM 2007]

A SÉANCE FOR A BLIND MAN

By the time I found Cecil Husk, he was paralysed and almost blind. In his youth he had been an opera singer, and his early mediumship was characterised by a singing John King. Perhaps because of his lack of success and because he was frequently exposed as a fraud, I had never been called to him before. The people at his séances attended more for the amusement of hearing him sing, coupled with the very likely possibility of seeing a medium disgraced, than from any real need to communicate with the dead. By 1918, he was over seventy. He rarely held circles and when he did so they were for a very few invited guests. Instead he eked out a living by managing the up-and-coming medium Etta Wriedt, who in return helped him to overcome the practical limitations of his disabilities at the few séances he did arrange.

When I first saw him, he was seated in his parlour with only two visitors, a couple in their forties, and Etta. There was no table. Cecil sat in his clunky, cheaply made wheelchair. Etta was sitting beside him in a small armchair and the couple huddled close to each other, seeking comfort from doubt and dread. I was watching from a corner of the room next to a standard lamp, a hideous fringed thing in purple, and no sooner had I arrived than the blind man turned to me and said:

'John King, thank you for coming.'

I replied with courtesy but he did not seem to register my response (Eusapia was unique in this). I moved closer to the couch and he followed me with his dead eyes. Obviously he really did know I was there.

The couple looked uncomfortable. They had no wish to hear a singing ghost, had hoped for some direct communication. Husk nodded at me again; I wondered if he might be senile. He was making no effort to speak to his clients and Etta Wriedt looked as if this was the usual turn of events. Then, suddenly, his head lolled to one side. It was genuine. Decades of witnessing fake trances mean that when you see a real one, you assume some medical emergency. Of course, the people in the room didn't see anything different from expected séance procedure but continued waiting patiently. The man now had his arm around his wife and she had turned towards him, as if to hide the two tears that chased each other down her face.

Husk began to speak. His voice was very different to the one delivering his earlier remarks. It was that of a professional performer and seemed incongruous coming from the drooping head, impossible, in fact, given that he was in a genuine faint of sorts.

'Billy is with me.' Husk remained motionless in his chair.

The woman looked up askance from her husband's shoulder.

'And how is he?' The male client was trying to take some semblance of control.

'His passing was a terrible thing.' Husk still did not move.

'Yes, he was only seventeen.' The woman spoke now, faltering.

'No, the actual passing was terrible. There was mud, so much mud, and the stink of sulphur, gasping for breath and finding only mud, in your mouth, in your throat, in your nostrils. Now at least there is nothing at all.'

The woman had broken down completely now and the man was holding her while he wept too. I was stunned. This certainly wasn't why people came to spiritualist meetings. The idea was to give consolation, not some hideous story that would devastate them with its horror. I concentrated hard on Husk, and for a few seconds seemed to be inside him, but what I witnessed was so awful that I withdrew again.

There was a wide field, all brown, all wet, incessant rain, the panic of men climbing, blinded by weather, over a parapet and as many falling as going on. A cry went out, I couldn't make it out, but there was fumbling. Some boys – and they were mostly boys, not men – pulling on heavy leather padded masks while they tried to drag their feet through the sucking, squelching ground. Others were coughing so hard they couldn't perform the necessary physical motions.

I had my own images of death and dying, but this was someone else's and seemed worse because of it. But whose was it? Husk was far too old and frail to have been anywhere near a battlefield.

'They told us he died an honourable death,' the man said. 'This is nonsense. What kind of monstrous charlatan are you?'

Husk still did not move, oblivious to the people in the room, caught there in that hellish place, watching boys struggle and die.

Etta placed several sheets of paper, supported by a leather blotter, on his knee and positioned a pen in his fingers. Without lifting his head, the unseeing Husk began to write. He filled a page, then stopped.

'He's at peace now. Billy says it's quiet there.' Again the theatrical voice, but now Husk's head moved upright and he wakened.

The man looked as if he wanted to kill him. The woman was distraught and pulled at his arm to get him away from the room. Husk hesitated then proffered the sheet of script. The man spat on him and tore the paper into pieces.

'If you weren't a fucking useless cripple, I'd make you one.' The couple left hastily while Husk was still orientating himself to his waking state, wiping off the globule of saliva that had landed on his arm.

'What happened, Etta?' he asked.

'You had the vision thing again, Cecil. I think it's enough now. It's the third time and you're not helping anyone, least of all yourself. You're too ill, you shouldn't be doing this any more.'

'I don't know what it is. All I know is that after years of carefully constructed séance activity, I suddenly don't need to do anything. But instead of people rushing to see me they can't get away quickly enough.'

'It's a difficult gift to carry at times, Cecil.'

Husk nodded at her; he seemed to be falling asleep. I was curious. Cecil Husk's mediumship was nothing but a sham; everyone knew this. Magicians had turned up at his meetings and replicated his tricks to braying laughter from the people gathered there. He was in his dotage now, seemed more like ninety than seventy-one, could not walk or see, and yet he was a percipient. He knew where I was in the room, even if he could not hear me, which was more than the successful and much lauded Etta Wriedt did, and he obviously had some connection with the dying. To write a death in the way he had just done – the scraps of paper that now littered the floor had told of one so carefully that it was like a historic recollection by an unknown and unseen witness – was an idea that appealed to me.

'Do you want to sleep, Cecil? I'll take you through to your room and call for Sam to help you.'

Husk's last year became my project. He would dream of the deaths I sent to him and then, when next at a séance, he would write them down. The people who attended the meetings grew fewer and less regular, bewildered and even angry at the irrelevance of the words he scrawled on page after page. But Husk did not care. He who had been a sham all of his life took great pride in the fact that he had something of import to record. The papers piled high; I do not know what happened to them all. Only a few seemed to survive the decades that followed, but they were a record of deaths – deaths in which I had been involved somehow, or which had come at fortuitous times.

It was an obvious thing. I puzzled that in the decades of spirit writing, I had only ever been able to make a scattering of recollections, enticing the Davenports or Eusapia to note my emotions, my desires, or trying more recently to get that charlatan in Brussels to copy my thoughts. I would have liked to write my life that way but it was impractical, the séances too short and too infrequent to compile a book, and I wasn't sure that Husk still had the capacity to retain a whole life in his mind and then convey it on paper.

Cecil Husk only lived for just over a year after that. I never again saw him invite people to his house, although I spent much time with him. He did tell Etta about me, and while she did not actually perceive me, she believed in me and would address a space in the room, although it was never where I was.

After Husk's death, I stayed on with Etta for a time. Despite his infirmity, shortly before his death he had arranged some Scottish sittings for her and so, a few weeks after the funeral, she prepared to head to Rothesay, where she made my name, John King, famous once again for a very brief time, but it was nothing but transparent fakery.

After the war the séances continued but I could not bear the clammy depression of the rooms, and instead I discovered another darkened space where I could while away a lifetime of hours. I went into one cinema, then another, and finally I stayed in one such auditorium while decades fell around me like so many dead leaves.

The East Finchley Picturedrome in north London was not luxurious. It was just a big hall with two blocks of seats, one more comfortable and consequently more expensive than the other. But when the lights went down, I found in the music of the piano, and those flickering human images of emotions, a new séance of sorts, and a place that I could hide. With Robert's death and then Eusapia's I felt as if the best decades of my existence were behind me. I hoped for someone to call me again, of course I did, but I was never sure if it would happen at all. I thought perhaps I might become as faded as the pictures that I watched for hours, days, and eventually years on end.

In 1924 the cinema changed its name to the Coliseum, although why a moving picture hall would be named after an arena of blood and slaughter, I never really understood. With the advent of sound, the figures on the screen grew more life-like, but seemed more distant to me. I often felt mute, silent, because I was not perceived. The new figures conversed and communicated as people do and I felt excluded from their easy interactions. Yet there was no doubt it was entertaining. From time to time, I ventured out. I left the smoke-filled auditorium and went into the thick fog that smothered London in wintertime. I found a séance in the house of an old woman, but these meetings were unplanned, shabby things. More and more frequently those looking for communication with another world went to a spiritualist church. These brightly lit halls with their atmosphere of cheerful resolution, tinted with heavy moralism, filled me with horror. There was nothing of the atmosphere of the séance room, the thing which allowed me to communicate, and in any case the religiously tinged banter and propaganda extolling the virtues of a happy hereafter repulsed me. There was none of the mystery.

I retreated again to my cinema. Supernatural figures, vampires, werewolves flickered in monochromatic narratives that compelled me. There were even films about my kind. Ghosts were immortalised in these reels of shiny black ribbon, but my name was still not called. Then, in 1934, I heard my name, Katie King, as if called from a great distance, and found myself in Canada, a country I had never even thought to visit.

The snow lay thick and crisp and brightest white over the town, a very different sight from the marzipan-coloured concoction that adorned the London streets I had left moments before. There was a wind which seemed as if it might be incessant and the people moved around the streets wrapped up so they were round bundles of clothes, but cheerily as if they enjoyed the season, despite its inconveniences. Yet their smiles and banter belied the shabbiness of the layers that protected them, and a long line of men waited, stamping feet and blowing gloveless hands and sheltering around the lights of glowing cigarette ends as if they offered warmth, outside an open shop front where a woman ladled soup into cups and passed them out. The Depression had hit Winnipeg hard. But as I moved on past the queue for the soup kitchen, I found myself in a more affluent neighbourhood, and eventually in a solid stone-built house with a snowman in the front yard, sporting a scarf and hat that some of the people I'd seen earlier would no doubt have been glad of.

Inside there was a bustling family home, except for two downstairs rooms which had a separate side entrance and appeared to be a doctor's surgery and waiting room. There were no patients there, but a medical man, Thomas Glendenning Hamilton, sat by his large desk in a room with drawn curtains and scant light, while a small, fair-haired woman with a ruddy complexion and uneven teeth was slumped in a chair across from him. She wore a pale green wool coat that was worn, with pulled threads; it hung open and a hand-knitted red scarf dangled loosely round her neck. It seemed strange that she had not removed them, but perhaps she felt cold during her episodes; it was a common enough effect.

'John King,' she moaned.

Hamilton leaned forward expectantly, but then the woman woke suddenly, lifting her head and looking bewildered. I watched and waited.

'Did anything happen?' She looked genuinely confused.

'Not much, I'm afraid. But I think John King was trying to come through again. Your sister had a very good connection with Katie King yesterday, did she tell you?' His voice had the same soft burr as Robert Dale with only a tinge of Canadian drawl.

'I'm sorry.' Her disappointment was obviously not feigned. The woman was either deluded or a genuine percipient, although her mind was completely opaque to me, so I favoured the former idea.

'No matter, here's your payment anyway, for taking the time to come.'

She immediately brightened at this and, taking the money from his outstretched hand, stood up to leave. 'I'll see that my sister comes tomorrow, and Euan, did you speak to Euan?'

'I did indeed. I spoke to him just before you arrived.' He gestured to a very smart-looking new black Bakelite phone that sat in the middle of his desk as if a display item rather than a useful instrument.

Euan was who I had been called for, I realised, not this woman or her sister, despite the brief muttering of my name.

'I'm meeting him later this afternoon, in the early evening, in fact. He seems to still have a job, a rare thing in these parts nowadays.'

'Euan works at the Ford motor plant, that's how Ed met him.'

The woman seemed to be hesitating. I realised she was waiting for another invitation and that the mention of her sister's next visit was meant to elicit it. It did not come. The doctor seemed to have lost faith somehow and he stood up and walked round his desk, ready to usher her out.

I remained there after her departure and watched the kind ministrations of the physician to the numerous patients who visited him. It was, as always, interesting to see the putrid rot that can set in to the most private of physical body parts, a very somatic corruption which earlier times had superstitiously and ridiculously seen as an outward manifestation of moral degeneracy.

At around five o'clock that afternoon, Euan arrived. He was not what I had anticipated at all – short and quietly spoken and as far from the showy type of medium that I was accustomed to as it was possible to be. He was entirely unaware of me. It was a very odd sort of meeting. There was no drawing of curtains, or particular preparation. Instead Euan stretched his hands across the table, forming a small circle with those of the doctor. In a few minutes his eyes closed and his hands fell from the doctor's. Hamilton lifted Euan's right hand from the table where it lay inertly and arranged the fingers around a pen. The hand took on a life of its own, and as Hamilton slid a sheet of paper under the nib, it wrote words in a delicate, feminine hand. It was uncontrolled and automatic; the handwriting was surprisingly ornate for someone whose eyes were shut. When the hand reached the end of a line, Hamilton moved the paper up and guided the hand to the start of a new line. Had he not done so the hand would have continued to write as far as it could reach and then simply formed the letters one on top of the other. At the end of two sheets of paper the hand fell to the table once more and Euan opened his eyes sleepily as if waking after deep slumber.

I glanced at the papers while Hamilton checked Euan's pulse and temperature. Hamilton did not look at them until Euan had gone and a follow-up appointment had been arranged, one that involved the participation of others.

Hamilton came back into the surgery and resumed his seat at his desk, lifting the pages as he did so. His manner was curious but with an edge of scepticism that impressed me.

But as he read, his mouth turned down. Tears gathered in the corners of his eyes, ran down his face unchecked, then splashed a pattern like raindrops on the ghost writing that had caused them.

I am intrigued here by the mention of the Husk papers. I have spent some time trying to trace any that might remain but have failed to do so. I understand that they are now in a private collection and not accessible to the public. Given this, it would be very interesting to see how they accord with the Cesenatico pages. It is sad too that this is the last of the typescripts. It seems inconclusive. [AM 2007]

The cinema in East Finchley still exists. I went with Peter last week, although the 143 bus journey from Archway seemed interminable and at one point I thought I would have to alight or vomit, although I managed to do neither. It's called the Phoenix now. I like the name. I imagine Katie rising from the ashes of Victorian spiritualism as a modern ghost, a philosophising spirit of our time. Is she still there? Or in the Italian bookshop? Why has she not written any more? Would that she might before I die. [AM 2012]

Influenza Spirit Writing
1932, Hamilton Collection

It is December 1918.

There is a small boy of perhaps two or three in a crib that he has almost outgrown. A Christmas tree has been set up by his bedside, a fir tree bedecked with baubles, and with a porcelain angel on top. The angel's delicate skin and silver dress, her white wings made from a bird's feathers, are a last attempt at wonder, from parents worn out by fretful care.

There is an enamel basin filled with steaming water from which emanates the smell of Friar's Balsam, and on the opposite side of the crib a tiny oxygen cylinder. His father stands beside this, his mother sits on a stool with the angel looking down as she weeps.

Arthur. His name is Arthur. He is pale at first but as I watch he turns a pink colour, an artificial-looking shade as if he has been painted. I have seen that colour before. I try to remember. It is that of heliotrope flowers, a hue of nature then, but not a natural one for human skin. He chokes on the mask that is helping him to breathe. His father first adjusts it then removes it in a final gesture of resignation. His mother looks up from her tear-stained hands; his father shakes his head. Arthur dies. The heightened colour of summer petals gives way to a face that matches that of the porcelain angel. His father's sobs fill the room while his knees buckle under him and he folds to the floor.

From: Lorna Gibb
Sent: 1 December 2013 16:24
To: Bob Loomis
Subject: Husk, Collation and Mysterious Social Media!

Dear Bob,

It was lovely to see you last week. I enjoyed our sandwich in the room upstairs at the Circle. Nice to see something else of the building beyond the library!

I was delighted to be able to get copies of the Husk papers, and to have the owner's agreement to use them in my text. They relate specifically to three of the deaths in the Cesenatico papers – the Koons child, Philip Crookes and Maskelyne's friend. I have inserted them in the relevant section and given them a distinctive typeface. Please let me know if you think this device works or if you can suggest something you think might be more effective.

Here is a draft of everything I have collated so far. I have, as you suggested, kept Adam's notes in various places where I think they add to our consideration of authorial identity. I have also, as you will see, kept some of his later remarks too, because I think they add a sense of other-worldliness that befits the collection. Do you think this is too much? Should I remove them? When you obtained permission from his partner, was it for all of his notes or only for the historical/typographical ones?

While I am pleased with the overall result of my collage (seems the best thing to call it really!) I am no further forward in finding out who the writers were, or, most intriguingly, how they knew each other. In anticipation of your amused snort, I confess it is almost enough to make me believe in ghosts (but not quite, I am far too cynical for that).

I assume the Twitter and Facebook accounts that have recently appeared for Katie King are also your doing and they amused me mightily. I was especially surprised, because you are so good at pretending that you are hopeless at internet social activities. Anyway, I hope you will not be too disappointed with what I have put together. I am attaching it to this as a large PDF file because that seems the best way of retaining the formatting that I used.

One thing I did want to ask, but please do feel free to say no, was if you might give me the contact details for Adam's partner, Peter? Adam's comments were invaluable and I should like to honour this. Having read so much of his work in the past year, I feel as if I knew him. If you think that a meeting would be too upsetting for Peter, I completely understand.

Hope to see you again soon,

Best wishes

Lorna

From: Bob Loomis
Sent: 2 December 2013 09:22
To: Lorna Gibb
Subject: Peter

Dear Lorna,

In haste. I am happy to give you Peter's contact details
but feel that I should warn you about some aspects of
the death of which you may not be aware. Adam took
his own life before the cancer did. Peter found him dead
in a bathtub in the flat they rented on the Adriatic coast
during Adam's last weeks. Terribly sad, and I prefer to try to
remember him as the fine young man he was in the years
before his illness.

I will text you the phone numbers.

I'm sorry I didn't mention the circumstances of his death
before, but it seemed disloyal somehow to an old friend.
The family made no mention of it in his obituary and so
most acquaintances assumed he had succumbed to his
illness.

In the same vein, am also attaching a PDF of the most
recent Cesenatico manuscript, number seven, which I
received only last week and which I found very distressing.
Please treat it in the strictest of confidences for now. It
seems too cruel to be a joke. The shop owner is a very
pleasant woman and I feel sure that she would never do
such a thing. I'm sure you will find Peter to be a charming
man. I remember him fondly.

Best

Bob

From: Lorna Gibb
Sent: 12 December 2014 13:13
To: Bob Loomis
Subject: Adam

Dear Bob,

As it happens, Adam's mother came to my meeting
with Peter. She was in London for a meeting with Adam's
solicitor. It was, as I'm sure you can imagine, a sad
occasion, with lots of reminiscences and an especially
poignant recollection of his last visit. Did you know
he returned to New Lanark a few months before his
death?

The last Cesenatico piece fits so perfectly with
everything else, but is, of course, awful in many ways. Is
there any possibility, even the slightest one, that Adam
wrote it himself? He was there in his last days, as you told
me before. I didn't mention it to Peter because I wasn't
sure if you'd said anything even to him about it. But
perhaps he would be able to shed more light on it. Or do
you think that would be unbearable for him?

As I was preparing to leave Peter and Adam's flat in
Islington, Adam's mother passed me a sheet of paper,
which I have scanned and attached to this. She found it
on Adam's childhood bed and, although it was written
in his handwriting, it was signed 'Katie King'. His mother
has become a committed spiritualist, although Peter
disapproves, and she wanted me to have a look at this. Of
course, it is just yet another sad consequence of Adam's
medical state, but because I know how fond you were of

him, I thought I would share it with you. In my book I could add it as an appendix after the final bookshop script.

I'm afraid I can't do coffee next week. Shall we meet up after Christmas?

Best

Lorna

SPIRIT WRITING

In the weeks that followed, I watched Hamilton's feverish obsession with his new protégé. I was reminded of my youthful
fixation with Robert Dale. Of course I still loved him, whatever
he might now be, yet still I could see that the lack of temper-
ance, the frantic longing that left swathes of time when I did not
hear of him without any consequence at all, was an immature
thing. The spirit who had left him in an asylum was wiser than
the one that who had craved glimpses after a decade of waiting.

Hamilton, despite his age, showed no restraint. He was
besotted with the younger man. Euan came daily after work;
Hamilton shortened his surgery hours to spend more time with
him; sheets and sheets of paper were covered with the ghostly
characters that now spoke of other, more famous, dead people.
Euan confused me. He was not a percipient, I was sure of it.
But he had some ability, some psychic gift that enabled him to
know what someone was thinking – a mind reader, then.

Again and again, he stunned the doctor with the accuracy
of his writing. He had little in the way of education yet could
write pages of Robert Louis Stevenson, a great favourite of the
doctor's, as if from memory. It was from memory, but not his
own, I realised that.

For me, learning that psychic abilities were fact was a small
thing in the face of the growing realisation that my own range

of communication and interaction was greatly diminished. Whether it was the years in the cinema or the lack of the séance environment where I was best able to be understood and interact, I did not know. But even the wishing of a dream, the disturbing of a night's sleep with a vision, which I had used so often – to guide the Davenports' travel, to bring Henry to Florence's aid, to get Husk to write for me – was no longer possible.

Euan claimed that the spirit who sent him the writing was the celebrated John King. This was undoubtedly what had drawn me to him, but I puzzled at a system of existence, of religion, of greater government – call it what you will, you may guess as well as I can – that would bring me to a place and a story that was not of my kind at all. With my arrival at Hamilton's home, I lost again the ability to move at will. I found myself locked into my own consciousness, unperceived and unable to communicate, attached to Hamilton by an invisible thread and learning nothing except that I had faded somehow.

In the summer, we went to London. Hamilton took Euan with him as well as his wife and family, and I accompanied them too, finding that I had no choice but to do so. Yet there was no comfort for me in the familiarity of those streets. The city of my former triumphs, where I had seen my mediums celebrated and adored, mocked the impotent creature I had become with memories. Hamilton was feted as the doctor of a thousand séances; Euan captivated an invited audience in the Wigmore Hall with his talents. I looked on as the enthusiastic crowd applauded me although I was not there at all. It was a small episode and a pointless one. When Hamilton returned to Canada, the unseen tie seemed to be broken and I was able to remain behind, with a city to watch, but still no one to hear me.

The greatest power of interaction I had known had been in the possession of a body and now I grew obsessed with them. I flitted tirelessly around the rented rooms that were popular in the period and spent weeks in a strip club. People searched for release in countless positions through acts of depravity and love, although it was not clear to me which were which, unless one party was unwilling. In their frantic couplings I imagined what I had known and regretted that I had not done more. I stared at the interstices in the joining of cunt and cock and mouth and arse and prick and tongue and willed my essence into them to no avail.

Occasionally, once or twice in the years that followed, the frustration that built up from my ineffectuality caused an event – a smashed window, an upturned wardrobe – happenings that brought me relief and hope as they signalled the possibility of intervention again. So I returned to my voyeuristic pursuits, hoping each time that I could build to that intensity more quickly, learn to control it somehow. But I never did. There were séance rooms again. But no one called for me, and despite the darkened rooms, so reminiscent of those of the previous century, I could not communicate with any of the mediums, or even do so much as raise a table.

By 1934 I'd observed much of backstreet human experience: clandestine joy, poverty and controlling riches, secret crimes, a gruesome murder, a backstreet abortion where the air was thick with the mother's fear and desperation, even once, in an alley behind a sex show, a child violated by a member of her own family. But it was in a cinema with laughter all around me at the antics of the Three Stooges that I lost consciousness.

And after forty years, I was once again aware of the living

around me, confused at first, then overwhelmingly sad that I had wakened, then finally, as I looked around me, surprised at how long I had slept.

The disorientation was compounded by the fact that while my surroundings indicated a passing of decades, the girl who stood beside me was occupied in dressing herself in a costume that was almost identical to that of Florence Cook in 1874. A man entered the room. They spoke together in Italian, obviously making arrangements for later that evening. There was talk of a crowd of men, of a circle of believers, then finally I understood everything. It was the centenary of the first appearance of Katie King.

I looked around, tried to move a rather ornate lamp that was placed by the dressing table, and found I could do so easily. The man and the girl looked at the lamp as it rose a short distance above the surface and was gently returned to its spot. He seemed completely unperturbed. The girl looked at him adoringly.

'It's Katie,' he told her, 'she's with us. Remember you are only doing this for the benefit of the audience. The spirits are always with us, even if they're not always guaranteed to perform for a crowd.'

He turned directly to me, and, with a slight bow, introduced himself. 'I am Fulvio Rendhell, Katie King, and I am very pleased to make your acquaintance.'

I sent a greeting to his mind but he did not respond. Someone who could sense my kind then, but not hear them, or perhaps it was that my powers, while undoubtedly improved, were still not what they had once been.

The theatre was modern, sleek and functional, without the ornate carvings and heavy velvet curtains of my past years. I perceived the transformation of the decades, of a century, and found it anachronistic that this public presentation of me was to be of something unchanging, locked in a Victorian image: a waif-like girl, in a dated long dress tinged with some substance that had the same effect as phosphorus. The stage was circular and around it sat the twenty-three invited guests, all men, their masculinity adding a hint of salaciousness to the event. Even now, in 1974, Katie might be an object of desire. I kept thinking of the actress who would play me. In her old-fashioned dress, her ringleted hair, I saw no hope of a future for the ghost of Katie King. Instead I saw this as an act of commemoration which would also consign me to the role of a well-loved figure from the past. The hope I had felt at the recalling of my name evaporated with the realisation that this would be a solitary night, an act of remembrance, and not resurrection. In my head, I was hungry to know and interact with the new world I had awoken into, but instead I found myself presented with the spectre of what I had been, with not even the faintest hint of what I could be now, of how I might be, in this new time.

The gathering was an informal thing: the men wore jeans, T-shirts and sandals. When the girl appeared she was beautiful, but she also looked like she did not belong at all, that this world had no place for her. I had been a spirit of the 1870s, it was true, but also of the 1840s, and of this new century too; I was still here; I had grown and faded and hoped to grow again. Katie touched the men. The men touched Katie, then lifted her high above their heads, as if to transport her away. A photographer flashed again and again to take pictures that would show the world the power of a twentieth-century medium, but also display the limitations of my being in a world that no longer had a place for me.

I did not share in the success of that night; my only comfort was in hearing Eusapia's language all around me again. I would not leave Italy until the twentieth century was past. I spent the long years in cinemas and darkened theatres, taking small comfort in music, in films and in the sight of the sea, which I found that I loved, as, like me, it did not physically change with the years but, like my thoughts, moved ceaselessly, incessantly. In the last decade of the century a bookshop was named after me: the Libreria Katie King, in a small town on the Adriatic coast, between Rimini and Ravenna, called Cesenatico. I settled there, made a home amongst the esoteric volumes and trinkets associated with the new ways people thought they might reach us. I liked the street outside the shop. Branches of trees on either side of the road arched over and met, as if embracing, so that there was shade on even the brightest of days.

Then after five or six years, my torpor, my acceptance of my consciousness and my interest in almost nothing at all, was transformed by a man who came into the shop one afternoon. He could not speak Italian; he asked Regina, the owner's daughter, who worked there from time to time, if she could speak English. His accent, his voice, was that of Robert Dale Owen, and with his simple request he brought my past back to me.

He wanted a crystal for his partner. He took one: a lovely, pale blue-tinged, multi-faceted thing that spun from a fine silver chain and dappled the walls with sequins when it caught the Mediterranean sun. I followed him. For the first time in years, I left the shelves of books and the clutter and went out into the sunlight, in pursuit of the glittering, glinting present and its recipient. His name was Adam, and the man who waited for him by the sea, who took the crystal from its paper bag, gasping when it caught the brightness of the day, was called Peter.

They walked around the town all day, delighting in the old-fashioned boats moored in the port canal. I accompanied them, taking pleasure in Adam's voice, in their easy relationship with each other. I expected nothing, finding diversion in the coincidence of their being there at all. Until, during dinner, a casual remark again reminded me that nothing is arbitrary. It began harmlessly enough.

'When's the train tomorrow?' Peter carefully lifted a fish skeleton from the flesh beneath it with his knife and fork.

'We need to get there before two if I'm going to get to the archive before it closes.'

'It's a spirit letter, isn't it?'

'Yes, a Palladino one, signed by the omniscient "John King", no less.' Adam smiled bashfully, as if acknowledging that their venture was a little silly.

'No complaints from me. Nice to have a free trip, courtesy of the Magic Circle.'

'Yes, but the bookshop wasn't on their itinerary.'

'The town is nice enough, it's good to be out of the bustle for a couple of days. Aren't you feeling better?'

'Yes, I think so.'

I sensed that Adam's reply was designed to please Peter. So he was ill. It might be of consequence. It might not. I had seen enough death over the decades never to take illness for granted though.

The surprise of hearing my name again had shaken me. So they were on some kind of quest for artefacts. From the conversation that continued through tiramisu and limoncello, I realised that they perceived it as a kind of jigsaw puzzle. Adam's job, as some kind of archivist, led him to search and bid for old documents and letters. At present, he was helping to build an archive about me for an organisation in London called the Magic Circle.

I stayed with them all that night, watched their gentle lovemaking, Adam's mouth cradling Peter's flaccid penis, feeling it quickly harden there. Peter washing out Adam's anus with a small plastic syringe and applying a lubricant before pushing inside him with some force. I was mesmerised by the incredible bodily intimacy of their togetherness.

They left the town the next day. Some limitation of my powers contained me there, in my bookshop by the sea, and I could not follow them, although I wanted to. I craved their interest in me and their easy tenderness. (I did not realise then how lonely it might come to make me feel.)

I thought of them often in the days that followed, wondering how I could add to the pieces of picture so that one day someone might recognise the whole of me. I puzzled too over the fact that, despite their interest, I was not able to be with them, questioned why it was so.

The answer came with a computer.

Regina, rushing to meet her boyfriend, left it switched on overnight after the shop was closed. It sat there, with its small red light winking at me in the darkness. With only a little effort I was able to make the screen light up. Just a little more and I could make the keys on the keyboard move. I had found my voice again. Finally my reduced abilities were enough to allow me to communicate through an electronic medium. I wrote all night, printed out fifteen or twenty pages and left them there, but did not save the computer file. In the morning, the owner, Gigliola, found them. She was amused, I could see, obviously thinking it some elaborate prank, perhaps by one of her two daughters. Nevertheless she read them. When the shop was quiet, which it was for much of the day, she flicked through the pages with an English-Italian dictionary by her side.

I wondered if she could make sense of that first onslaught upon my senses some two hundred years ago, longed to know what she thought of what I often referred to as my hibernation. The next night, she left the computer switched on again, and for many nights after. I ended with Palladino's death, did not at that time trouble her with my twentieth-century vagaries. She approached both of her daughters, and the weekend boy who helped out in the summer, telling each of them kindly that they showed obvious talent as a writer (if I was human this would warrant my blushing, I'm sure), and voicing her surprise at their English language skills.

Of course, they shook their heads and insisted that they did not know any foreign languages, beyond the politenesses required for the occasional passing tourist. Gigliola even sent the printouts to a publisher, a small Italian house who frequently fulfilled orders for the shop, but they did not reply. She was not a superstitious woman, still thought it some involved joke, but did not want to ignore the sheets of print, the story of a forgotten ghost, and so she sent an e-mail to a customer on her database, a young man called Adam who had visited the shop the summer before, and asked about the name, the connection with a ghost. Gigliola remembered him, although she was not exactly sure why. Perhaps it was the rarity of English tourists in the town, almost certainly it was the fact that he knew about the origins of the name of the shop, but possibly also because she thought him attractive, even if he was too gaunt, too pale.

Adam replied the same day and within the week was at the shop with an older man. Bob Loomis was a sceptic of the most absolute kind. I could see he was impressed by the reams of paper but obviously thought it was a clever trick on the part of the owner to gain publicity for her shop. Adam was much changed. He was quieter, even thinner than he had been before, and his hair, which had been thick and fair, was now short and clumpy. He was ill, progressively, inexorably sick.

Gigliola made a photocopy of my story for them and they took it with them on their way to Naples University, to find another letter, a spirit account of a death in a German river. It was mine too. I had written it when I was inside Eusapia years before, and somehow it had turned up in a house on the Via Tribunali, an antique curio, valuable for a collector, worthy of a trip to Italy.

Again, I left the bookshop and followed Adam and Bob to the train station, but this time I did not return. When I tried to follow Adam into the carriage, I found that I could, and so I haunted a man for the last time.

I had – and have – no understanding of what makes something happen at one point but not at another. I do not understand the vagaries of what you would call Fate. Adam was dying, and although he could not physically perceive me, he believed that I was real. He read the accounts from the bookshop, the spirit writings, everything he could find, and constructed my story as a history or a biography.

Adam's encroaching weakness mirrored my own. I envied him the inevitability of death, although I understood that for him it was still a dreaded thing. In his quest to know me, he went with Peter from Italy to New Lanark. Adam's parents lived nearby in a council estate, where the newest kind of mediums peddled hope in the form of mediumistic tuition for teenage boys and girls who sought a career beyond their surroundings. I watched his mother's next-door neighbour, a young girl who worked in Poundstretchers, hating her job, saving the little she earned, then handing it to a Circle of Believers, where a charlatan in a cheap suit told her she could learn to speak to spirits. Being a medium was no longer a way to rise up from the tedium of poverty; it had become a way to exploit the poor. Touting an unreal but better future by selling a skill they did not have and could not teach to anyone who wanted to believe they could learn it.

The television set that blared nightly in the cosy front room was filled with the opposite. This was an age of disbelievers. Atheism had become a religion in itself, its followers evangelical in their desire to bring the superstitious to their way of thinking. There was no place for me, except perhaps the bookshop in Cesenatico, a place that with the advent of the internet and electronic books, was as anachronistic as I was, except perhaps in the hope of a beautiful boy who was dying and wanted to believe in something.

Adam was in constant pain as the days passed. Their sex was discreet in Scotland, quietly satisfying needs, behind flimsy walls, on Adam's childhood bed, sparing his mother's awkwardness.

When they returned to London, Adam knew that he would not see his mother again.

They had a flat on Upper Street in Islington, North London, above an old-fashioned vinyl record shop. That shop was another outmoded trader, like my Italian bookshop, which would probably be rendered obsolete in time by the increased popularity of intangible music. This century metamorphosed the physical objects of books, vinyl, compact discs, into their substantive content alone. They were no longer talismanic; these virtual music and texts were the spirits of an age that had no time for ghosts.

The street hummed relentlessly like a jar filled with angry bees, but the flat was high above, with big Victorian windows and window boxes filled with red geraniums. The bedroom looked like a room from a Turkish harem, with dark wood wardrobes, printed fabrics and gold-embroidered cushion covers. Adam could not manage the two flights of stairs alone and so with Peter's help, once a day, he descended to the street and walked to the nearby fields of Highbury. They strolled together there, peeking in the windows of expensive houses where long-haired cats posed and walls of books reached up to high ceilings with ornate cornices, and a piano lay open, waiting for fingers on its keys. Their lovemaking was different now, rarer, and Adam did not have the strength to climax but took pleasure in masturbating Peter, in taking his balls in his mouth and stroking his cock, pulling the foreskin down so that he could lick the exposed tip. Their kind attentiveness was a balm that soothed me as much as it did them; my last lesson in tenderness.

While Adam was still able, they flew to Bologna, then caught a train for Cesenatico again. Peter humoured his wish to go there, so that he could spend his last weeks or days in sunshine. Adam was haunted by the place, although he never really told Peter why. They rented a one-bedroomed flat close to the Adriatic, and the Highbury Fields walks became promenades by the water, although Adam needed more and more support for even these short outings as each day came and went.

I had no idea of what would happen once he died. He was the first person to believe in me in decades and I despaired that he might be the last for as many years again, or even more. I prayed to something I was not sure existed, and certainly did not know the nature of, that I might die too. I was tired of endless watching, the loneliness and isolation that came with my lost abilities.

One afternoon, Peter went out to get some air, leaving Adam dozing in an armchair by a window overlooking the lapping water, the coarse, dark gold sand of the beach.

The drugs which eased the pain were working, but only because they had not yet worn off. There was always a terrible time between the effects of the medication diminishing and the time when it was possible to take more. Peter had left early so he would be sure to return before the crying began.

As soon as he had gone, Adam opened his eyes. I thought of him with a pity I had only ever felt for Robert Dale and then, when I did not expect it at all, I was inside a human being once again. The limbs were aching; his head felt muffled and his mind was attenuated, pulled tight, able to focus only on when the pain would return. So there was no real respite then. I had thought those moments after the medication brought a drug-induced reprieve. In fact all they heralded was the difference between pain and waiting for it. I also knew Adam's despair; the inevitability that Peter would see him fail further still, become an infant before his death, that it would tarnish his recollections of their time together irrevocably. And then there were the thoughts of suicide. Rather than shy away from the impending inevitability of dying, Adam longed to control it, to precipitate it, to cheat hurting, suffering and degeneration out of their last hours. There was a list of activities he could still do circling in his head, each one coupled with another phrase, which was 'when I can no longer'. Then. But his mind finished the sentence in so many different ways that I couldn't keep up. The only resolution seemed to be that he had to bring about his own death while he still had the physical capability to do so.

I wondered what might happen if I was able to be inside him as he died. Could I die too? What would I see afterwards? I imagined passing out of consciousness with him and never waking up. But my entry into him was a brief moment and I had not controlled the experience in any way, so it was a vain hope rather than a plan.

When Peter returned, Adam was once again dozing and I left both of them preparing for bed. Peter cradled Adam as he led him through to the high-ceilinged white bedroom and the iron bed with a crucifix above the headboard. Out on the street, I passed by the canal as the sky turned violet then purple, the aftermath of the earlier rain, the colour of a bruise. Local residents walked out, dressed for the evening *passeggiatta* in soft, worn linen jackets and chinos, in short skirts and high heels, in carefully cut silk dresses that hung in folds over curved hips and breasts. Sails displaying the emblems of fishing families billowed, dark ochre and claret and cream in the breeze.

I watched the street lamps along the canal, reminiscent of a hundred years ago in their shape and style, as they lit up. I did not want to return to the apartment again. For the first time

I could remember, I felt that I was encroaching on something that was too intimate for observation. I had seen a thousand couplings and as many partings, countless deaths, so many ways of dying. Yet there in Cesenatico, after the rainfall of the afternoon, faced with my own impotence and the lovers' avalanche of tenderness, the sad solicitousness of their caring, I no longer wished to intrude.

So I returned to the familiarity of the bookshop which had come to be my home in the years before. It was unchanged. The computer was still left on overnight, even though I hadn't written anything there for more than a year. A superstitious hope, I think. I wrote a little then, wondering if I might end my story, or if the decades would stretch on as I kept leaving little piles of paper, until that too was no longer possible for me, or until the technology was replaced by something else.

In the morning, I returned. During the night they had thrown the sheet back and the two men lay, spooned together. Adam was curled inside the curve of Peter's stronger, healthy body and looked almost foetal. Peter's arm came over him, reached round to his genitals, which he cradled in his hand. I felt more alone than I could remember feeling. I wanted to wake them by moving something noisily, or give them dreams of me. I concentrated. A solitary sheet of paper drifted noiselessly from the dresser onto the floor. The men did not even stir. Adam's conviction that I existed was not borne out by any real perception, for I knew that he had no physical sense of me. It was an unknowable thing that he somehow knew. Just as I was sure he would be the last of my believers.

The figures in the bed moved restlessly, then woke. Adam was already weeping before Peter had a chance to bring some medicine and water to him. He took the pills and lay back again. Peter covered him with the sheet then dressed himself carelessly.

'I'm going to get some food. We don't even have coffee any more. I'll walk to the Conad on the edge of town, won't be more than a couple of hours, less if I can.'

'I'll be fine. Don't hurry back for me. It'll do you good to get out of the house for a while. I'll sleep some more.'

Adam closed his eyes and when Peter left shortly after, he turned the lock slowly, almost silently, putting his shoes on only when he was out in the hallway and the door of the flat was tightly closed behind him.

But within minutes of Peter's departure Adam levered himself up by his elbows and then slowly pushed up to a sitting position. He seemed alert, almost animated, a manner that was in absolute opposition to his almost skeletal body and grey-tinged skin.

'Katie,' he said. 'I know you're here.'

I had thought I would never hear anyone speak to me again, and although I did not know – would never know – if he was deluded or percipient, I tried to reach him any way I could.

Nothing moved. No light switch flickered. No table levitated. No thought passed through his mind that was not his own. I wished for a computer and a printer. I wished for a séance from a hundred years before.

'Katie, can you give me a sign?'

I could not. My sensation of isolation was defined. He didn't see me because there was nothing to see, could not hear me because I was not in his head. I could not protest until now, printing onto this paper, when it is already too late.

'I sense you, even if you can't communicate. I know you're real.' I listened hard for some hesitancy in his voice which might demand reassurance that I could not give, but there was none at all. He knew I was there although his senses told him otherwise.

'I've finished your book, you know. I completed it before I left London.' He spoke to the empty room with no expectation of reply.

He had started to make his way to the bathroom now, walking shakily, leaning on furniture as he went. He sat on a wooden three-legged stool; it reminded me of a milking stool. Peter had moved it from the hallway and into the bathroom the week before so Adam didn't have to stand while doing his ablutions. It was a bit too low for the mirror, so a small vanity mirror was propped up against the back of the sink at the right height. He leaned over from the stool and started to run a bath. Water gushed out of the wide tap.

'You know what I'm going to do, don't you?'

I thought I did. The tub filled quickly.

'Will you write this down, Katie?'

Adam sprinkled some bath salts, and the scent of hyacinths and a hundred memories crowded the steamy room.

'This smell reminds me of my mother, you know. She used to grow them in the garden then bring huge flowering pots of them into the house in the springtime. It brings back my earliest memories; now they will be my last ones, I guess.' He looked a little awkward at this, self-conscious, as if he had said something stupid or melodramatic.

He stood up to reach for the razor blades which were kept in the mirrored cupboard over the sink. He turned off the taps and clumsily clambered into the bath, using the furthest wall for support, still holding the blade in his free hand.

'No music for me, Katie.' He gave a half smile.

The swiftness with which he drew the razor blade down, not across, his wrist surprised me. He was meticulous and only winced slightly as he carefully cut along the blue line of vein. He used a second razor blade for the other wrist, dropping the first in the bath.

The gush of blood was a sudden, flowing brightness in a room of white and grey.

He leaned his head back on the rim of the bath and closed his eyes.

'Thanks for staying with me.' He sounded sleepy.

I had never tried so hard to be with someone, not even Robert Dale, as I did then. But nothing happened. I watched, I waited and I envied, yes, envied the stillness, the nothingness that fell over him. It was a sleep so deep that I knew he could not be found and I wanted it for myself.

I left to watch the sea washing over the shingle, the bustling market place on the Piazza delle Conserve, the slow-moving traffic kissing nose to tail, then finally went back to my bookshop to wait, for what might be an eternity.

While I have the strength I summon up the life I have not lived.

The images flit past, chaotic in their chronology and geography.

The copper-coloured cobwebs of the desiccated branches of pine trees close around a ruined house. It is the end of the rarest season, a dry summer in a valley usually hidden by misty rain and dominated by torrential, fast-flowing water. The upstairs room with the bed where Robert Dale lay as a child, close to death, has no roof and no floor. There are piles of decaying leaves, a carpet so dense that the remains of the hearth of the downstairs parlour fireplace are only half visible. I look up. I see sky, crumbled supports that held the surface he walked on, moss-covered walls that surrounded him, a stone curlicue, an architectural remnant of those days.

The walls disintegrate even as I stand there, fine layers of dust, floating down onto the leaves. I see him with his family, but it is my imagination, nothing else. Braxfield House is a derelict shell without a spirit. He might be in Naples, or New Harmony, surely there, or perhaps nowhere at all.

This is now the quietest of places. Where there were the games and laughter of children, the chink of glasses, the clatter of cutlery, the noise of servants emptying slops and gossiping, there is nothing. The stillness of the day means that even the leaves do not rustle, and I am too far above the river here to hear it. It seems that even the birds don't chirrup, but of course they do, I am a silly spirit, listening so hard that I can no longer hear what is around me. Silence is never really absolute in a countryside place such as this.

I am a ghost hoping to see a ghost.

Narrow ribbons of sky shine cerulean above the decaying grandeur of a Neapolitan street. There is a patch rubbed smooth by passing pilgrims on an aged brass skull that adorns the wall of the church opposite the house where I first saw Eusapia.

I am reminded of a philosopher and his notion of hauntology. He asked, 'What does it mean to follow a ghost? And what if this came down to being followed by it, always persecuted perhaps by the very chase we are leading?'

This time that I am now in perplexes me, yet somehow I think it should not. The world of technology, the one within which I have written so much, is disembodied too. I could live inside a game, inhabit its creations perhaps, but I am afraid of an eternity that becomes an endless repetition of empty gestures; of being the ghost in the machine when I have been a spirit that inhabits humanity.

I am obsessed by my desire to find a sign of what I have known, a trace of my existence.

A snake slithers across an untended grave, in a wooded clearing, as dawn light dapples the headstone.

A sail from another age unfurls and a burgundy seahorse rises over a canal lined with pastel-coloured cottages.

In total darkness, I am able to see a pocket watch encrusted with coral, on the powdery bed of a Cuban sea.

In Flanders fields the poppies grow.

People read names to commemorate the dead, to show they are not forgotten; I am afraid I will never hear my names spoken again.

I remember.
'John, tell us what we should do.'
Oh, what it was to make them listen, even when they could not hear me.

'Dirty old lecher, wants his hands all over me, wants to push that fat, slimy tongue between my teeth, makes me feel like retching, best not to think about it.'
The rancid smell of unwashed crotch when the pale, carefully manicured hands of gentlewomen stripped a young girl naked.

'Lift the table.'
'Getting fucked by a ghost might be enjoyable.'
Eusapia, mi manchi davvero tanto.

'Katie, I know you're there.'
That last unwavering conviction that I would have rewarded.
That briefest of moments when I was inside him and felt all of
his sickness, the heaviness of carrying a body so full of hurting.

My acknowledgement could have been a final benediction: an
entering into him, a last act of grace.
For both of us.
Yet I could not make it so.

Then, outside a smart London town house a boy is waiting in a
hooded top, rocking his head to music I cannot hear. I look again,
initially puzzled by an unfamiliar place. There is a satellite dish
and Venetian blinds, and a yard with an overflowing rubbish
bin, but in fact the house is unchanged, the Dalston street looks
much the same, and I half expect to hear the rustle of Florence
Cook's cape, catch a glimpse of her pristine white gloves.

I try to speak. But I have no voice any more. I do not know what
I would say in any case.
A young girl approaches the boy and they kiss.
I think of breathing.
The slight chafe of unshaven skin.
The tenderness of lips.
The inside of a mouth against a tongue.
The taste of another.
Of desire.

But then, unasked for and unwanted, there is the sight of red,
red blood flowering in water. It seems like the end of the arc of

my evolution. The rise and fall of me descended into a memory of bleeding out.

I can only know my own consciousness; so many eyes have passed over me and through me with no recognition at all.
I have to believe in spirits. I know that I exist.
It seems I have more in common with the living than I thought.

ACKNOWLEDGEMENTS

My dear agent Peter Straus and editor Max Porter made this book possible with their faith. Peter arranged for me to meet Max for tea and that first meeting heralded the beginning of what has become an inspiring and enjoyable collaboration, continued over lovely lunches and including first editions, shared books and the Seventh Kingdom. Thanks to all the team, and it really is a team, at Granta who made it reality.

Thanks to all of the archivists and others who helped with research, including staff at the New Lanark Archives and the Harry Price Library, Paul J. Gaunt at the *Psypioneer Journal* and Professor Richard Wiseman.

A triumvirate of kind friends who are fellow writers commented, criticised and suggested improvements. Charles Palliser, Michael Newton and James Charlton, your advice was of great value to me. I hope you're not disappointed with the result. A fourth, David Rain, made reading suggestions that were outside my usual sphere and which really changed the way I saw the narrative.

Alessia Bianciardi, from my Ventimiglia years, was enormously helpful with the Italian research, while Andrew and Amanda Gallagher, just over the border, shared their lovely home in a beautiful place as a refuge in the final months of editing.

Bob Loomis and Ian Keable welcomed me to the Magic Circle Headquarters and guided my research into the world of illusion. John Kavanagh and Duglas Stewart were obliging sources of musical history and Jim Burns cheerfully rescued me from IT mishaps.

Gigliola Ruscelli at the Libreria Katia King in Cesenatico was kind and welcoming. Shirley Tinkham moved and delighted me with her haunting images of the Koons' Ohio.

I am very grateful to Old Possum's Practical Trust for the award of a grant to help me undertake research in Naples.

Finally, most importantly, thanks and love to my husband and my mum, who have put up with me and Katie and John for quite a while now, with their usual, much appreciated mix of love, perseverance and patience.

Keep in touch with
Granta Books:

Visit grantabooks.com to discover more.

GRANTA